APRONS & VEILS
BOOK FIVE

The Courting of
Miss Cady

GRACE HITCHCOCK

VALMONT
HOUSE PUBLISHERS

The Courting of Miss Cady © 2025 by Grace Hitchcock

Published by Valmont House Publishers

GraceHitchcock.com

Names: Hitchcock, Grace, author.

Title: The Courting of Miss Cady / Grace Hitchcock

Other Titles: the courting of miss cady

Series: Aprons and Veils; book 5

Identifiers: Large Print 979-8-9912707-8-6 | 979-8-9912707-1-7 Paperback | 979-8-9912707-2-4 Ebook

Subjects: Christian Romantic suspense fiction

All scripture quotations, unless otherwise noted, are taken from the King James Version of the Bible.

Cover design by *Carpe Librum Book Design*

Editor Chantelle Mills

Author is represented by The Steve Laube Agency

For those who believe that
love at first sight exists,
this story is for you.

"God is love; and he that dwelleth in love dwelleth in God, and God in him. Herein is our love made perfect, that we may have boldness in the day of judgment: because as He is, so are we in this world. There is no fear in love; but perfect love casteth out fear: because fear hath torment. He that feareth is not made perfect in love."

1 John 4:15-18 KJV

CHAPTER 1

$\mathcal{N}$ew York City
December 1898

JANE CADY SQUINTED through the tulle of
her wedding veil as she waited in the foyer
of the church on Fifth Avenue. Her pulse
pounded in her ears as the organist began
the first notes of the Wedding March. Jane
glanced about for her father, her heart sinking. He was always flighty and had his head
in the clouds with each new business venture that absorbed his every thought until it
was followed through, but this—this was a
new level even for him.

She pushed the double doors leading into the sanctuary open a crack. The pews were filled, the lovely chapeaus of the elite society ladies creating a meadow of fake blooms that basked in the morning light streaming in from the stained glassed windows. Reverend Hall stood at the top of the aisle, between the massive flower arrangements featuring orange blossoms, speaking with—she averted her gaze, even as her heart skipped a beat at the sight of her handsome groom. She didn't want to see Graham Bank until the very moment she was to be his wife.

The church bells sounded ten times, announcing to all of New York City that she was about to be wed. Outside the front doors, the crowd gathered cheered for her. She danced from side to side, trying not to pick at the orange blossoms of her enormous bouquet. *Where is Father? He reads the news sheets, and the time was printed on every single one!* The guests were waiting for her. Could she walk down the aisle without him? No. It would cause nearly as much scandal as her being late to her own wedding.

The front doors of the church burst open, shouts and sounds of the city spilling inside for a moment as the doors shut. Father ran to her, panting in his wedding suit. "Daughter, we must speak. There has been a development with my ships from the—"

"Father! Thank goodness you are here." She seized his arm and straightened Father's silk top hat and patted down his graying beard. He was disheveled, but at least he was here. "There is no time to waste, Father. The bells have already sounded the hour, and we are already late."

"But, Janey, you see, that is why I was tardy. You need to know—"

She placed her hands atop Father's shoulders and steered him to the doors. "We can speak *after* the ceremony. Nothing—I repeat, *nothing* is as important as my marrying Graham at this very moment." She nodded to the footmen who pulled open the double doors, the blasting notes of the organ vibrating through her and sending anticipation humming to her very fingertips. After years of waiting for the right man, being judged for waiting until she was nearly four and twenty to accept a suitor, she would be Mrs. Graham Bank.

With her head held high and the demure smile that Graham liked so much, Jane attempted to glide up the aisle, but her father's steps were gratingly slow, as if he were dragging his feet. *What is he waiting for? He's not the one getting married, and I certainly know that he isn't mourning my loss.* She pulled against his arm, ever so slightly, urging him forward. *Please, please don't make a scene for once, Father. Please, let me have this moment.* She smiled at the snobby Miss Carol and the Montgomery sisters—*Wait, is Kitty Montgomery dressed in mourning over Graham?* She stuffed down her ire. No, not even the presence of her social enemies at her wedding would stifle her joy.

"Janey, I must speak with you," he whispered. "It is of the utmost importance and relevance."

She forced herself not to cringe. To everyone else, they would likely imagine his murmurs as sweet reassurance instead of his barely veiled panic. "Father, you know I love you," she returned through her pretty smile. "Please, wait to deliver this message. Don't ruin this for me."

He patted her arm and muttered something about the groom maybe not hearing the news. "Still there. That's a good sign. Perhaps it will be well."

She ignored Father's nonsensical mutterings. He often talked to himself, mentioning only fragments of sentences on his mind, making it nearly impossible to understand him most days. Behind her, she heard the heavy sanctuary doors scrape open again, but she didn't turn to see who could be entering so late and rudely interrupting her procession. Nothing could bother her today, though. She lifted her lashes and focused on Graham. Her handsome soon-to-be husband stood well over six feet, and his golden hair was brushed into a dashing pompadour. She could hardly believe that Graham was to be *hers*.

He had been named New York's bachelor of the year, and she had caught him. Certainly, her inheritance was enough to draw nearly every suitor to her door, but none had captured her attention like Graham Bank. From his deep, baritone laughter to his intense gaze never leaving her face as they conversed, Graham was a dream come true. He found her lovely and interesting and not silly at all. And his heart was hers.

From the corner of her eye, she spied a man in a simple brown suit with a bowler hat atop his hair, racing along the side of the church, as if he were trying to sit in the front. *Is he family?* But he did not stop at the front pew. He hurried straight up to Graham. Her heart pounded and her steps faltered. Was someone ill? His mother hadn't been able to make it this morning to the ceremony. Surely, she didn't pass? *No, not dear Mother Bank.* She had been so kind to Jane—far more tender than even her own mother had been.

"Oh dear. Oh dear. No, no, no—" Her father's pace slowed. "It's happened."

She tugged Father forward but nearly stumbled to a halt all together when alarm flitted across Graham's face and his eyes met hers.

Whatever it is, my darling, we will bear it together. She silently sent him the message from her heart to his. As in love as they were with one another, she was confident he would understand.

Graham staggered down the step that separated them. His large, smooth hand grasped her gloved hand. "My darling, did you know?" He bent and whispered in her ear.

"Know? Know what? Graham?" She returned, squeezing his hand. "What's wrong? Tell me."

Graham shook his head. "I-I cannot do this."

"Is it your mother, Graham?" Her chest tightened. "Is she worse?"

"No. It is other news . . . from Mother."

A *message* from Mother Banks? Surely, she would have wished the news to wait until after they were wed. *Unless it is truly terrible news?* Would Graham insist on pausing the ceremony, or would he wed her, since it was all arranged and leaving her at the altar could hardly be less than a scandal?

"Mother is fine."

"Thank goodness." She moved to press her hand to her heart but then remembered her bouquet.

His gaze landed on her father with a scowl. "But I cannot say the same for us."

Us? Her heart sped and the room seemed to shrink, every curious eye scalding her skin. "What do you mean? I don't understand, Graham."

Father's face reddened. "At least, have the courtesy to tell her in private, Bank."

"Something *you* should have done." Graham cradled her hand and slid it through his arm, pulling her back down the aisle, keeping his gaze firmly on the exit.

From the corner of her eye, she caught the flurry of black tulle as Kitty lifted her mourning veil, hope in her features. The already curious guests erupted in murmurs as Graham practically dragged Jane to the foyer, shoving the double doors closed behind them. Her groom released her the moment the doors closed behind them.

"Graham! What is going on?" She flung the veil away from her face—desperate to see Graham—to understand. She adjusted the chocolate curls framing her face and ran her fingers down the front of her exquisite wedding gown with its ornate pearl beading and diamond clusters.

He paused in his pacing, his frown softening for a moment. "You look stunning, Jane. I always loved it when your cheeks blushed." He sighed.

"T-thank you, but couldn't you have waited to tell me after the ceremony? Father was so insistent to tell me something too, but I made him wait." She refrained from twisting her hands. Graham hated it when she fidgeted. It was a horribly difficult habit to give up—fidgeting. "What happened?"

"There isn't going to be a ceremony, Jane." His gentle voice pierced her heart.

His words sent her staggering, as if he had struck her. "W-what? What do you mean? Everything is arranged. My things are awaiting me at our new home on Madison Avenue." She gestured to the closed doors. "The New York Four Hundred are seated inside as we speak and the rest of New York is awaiting our departure from the church just outside. The streets are lined with well-wishers. Surely, whatever it is isn't important enough to delay our ceremony. It will take a half an hour, and we will be wed and then, you can deal with whatever it is that needs your attention." She grasped his hand. "My dearest, please do not delay our wedding any further. I can only imagine the gossip that is spreading—"

"It is not a delay that I am seeking." He moved away from her touch, crossing his arms. "I cannot marry you. We are no longer *compatible* as our values do not align."

Compatible? "Did the messenger carry a false tale about me? I have been true only to you, Graham. I vow it. I've never even kissed anyone before you proposed to me." Her cheeks burned at the thought that *he* could not claim the same. But she had forgiven him for his momentary lapse in kissing Kitty Montgomery the very hour before requesting to court Jane. "What could that man have possibly said that would see you break my heart in front of the New York Four Hundred?"

"For that, I apologize. I would have avoided your humiliation if I had known." He shoved his hands into his pockets, remorse filling his gaze. "My mother sent the messenger. She said that if I go through with the wedding, she will disinherit me, and I will lose everything."

She gripped her stomach, her fingers rolling over the pearls sewn in patterns of orange blossoms. She couldn't breathe. Why couldn't she draw a full breath? "B-but Mother Bank was the one who championed our union. This makes no sense. And if her withdrawal of funds is stopping you, then I have more than enough to see us through."

Graham lifted a finger and pointed at the sanctuary doors. "See, there is where your father is a liar. My mother just read in the papers that your father is *ruined*."

She rested her hand on the wall, holding herself up as the room spun. *No. It can't be.* Was Graham breaking it off with her? Or simply informing and secretly desiring her to plead? She had pride, but this—this beautiful first hope of love being torn away from her because of her father's investments was something her pride could never come back from. The bouquet tumbled from her grasp as she folded her hands to her chest. "Graham, please don't do this. I'm begging you. Surely, there has been some kind of mistake—"

"No, there hasn't been a mistake." Graham raked his fingers through his hair, ruffling his perfect pompadour. "In fact, at this very moment, all your assets have been seized to pay for the debts Mr. Cady acquired for this latest venture. No doubt, they will be requiring even your wedding gown to pay back his debts."

Did Graham not know of her trust fund? A single butterfly of hope flapped its wings in her belly. "I have millions in my trust fund, Graham. Millions of dollars do not simply evaporate." She reached out to him. "There is no need to call off—"

"Not anymore. Your father had access to your funds and sank *everything* into a venture that would have seen your family the wealthiest in America. But the diamond ships sank, his venture failed, and you are without funds." He grasped her hand. "I'm sorry, Jane. I truly am. I was fond of you."

"Fond?" His once endearing touch that she had craved felt cold and a hint clammy even through her glove. "You said you loved me, Graham Bank."

He shoved his hands in his pockets and rocked back on his heels. "Love is such a funny word—it can mean so many different things. For instance, I love chocolate and horse riding."

"It is not a funny word," she ground out, her anger melting into a broken heart. Tears spilled down her cheeks. "It is a most sacred word when used by a man who wishes to wed."

"Well, whatever it is, I, in fact, do *not* love you, Jane Cady." He cleared his throat. "I wish things were different, but I must, based on my mother's message, step away from our commitment. I wish you luck."

Her knees buckled and she sank into a cloud of white as her world faded into blessed nothingness.

Murmurs filled the corridor. She could

feel the cold stone seeping through her pretty silk stockings. Her head hurt. Why hadn't Graham caught her? Why hadn't he at least carried her out to the awaiting carriage and away from all the shame while she was unconscious? She didn't dare open her eyes to see how many people were staring at her, memorizing her humiliation to spill over high tea and rejoice over the great parvenus Cady family being brought low once again.

"We are ruined, Mildred." Father's voice came from her side. "There is nothing left for us here now."

"What do you mean, Benjamin?" Mother replied with a nervous laugh, as if trying to cover up her husband's troubling words and hide the fact that their world was imploding in front of the New York Four Hundred. "You aren't making any sense. Darling, can you see what is keeping Graham?" She pitched her voice to carry to the nearest guests who might spread her words, "Surely, he is fetching the doctor for our daughter, whom Graham knows so well that he anticipated her faint, which is why he pulled her from the altar!"

Poor Mother. She hated not being in control of a situation.

"Can we please leave, Mother? Everyone is staring. Father, can you lift her?" At twelve, Jane's sister Theodora was at least bold enough to tell her father what everyone else would not.

Father placed his hand under Jane's shoulder and lifted but dropped her immediately, her head thudding against the stones. She swallowed back a grunt at the sore spot being struck again. If it hadn't been for her ornate coiffure, she surely would have been concussed. She was going to have to open her eyes, wasn't she? She was going to have to face everyone as she fled the church.

Another, gentler, hand grasped her own. She nearly sagged in relief. Meg was there. Her best friend would see Jane out of this situation.

"Mr. Bank, there you are!" Meg called out to him. "Did you find the doctor?"

"No . . . ?"

"Then we must see her home to be attended to by her physician. Please, help our dear Jane to the carriage," Meg instructed.

A pair of strong arms lifted her and the sound of the large front doors swinging open were no sweeter than a choir of angels at this moment. Cool air kissed her scalding cheeks. The crowd outside cheered and faltered, no doubt at the sight of her supposedly unconscious form. They murmured and cried out, but she blocked the crowd out. She had only to survive until she was alone and then, and only then, could she fall apart. She felt herself gently deposited on a tufted leather seat.

"Just because I can't marry you, doesn't mean I wish you ill, Jane Cady. I did love you in my own way," Graham whispered.

So, she hadn't fooled him. She opened her eyes and glared at him through her long, dark lashes. "And yet, you have caused me the greatest pain of my three and twenty years, Graham. You are right, love *is* a funny word if this is what you think it means." She sat up and shoved him out of the carriage and slammed the door, rapping her fists on the ceiling. Her family could take the other carriage home. She had to get out of here. "Take me home, Oswald."

New York City blurred through her unshed tears for the short drive home and not even the sight of Central Park brought her peace as nature usually did. Nothing but further humiliation kept her tears at bay until she could be truly alone. As soon as the carriage rocked to a stop in front of her four-storied stone home, she gathered up her voluminous tulle and silk skirts and bolted out the carriage and up the steps into her home.

Men in bowler hats and dusty jackets paused to stare at her. She whirled, but they swarmed her estate, each bearing some sort of treasured collection from her home tucked in their arm, and all had notepads and pencils out.

The butler gasped and rushed to her side, his eyes wide at her sudden appearance when she was supposed to be getting married, but in his kind fashion, Smithy didn't question her. "I couldn't keep them out, Miss Cady," Smithy whispered. "The debt collectors had the police let them in—they had a warrant. There was nothing I could do. They haven't gone up—"

She nodded through her tears. She avoided eye contact with the strange men who scattered out of her path, like cockroaches being frightened by a lantern. Jane kept her head down as she raced upstairs to her room, tossing the veil over the side of the railing as she ran, sobbing for the life that had been promised to her—for the man who she thought was her dream. Father was right. She was ruined, and there was nothing left for the family in New York except humiliation.

THANKFULLY, her family did not seek her out after they returned from the church. With Mother's wailing filling the house and Father's shouted promises for a brighter future, even little Theo kept herself hidden away, so Jane allowed herself to wallow. She rested her cheek on the Parisian carpet beside her bed with her small wooden memory box next to her, the letters that Graham had written to her during their courtship spread about her feet like a fan. She had searched his letters for some sort of indication that he had not loved her . . . he had said all the right things.

Her door pushed open.

She couldn't let the servants see her like this. She sighed and pushed herself up to sit back on her heels as her dearest friend in the world poked her head inside.

"Janey?" Meg crossed the room in her bridesmaid's gown and knelt beside Jane, pushing aside the mountain of Jane's wedding tulle to sit. "I came as soon as I could, but I only just managed to keep the Montgomery ladies from calling upon you." She shivered. "The pair of them are still as spoiled and rude as they were when we were young girls." She grasped Jane's hand. "I am so sorry."

Her tears rose once more. "I'm sorry too. My father convinced yours to invest in the prospect as well."

"Yes, but he only gambled a half a million." Meg retrieved her handkerchief and gently dabbed away Jane's tears. "My dress budget will only suffer for a season, maybe two, but that matters not one whit to me. I only care about you and the fact that Graham treated you like . . . like—"

"Like a business deal gone poorly?" Jane lifted her favorite of all of Graham's letters —the very first he had sent her. She pointed to his little sketch of her at the ballroom when he first beheld her. She looked radiant in the sketch. She thought it captured how he viewed her. She felt special that the most desired bachelor of the season had singled her out. If her father's venture had been successful, their family's wealth would have surpassed even the Astor's and Vanderbilt's. "I thought he loved me."

Meg squeezed her hands. "You will find true love again, Jane. I know it." She shook her head. "Though, I highly suspect that Graham never truly loved you. And to be honest, I always thought him undeserving of you."

Jane released a short laugh. "I am inclined to agree. But what do I do now? How will I find a real love? No gentleman in this city will ever look at me again, much less wish to court me without money to my name."

Meg sighed. "I wish I could disagree, but you and I both know the types of people our set belongs to. For the majority, we fix our gazes on obtaining more and more wealth. I believe in another city, though, you may have your knight in shining armor awaiting you."

Jane released a short laugh, laced with the bitterness of the day. "What other city? Are you spiriting me away on a Grand Tour?"

Meg shook her head. "I wish that I could, dear friend. I wish that my money belonged to me and not to my father until I wed because I'd give it *all* to you, dearest Jane. I could beseech Papa, and he *might* say yes, but he is quite put out with your father at the moment. But I was referring to the message from one of your wedding guests that your father received while I was downstairs and—"

The door burst open once more, and Mother pointed to Jane on the floor. "You see? This is what your risk did for our family, Benjamin. And you expect me to abandon everything to move *West* in a matter of days? West!"

Theo's pale face appeared in the doorway, her body poised as if ready to run, if necessary, but curiosity over their fate, no doubt, compelled her little sister to listen as it did to Jane.

"We have no other choice, Mildred. And we have a week. Thankfully, I know the bank owner."

"Well, thank goodness for small mercies," Mother retorted. "A week to say farewell to a lifetime of friends? To my family?"

"They won't miss us that much for it is your parents who will not give me another dime."

"Because that portion of the family fortune belongs to my elder brother. You had my inheritance of millions, and you *gambled* it all away, Benjamin." She pressed her lips into a thin line.

"It was supposed to be a sure thing, not a gamble. How was I supposed to know that the diamond mines that I just purchased would dry up and that the diamonds I did manage to collect would sink along the coast?"

"But why did you have to send *all* the merchant vessels on this speculation? You should not have invested so heavily, Benjamin." Mother clenched her fists, her curls trembling in her effort to remain calm. "You even took the trusts that I set aside for our daughters. How did you even manage to access the funds without my signature?"

"I forged it, as I have done for years, but what is done is done. We are moving and that is final." Father nodded to Meg and had the decency to appear chastened, no doubt for what he had done to her family as well. "Please apologize to your father, Meg. I did not plan on this going so poorly." He turned to Jane, determination hardening his expression. "Plan on saying your goodbyes to your friends this week, Jane, but first, give me the ring."

Her eyes widened as he impatiently wiggled his fingers at her. "M-my ring?"

"Yes, the engagement ring. Because

Graham broke off the engagement, the ring is ours to sell, and we desperately need the funds for travel."

Meg gasped but she remained silent with her gaze on Jane, as if asking Jane if she would relinquish the one thing that could see her future secure.

Jane twisted the lovely pear cut sapphire with tiny pearls surrounding the gem in the light. It had given her such joy and pride when Graham had presented it to her. She almost protested that she wished to give it back to Graham, but what was the use of fighting her father when he had that gleam in his eyes? Years of experience dictated no other opinion would win but his. Numb, she slipped it from her finger and dropped it into her father's awaiting palm.

"There's a good girl. Tomorrow, sift through your things and pack whatever you can fit into two trunks. The creditors agreed to that much, as well as one heirloom jewel each and the possession of our oldest horse. The rest of our belongings and stock will have to be sold off. We leave in one week."

The knot in her chest eased that at least her old gelding, Phantom, would not be taken from her too. "Can we leave sooner?" Her cheeks burned at the thought of being in New York that long—receiving guests and well-wishers and gossip mongers alike. *Lord, help me bear it.*

"I wish we could leave at once, but in order to get the best price for our things, I need to set up an auction," Father patted her awkwardly atop the head. "You must be brave for a little longer, Janey."

Meg pulled Jane to her feet and embraced her as Mother and Father departed as soon as they appeared, slamming the door behind them. "You see?" Meg whispered, her voice trembling. "It could be the new beginning you need, dear friend. Maybe you will find a life away from your father after all."

"A new life." Jane pulled away and ran her finger over Graham's miniature picture. "I was going to have it with Graham."

Meg rested her hand atop Jane's, covering the miniature. "I know this is not what you want, but perhaps the Lord is sparing you from a life with a man who values money more than his bride." Her gaze flitted to the door.

Like my parents. She lowered Graham's picture into the box, packing away his letters and tokens of affection, her tears smearing the ink on the final letter—the one where he admitted his intentions. Her heart grew too heavy, and she leaned into her friend's arms once more. If this was what a man's love was like, she wanted nothing to do with it ever again.

CHAPTER 2

*L*as Vegas, New Mexico

JANE CADY GRIPPED her gelding's reins as she stared up at the ramshackle house on the edge of the dusty western town that was to be her home for the foreseeable future. It had only taken the morning of the wedding that never happened for her world to completely change. She, like her sister and Mother, stayed isolated during the waiting to leave, but the papers had taken the story to new heights and even fleeing west by train did not keep her safe from humiliation. The newspapers along the railway all bore headlines boasting of the Cady family's fall from society. It was a relief to arrive to their new town before it awoke—at least no one had stared at them while they rolled up to their home with all their earthly possessions piled on the back of a wagon that followed the questionably old hack.

The sunrise, though she normally considered it romantic on the balcony of their Newport cottage, did nothing to improve upon the abandoned house. It could have been beautiful a long time ago, save for the pieces of gingerbread molding hanging by a thread from the porch roof and broken steps leading up to the house that made it appear more suitable for ghosts than a family of four. But it was cheap, and the owner, Mr. Brady, had been more than happy to rent it out to them—at least that was what the current House Manager of the Harvey House's Castañeda, a Mr. Perkins, had said in his telegram. Hopefully, the inside of the house was better—it was certainly no mansion on Madison Avenue . . .

where she should have been living with Graham. *No.*

She pushed away the thoughts of what should have been, but it was hard to accomplish given this morning, only ten days after her wedding that never happened, was supposed to be the voyage of her wedding trip to Italy. Would she ever see Venice again? Her grand tour was two years ago, and she had always planned to return for a wedding trip with the groom of her dreams.

But, as the days between her disastrous wedding morning and the present stretched, she found that she did not *miss* Graham like she thought she would. She missed the freedom that a marriage with him could bring. Certainly, her ex-fiancé had been handsome and she the envy of the season, but had she really known Graham? *Apparently not, given his flight from the altar— No! Do not mourn what you lost. Don't think of the darling villa in Italy. You are lucky to have a holey, haunted roof over your head at all.*

She forced a smile and, fixing Phantom's reins to the hitching post, turned to help her mother from the hired hack as Father helped with the bags while Theodora crossed her arms, refusing to remove herself from the bench seat, her opinion of their new address stated plainly on her face. Jane sighed, willing her smile to brighten. When Theodora took to one of her moods, it was best to be the voice of reason and hope.

"I'm thankful the journey is over. Aren't you, Mother?" Jane questioned with forced sunshine coating her words. "This has been quite the adventure thus far, hasn't it, Theo? I wonder what we shall find inside? Perhaps some forgotten treasure, or perhaps some new bugs for you to study?"

Theo's brows lifted and she assessed the house once more, interest brightening her countenance as she gripped the side of the buggy and swung herself down. "You think so?" She plunked her hands on her hips and stared up. "Well, it couldn't be more boring than the train."

"I'd rather we were still on the Atchison, Topeka, and Santa Fe railroad than here. What a fall in status. From Fifth Avenue to a glorified shack on a street without a name,"

Mother muttered, lifting her lace handkerchief to her nose as she gripped Jane's arm and stared up at the house, her frown deepening. "Your father painted quite the field of wildflowers of this place, didn't he? He even compared it to our summer cottage in Newport with its sprawling front porch— sprawling, indeed. Why, our garden sheds are in a better state than this."

As usual, Father exaggerated. What else should we expect? But Jane swallowed back the unkind truth that would do nothing but bring down Mother's mood further. "With some work, it will be lovely, I'm sure." Jane wasn't sure, but what else could she say? It was better to burn the place to the ground than risk falling through the floorboards of the second floor?

Jane held Mother's elbow and assisted her up the steps that still bore flecks of white paint. With a fresh coat of paint, the house might be somewhat pretty again, and being on the outskirts of town, the porch did have a lovely view of the town of Las Vegas with the Gallinas foothills behind it. Jane maneuvered Mother away from the broken step and tried the doorknob. It swung open. She scrunched her nose at the musty odor. A broken window in the corner allowed morning sunlight to spill inside to reveal dust coating every surface and droppings in the corners of the room. She'd have to clean the droppings before her mother saw them.

The hackney driver and his assistant dumped their trunks onto the porch. "Well, if I can't convince you folks to stay at the Castañeda in town, I'll be on my way. The missus makes a mean batch of flapjacks, and the boy and I don't like 'em when they get cold."

"Oh, I'll be at the hotel shortly. I'm the new manager there." Father clasped the driver on the shoulder as Mother cringed at the mention of the Harvey House, as she always did at the reminder of their fall. Father pressed a dollar into the man's hand. "I thank you for your service. Enjoy your roast."

Jane barely hid her grimace at Father's extravagant tip. This fall from grace and fortune would take time to get used to for them all—including adjusting their habit of tipping so generously.

"Flapjacks," the man muttered, but grinned at the dollar and tipped his hat to him.

Jane strode inside, her skirts dragging across the wood floors, which lifted a cloud of dust that set them all to coughing, but Theo lifted her hem to cover her nose and ran straight up the stairs.

"For goodness sake, drop your hem and use a handkerchief, Theo." Mother cried after her. "And take care not to fall!"

Father whisked out his handkerchief and handed it to Mother. "I know it needs a little cleaning, Mildred, but it'll be as good as new in no time."

Mother pinched her nose shut with the handkerchief, disgust exuding her nasally voice, "Benjamin, there are more cobwebs than surfaces visible."

Father moved to the interior shutters and unlatched them, swinging them open wide. Light burst into the room making it less scary and more hideous all at once. "I know it's a tad bit messy, and I'm sorry. Mr.

Harvey offered to hire a girl to clean any place we decided to rent, but I told him that, uh, we had made other arrangements."

"Meaning, we couldn't even afford to hire a girl, much less pay for this horrid little hovel," Mother muttered.

"There is only so much of my old friend's generosity that I can accept, Mildred," Father ignited the match and, with shaking hands, lit the wick. "Mr. Harvey did arrange for a crate of cleaning supplies to be left in the kitchen."

"A crate of—You were on the board that gave Fred Harvey permission to run his establishments on the railroad in the very beginning!" Mother sputtered. "If it hadn't been for your vote—"

"Yes, but that was a long time ago. Fred was the one who made it a success. It was kind of him to offer me the job of House Manager when he saw what happened in the church—" At Mother's trembling lip, he amended, "Well, it was kind of him to offer me the job when he already had a perfectly good manager in place." Father opened two more shutters.

A pounding on the stairs sounded and Theo burst into the parlor, her nose wrinkled in disgust. "It's worse upstairs. Why couldn't we stay at the Castañeda while this place is put to rights? Surely, the rooms can't all be reserved in a town this size."

"You know how I feel about that place, Theodora. It is bad enough that your father is forced to *work* such a menial job to see us through this rough patch, but to stay there and have everyone know who we are and *why* we are there—it's all too much for me to bear."

Theo ran her finger over the remaining rippled wallpaper that had large sections ripped away. "And where are we supposed to sleep tonight?"

Mother lifted her chin. "Yes, Benjamin. I can't imagine there being beds with fresh linens ready for our use? You know how exhausted I have been lately."

"That was when you were planning the wedding," Theo interjected. "You shouldn't be so tired anymore." She glanced at Jane and grimaced, as if realizing her insensitivity. "Sorry, Jane."

Jane shrugged. "I can consider it the one boon with this adventure—Mother can recover in peace."

Mother blinked. "In peace *where?*" She gestured to the single piece of furniture in the parlor, a chaise lounge with a spring dangling out of the middle and tufts of cotton and straw sticking out of it.

"There are mattresses on the floor upstairs," Theo piped up.

"I can secure a few pieces of furniture in town," Jane interjected. "But, with so little furniture, it shouldn't be too hard to prepare the house for our occupancy."

"It will take some cleaning, but, uh, I am afraid I cannot help." Father lifted his bowler hat, flapping it before his cheeks, though Jane couldn't imagine how he could be hot in the freezing home. "I promised to arrive at the Castañeda as early as possible, and the new shift of Harvey Girls take over at six in the morning."

"And who is going to do this cleaning while you are surrounded by these waitresses, *Benjamin?*"

Theo darted back up the stairs and Jane

escaped onto the front porch as they both sensed Mother and Father were about to have a rather loud discussion. Jane leaned against the railing and stared out at the little town of Las Vegas with the sun glinting off the tin roofs. *Lord, I know this is not what I dreamed of, or my family, but maybe this is for the best. Will You give me a new dream? Something even better than I imagined with Graham.*

The gentle trill of a robin in the cedar tree to the right of the porch soothed her heart. Perhaps she packed the bird book in her trunk? If there weren't many socials out here, perhaps she could study birds. *And when I tire of that, I can start my collection of cats.* She lifted the lid of her green trunk and rifled through the contents, pausing when she found Meg's departing gift that Jane had promised to open in her new home.

Pulling away the pretty red paper, she found a dictionary of flowers. On the inside cover, Meg had slipped a note.

Dearest Jane,
These dictionaries have become all

the rage in London. I meant to give this to you as a wedding present so we could speak in code through our letters, as Mother still insists on reading every note from you, but consider this an early Christmas present. Use this to interpret the silent meanings of your score of suitors' bouquets and write me back using blooms as a way of letting me know how you are and if a gentleman has caught your eye. As for me, I am hopeful of meeting a count on my grand tour. May we have a gladiolus moment! Our futures are bright, dear Jane.

Take heart,

Meg

Jane flipped through the dictionary and felt her somber mood fall from her shoulders as she looked up the flower in Meg's letter, giggling that it meant, "Love at First Sight." She snorted. *As if that would ever happen to me.* She closed the book with a sigh. *Flowers from suitors seem like a lifetime ago already.*

Father burst through the door, slamming his hat atop his head as he muttered something about divas under his breath and charged down the road without even a glance to Jane.

Straightening her shoulders and pushing herself to standing, Jane closed the lid of her trunk and resolved to stay strong as she set about for the kitchen, but no crate was atop the counter or wooden table with its single remaining chair. Opening a few cupboards, she found a cluster of abandoned cans of food, excessive mouse droppings and tufts of dust bunnies. At the fifth cabinet, she discovered the crate with its promised rags and soaps, along with a sturdy bucket. She twisted about and found the hand pump in the kitchen, but as the stove was dormant, she'd have to do her cleaning with cold water.

Pumping the water and carrying the supplies up the stairs had her in a sweat before she even began cleaning the master bedroom upstairs. She planted her hands on her hips and surveyed the room. It was far smaller than even Theo's room back home, but at least it would take less time for her to clean and make certain that Mother would have a decent place to rest and escape the dust.

The room took hours to clean, and she was nearly finished with her and Theo's bedroom when a cry made her almost drop the bucket of water she had just hauled upstairs. She set it aside and sped to the second-floor landing, leaning over the railing to find Mother standing at the front door with a basket on her arm and a hand pressed to her lace jabot.

"Mother? What's wrong?" She gritted her teeth. *Please don't say you saw a mouse.*

"Your father forgot his lunch."

Jane sagged on the railing, the fear draining her limbs, leaving her exhausted and strained. "Mother, he is working at the

Castañeda. They have the finest food in the West."

"Yes, but this is the last of the cheese he loves with those fine imported crackers." Her cheeks pinked as she dipped her head. "And, well, I don't like how we parted this morning."

"Then, why don't you bring it to him and tell him yourself?" Jane gestured back to the room she had been cleaning. "I have so much more left to do."

"In my condition?" She ran a hand over her skirts. "I have been travelling for two days to get here, and you haven't even drawn the hot water for my bath."

"The stove is dormant, Mother." She worried her bottom lip. "Maybe Father knows how to start the fire, and you could take a bath when he returns."

"Even if I didn't bathe, it would take me hours to prepare myself with a cold sponge bath. No, you must go into town on my behalf to convey my regret."

"Regret . . .for?" Jane prompted. *Sending me to a restaurant with a basket of far inferior food?*

Mother pinched the bridge of her nose. "Jane, it is enough that I am conveying any sort of regret after how your father lost all our funds and dragged me away from my family and friends. I am getting angry again just thinking about how he lied to us, manipulated me, and—"

"Very well." Jane sighed and clomped down the stairs. "I will bring him the cheese and crackers."

"Thank you." Mother handed over the basket. "And be sure he eats. He gets so caught up in whatever shiny task that has caught his attention and forgets such tedious, mundane things as eating." Though her words were harsh, her tone betrayed her affection for Father. "And we know how cranky he can get when he doesn't eat. We would not want him to embarrass himself with his staff by speaking words in hunger that he would regret later."

"Certainly. It is not as if bringing cheese to a country-wide lauded restaurant is humiliating or anything of the sort," Jane muttered as she collected her hat from the kitchen.

"And if it is, you have been through worse," Theo supplied from the kitchen where she was rubbing the soot from the windows.

Jane forced a smile. "Yes, Theo, I've been through worse. Thank you for reminding me."

Theo dropped her arm, twisting the filthy rag in her hands. "I wasn't trying—"

"I know." Jane lifted her hand, staying her little sister's apology. While she was a little spoiled, Theo did love her. "Thank you for cleaning without being asked."

Theo shrugged. "It's fun to do something I was never allowed to try at our old house."

Jane laughed. "Well, if you think this is fun, you should finish cleaning our bedroom while I see to this."

Theo's eyes sparkled as she shot to her feet. "I won't let you down."

Jane kissed Theo's cheek. "I know you won't. Besides, neither one of us knows how to clean, so you will likely do just as good of a job as me." She wove her hat pin through her chapeau and snagged the basket from Mother as she rushed out the door.

Phantom stamped his foot at the rail and her heart sunk. The gelding had been tied up for nearly four hours.

Her stomach sank at her accidental neglect. She darted inside and retrieved the spare wooden bucket and pumped water into it, hauling it outside. She grunted from the effort and set down the sloshing bucket before the horse and made certain the reins were long enough for him to drink. "Sorry, my boy." She shook her head. "I am too used to servants seeing to our needs, I suppose I neglected to remember that you would need care by me." She ran her hand over his mane. She ached to ride Phantom over the foothills in the distance, but her mother's errand stilled the desire. She was no longer the carefree heiress of last week. "I wish I could ride you, but I don't have time to change into a riding habit and saddle you up. I promise to find you oats and a good brushing when I return. I will ask Father where to bring you for your care." She kissed his nose and trailed her fingers down his spine as she hurried down the dusty road toward town.

They were only a few minutes' walk to the first building on the outskirts of town, and she could see that Las Vegas had already come alive since they had driven through it. A few women walked along the boardwalk, children in hand. Jane nodded to each in passing, thinking it must be the small-town thing to do and was met with warm smiles in return. She stepped off the boardwalk into the main street, trying to recall the direction they had come from this morning.

All she had to do was find the railroad and its brick platform, and then she would find the Castañeda. It was directly behind it. She remembered passing a saloon, which had still been going strong at that early hour. The tinkling keys of a piano drew her attention when the thundering of hooves sounded and she whirled around as lowing filled the air, dust swirling and rising above the roof as sharp whistles split the air.

Horns rounded the corner—attached to massive cows. *Or are they called steer?* But the steer didn't veer away as she expected. *The cattle are allowed on the main road?* She gasped, scrambling to gather her skirts in one hand, while keeping the basket upright. She tried to dodge back toward the safety of the boardwalk, but the massive cattle with long horns were already upon her. *One day. I lasted one day in the Wild West.* She side-stepped left and right in the most compli-cated diamond of the first water dance of her life, weaving until one of the cows stepped on her hem. She jerked back, at-tempting to wrench her skirts, and the long-horned beast beside her knocked off her pretty hat. She screamed. *Lord, de-liver me!*

A strong hand grasped her under the arm and jerked upward. She was suspended in the air for a breath, then two, until she was slammed into something hard, yet gen-tle, as a strong arm wrapped about her waist, securing her to the rider. She twisted to look up at her rescuer. The sun shone down on a Stetson, bathing the man in a heavenly glow. She blinked, finding a cow-boy, a *real* live cowboy, bearing a fierce scowl. He was the most ruggedly handsome man she had ever seen. With piercing blue eyes and dark hair curling out from his tan hat, he could have easily been on the cover of her sister's dime novels.

The steer charged about his horse, and he expertly wove his steed through the beasts, cutting and releasing whistles until they were at the back of the herd, the dust finally settling and he turned his full, remorseful gaze on her.

WADE STERLING GAZED down at the woman in a turquoise-colored gown draped over his lap atop the saddle. He swallowed. With her chocolate curls with a hint of red cascading out of her low coiffure, she was the most beautiful woman he ever beheld—and his brother's newly purchased cattle had nearly run her over. "I am so sorry, miss. My brothers cleared the path—I thought they did anyway. Are you hurt?"

"No, thanks to you, sir." She offered him a small smile and lifted the basket from her lap. "Not even my basket was harmed. Though, I did fear the worst there for a moment. How did you lift me with one hand and from your position atop your mount?"

He shrugged. "You are a little thing. Weren't hard to do."

Her cheeks tinted at his words.

Did he say something wrong? She *was* little, but he had practically no experience talking with a lady. "Did I hurt you? I'm used to hoisting up my dog, but uh, I ain't never done so with a woman." He glanced down at his blue coonhound, who circled back from the herd and sat on his haunches, his tail wagging as he panted.

"You were surprisingly gentle." She smiled up at him.

His heart stuttered. "Uh, good."

"Though, I feel rather foolish for needing to be hoisted up in the first place, but I'm ever so thankful you were there."

"Me too." He slid off the saddle and reached up for her. Her petite hands splayed on his shoulders, and he lifted her from his horse's back. "My brothers shouted the warning. Did you not hear it or the hooves?"

Her cheeks tinted again. "I was too distracted with trying to find the railroad tracks to notice."

His brows lifted. "You from out of town?" *Not that I would know or recognize half the folks in Las Vegas.* But, if he had ever seen her before, Wade would have remembered.

She nodded. "I was trying to find the Castañeda."

He pointed down the road. "That way. It's right by the railway that runs parallel with the mountains. We were bringing the herd from the station by an unexpected route. There was something blocking our original path. I can walk you to the hotel. Is that where you are staying?"

She shook her head as she fell into step with him.

She sure was quiet. But maybe she took after his new sister-in-law Corinna, who was quiet at first and slowly opened up as time passed. He caught her eyeing his horse. "You like horses?"

"Like?" She shook her head. "No, I live and breathe horses."

"Me too." He ran his hands down Lone Star's mane. "I'm a horse rancher and live up the mountains." Why was he offering so much information? He never did so. But this little bit of a woman had him stumbling over himself. Was he boring her? He clamped his mouth shut. He pointed to the massive brick building. "There it is. Have a good day, miss, and I'm glad you didn't get trampled."

CHAPTER 3

*J*ane Cady stared after the cowboy—still taken aback by the raw strength and power of the man. *So strong and yet so careful with me.* She straightened at that thought. *Good gracious. Left at the altar one moment and in a romance novel the next.* She giggled at her momentary flightiness. *Perhaps Meg was right—I'm not immune to all men after all. At least I'll have something to write to her about. Gladiolus moment indeed.*

Jane had thought herself incapable of such a reaction after Graham . . . and yet, Graham had never ignited such a feeling in her before. She pressed her hand to her stomach to still the long-forgotten butter-flies inside. She didn't know the cowboy. He could be a scoundrel, a rogue, or a ne'er-do-well. *But the way he looked at me with such kindness*—Her romantical side had caused nothing but trouble for her. No, from now on, logic was to be her guide. But she didn't turn her gaze as she watched her hero dis-appear around the corner.

With a sigh, she glanced up at the red brick Harvey House that was built in a Mis-sion Revival style. It was charming. Even with its two wings jutting forward on the north and south sides of the main building with a slate roof over adjoining arches that created a wraparound covered porch, it couldn't possess more than forty, maybe forty-five, rooms. But some of her favorite holidays had been at smaller, quaint hotels. Between the wings was a courtyard with a single live oak in the middle with a bench beneath it. It would be quite the cozy spot for her and Theo to read while they waited for Father to finish his shift. Just behind the courtyard, adjoining the north and south sides of the building, there rose a bell tower with a black sign with green trim. The sign's painted gold letters read, *Hotel Castañeda, 1898.* So it was not even a year old. At least her mother couldn't complain about Father's new place of work as being derelict, as well as a step down from their standing in society.

Through the windows of one wing, she spied the dining room with a crimson and white tile floor where women in black gowns and pristine white aprons bustled about with plates of food and steaming pots of tea and coffee. The linen covered tables gave the restaurant an air of refinement as well as the fine white china atop each table. Even from the porch, she could smell the rich food within, and it made her stomach awaken. *How much does a meal cost?* She worried her bottom lip. She never used to pause over such things, but she only had eleven dollars in her reticule. Her father had asked to borrow the hundreds she had set aside for her wedding trip . . . and she had seen no other way out but to allow him to borrow the funds. But, oh, the scent of smoked meats was enough to make her knees weak.

She glanced down at her basket. Why did her mother have to insist on this errand? The hotel had chefs brought in from Europe. Not only was it insulting to the staff but humiliating for Jane *and* her father as well. She sighed again. But Jane had promised Mother and promises must be kept. *I wish someone would have taught Graham that lesson.* She shook off the uncharitable thought, determining to put him out of her mind.

She checked her skirts, which were remarkably free from dust, save a single hoof smudge on her hem that had a slight tear. Hopefully, no one would notice. She rolled back her shoulders and strode through the doors of the hotel. A clerk behind a massive, ornately carved desk greeted her with a smile. "Good morning, miss. How can I help you?"

Now, *inside* the building, the smell of food made her stomach audibly growl. She hadn't eaten anything since yesterday on the train and that fare had left much to be desired. *Maybe I can order some food to bring back home to Mother and Theo.* "I am looking for my father. My mother wished for me to deliver this to him." She lifted the basket.

The clerk kept his smile steady—not understanding. "And *who* is your father, miss?"

"Oh," Her warm cheeks turned into an inferno. "My father is Benjamin Cady. He's the new House Manager."

"Ah, yes. Mr. Cady." His brows pinched, as if he were unhappy at the reminder. He motioned for her to follow him. "He's in the dining room, Miss Cady."

She followed the clerk into the large dining room with its wall of windows that boasted of a lovely view of the Gallinas foothills beyond. It would be a splendid view in spring when all the wildflowers bloomed, but even in the dead of winter, the view of the distant mountains sparked wonder. The clerk led her to a table in the corner where Father had a plate of steaming pasta before him and a plate of steak to the right of the first dish. *Two entrees?*

"Janey! Have a seat, my dear." He smacked around his mouthful of steak. "Mr. Perkins, will you see to it that my daughter is brought another setting?"

Mr. Perkins? Her eyes widened that the man she had assumed was the clerk was in fact the former House Manager. *He is still here?* Shouldn't Mr. Perkins have been gone by now to his new position at the prestigious Montezuma Harvey Resort? And here, Father was treating him like a footman. She offered him a polite smile as she took the seat Mr. Perkins held for her. "Thank you so much for your assistance, Mr. Perkins."

"Of course, miss. Would you like me to take your basket?"

She cradled it to her stomach. "Oh, no thank you. I need to hold on to it."

"Very well." Mr. Perkins snapped his fingers at a nearby Harvey Girl in a black uniform. "Miss Dolly, please see that Mr. Cady's daughter has a setting."

The waitress's pretty red hair was arranged in a bun with a white bow atop it and bore a little bronze badge with the number "1" engraved on it. Miss Dolly gave Jane a brilliant smile and whisked away to the back of the room. Within moments, the waitress returned with a stack of gleaming porcelain and silver, setting Jane's place efficiently and perfectly. "Good morning, Miss Cady. Would you prefer coffee or tea?" Miss Dolly folded her hands before her large white bib apron.

"Tea, please."

"What type do you prefer? We have green, black, white, and rooibos."

Jane's heart was racing too much to order her favorite black tea. It was best to choose a calming brew. "Green."

"Lovely choice. Our green tea today is Sencha Kyoto, a delicate tea composed of cherry blossoms that I find light-bodied, sweet, and refreshing." Miss Dolly turned the cup in the saucer so that the handle pointed a specific direction. "And for your order? Did you have a chance to look at the menu?"

Jane shook her head and looked to her father, but he was cutting into his steak with too much gusto to notice her. It had been a long time since they had a filling meal. Mother was too averse to train fare to allow them to purchase more than fruit. They finally stopped at the Topeka Harvey

House after all three of them attempted to persuade her and she had allowed it merely to keep Theo from complaining. *Do the Harvey Houses even have the same menus?* "Do you have any recommendations for a seafood entrée?"

"Oh yes, all our seafood is delivered fresh on the train in crates of ice to keep it at the height of quality. I particularly enjoy Shrimp à la Marquez. It has a nice heat to it and served with wild rice."

Jane's stomach growled, but in the din of the busy dining room, she hoped the waitress would not hear. "I'll have that, please."

Dolly nodded. "And for dessert, may I suggest Peach Alexandria?"

She had not intended on dessert, or even lunch, but her stomach rumbled again, so she merely nodded.

"We will *both* take that, thank you, Miss Dolly, as well as the chocolate cake," Father interjected. "I need to be well versed on what we serve here in order to better recommend it to travelers." He turned to Jane, effectively dismissing the waitress. "Why are you here, Janey?"

Jane smiled her thanks to the Harvey Girl, but Miss Dolly was already heading to the kitchen. Another girl poured her tea and was gone before Jane could thank her. She lifted the cup and inhaled the sweet beverage. By the color and scent alone, she knew it was perfectly brewed—not too strong as to muddle the taste, but not so weak as to taste like water. "I came because Mother insisted you have your last bit of cheese as her way of apologizing."

Father barked out a laugh, drawing attention. Her cheeks heated. Her father never was one to remain in the shadows wherever he went. How would he adjust to being a manager if he did not curb his boisterous self?

"I take it, she is feeling remorseful for her sharp words this morning." He scooped up the pasta, tasting it with rapid smackings of his tongue. "Marriage is about being quick to apologize. I shall send her some flowers back with you." He pointed to the vase of pretty blooms on their table. "Take those back with you."

Take the flowers from the table? "I couldn't.

Besides, Father, don't you think she would prefer a note?"

"And what do you know of marriage?" Father chortled. "Graham Bank jilted you. What is your plan now?"

She nearly choked on her tea and glanced about. Thankfully, no Harvey Girl was near enough to hear his words. "Why on earth would you ask me such an insensitive question?"

Father returned to his steak, nodding at the taste as he dipped another piece into the juices pooling beneath it as he chewed with an open mouth, little flecks of steak getting caught in his mustache.

"I'll be back in ten minutes with your dessert." Dolly placed the entrée before Jane.

"Thank you," Jane whispered, forcing back her tears of anger at her father's poor choice of words.

"Bring it now," Father commanded without even looking up from his plate.

Despite her anger, Jane's stomach was growling too much now to ignore her plate. She took a bite of shrimp and closed her eyes at the burst of flavor. It was fine enough to give Delmonico's competition.

"Because, you have spent your life preparing to wed a man. We have no money now, so how do you suggest you support yourself? My wages can hardly keep you in the style you have grown up with." Father pointed his silver fork at an open telegram on the table. "I received an interesting proposition this morning from my old associate, Hyde Austin. He was sorry to hear of your jilting but wished to offer for your hand."

"Mr. Austin, as in Graham Bank's best friend, wishes to wed me?" She shook her head. "But he doesn't even know me. We met once before his trip to Europe. Why would he—" Jane paused as Dolly deposited the desserts and whisked away.

"True, he was in Europe for the entirety of your courtship with Graham, but he returned home to attend the wedding. He found you enchanting and he was appalled by Graham's behavior, as we all were. Austin wishes to make amends for his friend's actions by marrying you himself."

Her brows rose as indignation filled her over the idea of a man merely picking her out of a crowd because he thought her enchanting and saying he would marry her. *But Mr. Austin was always kind and respectful. He wouldn't be so callous.* Suspicion rising, she narrowed her eyes at Father. "He said *all* of that in a telegram?"

Father shrugged. "I embellished a bit, but the sentiment is the same. So, I told him to come meet you."

"What?" She blinked. He did all that in the few hours he had been gone from their new home? "You asked him to come to Las Vegas? Without consulting me?"

"Why would I? You have prepared your whole life for *one* objective—to wed and wed well. One gentleman is as good as the next."

She suddenly wasn't hungry at all. She pushed away her plate. "I cannot even begin to explain how that makes me feel."

"I can tell you how I feel." He finished off his dessert and rested his hands on his stomach. "Relieved that this position is not forever. Granted, we will likely be here for a few months. This hotel will prove a boon with you taking over the cooking at home until you marry Mr. Austin and see us returned to our rightful place in high society."

She set her teacup in the saucer, gripping it so hard between her hands that the brew trembled within. "You should have asked me, Father."

Father returned to his pasta, picking out the oysters and popping them into his mouth. "You would have agreed . . . eventually."

She lifted her chin, biting back her answer as another Harvey Girl topped off her tea. "Thank you, miss." She forced her smile, though she imagined it was strained. She let it drop the moment they were alone. "Well, I won't do it."

"How else do you suggest you support yourself? And this family?" He pointed his fork at her. "I already said that I can't keep you in the fashion you are used to. I grew up working, but you, you were always kept a lady and don't know how to do anything but dance, ride your horse, and look fetching."

Because Mother refused to allow me to do anything else with my life while I waited to marry. "I-I don't know how I will support myself, but I won't rush into a marriage to suit you—not again."

His eyes flamed. "Ungratefulness does not suit you, Jane."

Hurt flared in her belly. She had done *everything* her father had asked her for years and this was how he saw her after *one* time of refusing to do his bidding? "That isn't fair, Father."

A scream from the back room brought Jane to her feet, clutching her lace jabot. Was the hotel under attack from outlaws?

Miss Dolly rushed out from what Jane guessed to be the back corner staff door, her cheeks pale. "Mr. Cady, one of the girls fell off a stool and snapped her ankle."

Mr. Cady shot to his feet, dropping his napkin on the table. "Did you send for the doctor?"

"One of the cooks, Monsieur Pierre, ran out the back door to fetch him." Miss Dolly twisted her hands. "This has never happened before. Oh, poor Jenny. She has been with us since we opened here and worked for the—"

"Yes, it is a shame. I am under the impression that we only have enough staff to cover the shifts, and no extras at this point, given one of the girls, a Miss Corinna Victoria, was dismissed from her position weeks ago and a replacement wasn't summoned?"

"No sir."

"Why didn't you replace her? You've had ample time." Father frowned.

"We had two new girls arrive before she was fired and I was hoping Corinna could return, but she married instead and—"

"So many words for a simple question." He pinched the bridge of his nose and sighed. "Will we have enough staff for the Christmas dance that Mr. Perkins informed me about this morning?"

Miss Dolly's expression hardened as she shook her head. "No, sir. We barely have enough as it is. I need permission to send for another girl in Topeka."

"Something that you should have done when Miss Corinna was first dismissed. But it will now take too much time to replace Miss Jenny." He threaded his thumbs in his vest pockets.

Miss Dolly cleared her throat. "I understand your frustration, sir. But we have a system in place. It won't take that—"

"The girl will not be here in time for Christmas." He turned to Jane with a measured smile that she did not like. "Jane here can be trained to take Miss Jenny's place."

"What?" Jane exclaimed in unison with Miss Dolly.

"Respect the dining room, daughter." Father lifted a friendly hand to guests and gave them a patronizing smile as he gently grasped Jane's elbow and tugged her behind the potted palm that seemed to separate the dining room from the Harvey Girls' workstation.

"Father, I am hardly equipped to become a waitress," she hissed. *What are you playing at?*

Father nodded. "Agreed, but maybe some hard work will soften your heart to the idea of Mr. Austin coming courting."

She stiffened as Miss Dolly joined them.

So, that's how he wishes to play this next round? Her father was skilled in the art of manipulation, but she was done. Done playing his game. He thought she was afraid? That she would fail? He seemed to forget that she had inherited a healthy dose of stubbornness from him. "Very well. I accept the position."

"This is highly unorthodox," Miss Dolly muttered. "We've only made an exception to the rule a handful of desperate times. It takes weeks and weeks for a girl to train properly, Mr. Cady. And with us not having enough staff, I'd have to train her myself and I am stretched as it is."

"And yet, Fred Harvey himself gave me this position of authority to make just such a suggestion. Trust me in my appointment of this young lady. Getting a girl from Topeka will take at least a couple of days. Jane is here. She will work hard and, as I am in charge of this establishment, what I say goes." He clasped his hands over his stomach. "And she is to sign a contract at once. It must all be legitimate. I believe there should be a few in my office?"

"Those are the reference contracts, but I

suppose those will be just as binding." Miss Dolly's gaze softened as she caught Jane twisting her hands. "Miss Cady? Do *you* want to be a Harvey Girl?"

She blinked. *Want?* No one had asked her what she had wanted in such a long time. Certainly, her family had showered her with gifts but never had her father or mother asked her what she wanted in life. She had thought she wanted a life with Graham, but the way he treated her had wounded her girlish thoughts of love. She wanted something true and real. Perhaps, this position could be the first step to building a life away from the manipulation of her father . . . even if he was the one manipulating her into accepting it. But she could earn a wage and maybe, just maybe, she could build a life away from her father's thumb without needing to marry. Her heart sped at the thought of escape. "Will I be living in the dormitory with the rest of the girls?"

Miss Dolly's eyes lit with surprise. "Of course. It is policy. But I'm certain we can work out for you to live with your family since they are in town."

Jane shook her head. "No. I would like to stay in the dormitory. I would love to become a Harvey Girl. When do I start?"

"You would?" Father uncrossed his arms, surprise coloring his tone.

Jane met his gaze. "Absolutely. It would be an adventure."

Father pursed his lips as if he wanted to say something but couldn't given Dolly's presence. "Good. Good. It's high time you make yourself useful. Let's head to my office and you can start training today."

"I need to let Mother know. She will worry if I don't return within a few minutes." She glanced at Miss Dolly. She didn't dare voice what Mother would think in front of the head waitress. "And I will need to make sure Phantom is taken care of."

Some of the spark in Father's eyes dimmed as if he had not considered his wife's reaction. He never did, and Mother would let him know it. "I'll see that Phantom has a stall in town. Contracts first. We must make it legal." He laid a gentle hand on her arm and guided her through the dining room threshold, toward the clerk's desk, and striding behind it, continued on to the hall, pausing at a door with a transom above it. In gold letters with black trim, it read, *Manager.* "Inside."

Miss Dolly followed them into the small room as she chewed on her lower lip.

He flung open the top drawer, riffled through it and, with a smile, retrieved a rather rumpled and coffee-stained stack of papers and tossed them on the desk in front of Jane.

Jane lifted the top page, her gaze roving over the points, pausing on the words *Marriage Clause.* Her lips parted as she read the rule stating that no Harvey Girl could marry during her contract. If a waitress did so, she would forfeit at least a month of pay. *No worries there. The man of my dreams is just that—a dream and never will be a reality.* She ran her finger down the third page where two lines were blank. She signed her name with a flourish and spun the papers around for Father.

He signed his name as well before folding the papers and handing them to Dolly. "Miss Dolly, have this mailed to the

Topeka office with a note of explanation, citing that it was my express orders."

"But, sir, I'm only the head waitress. Don't you think that you should write it, or at least, have the House Mother, Miss Trent, write it before she leaves on her trip—"

"There is no time. You write it and mail it at once. I will return with my daughter to fetch her things from home and will be back within the hour. Have a room at the dormitory assigned to Jane by then and inform Miss Trent of all that has occurred."

Jane followed her father out onto the street. As usual, he strode ahead of her, and she had to fairly trot to keep up with him. It was not in his nature to wait for anyone— no matter the consequences. Despite how it all came about, a zing of excitement coursed through her veins. For once in her life, she was about to have an adventure outside the stuffy parlor of her home—to do something beyond watching her life pass by behind the lace curtains of the drawing room as she waited for each house guest to come and go. Her mother hadn't even allowed her to take part of charity work for fear she would get sick. She had been trapped for years doing what she was told.

Jane supposed a large part of her disappointment in not being married was the fact that she wouldn't be able to control her days. A small smile bloomed. She was about to be free. She could have a life away from everyone's control. Certainly, she would be *working* for her father, but she doubted he would last long as manager. It wasn't grand enough for him and he was distracted easily by the next shimmering business idea. But she could stay at the Castañeda. Jane only had to prove herself. She would work until she dropped if that was what it took to break free from her father's household.

Father climbed the steps to the house where Mother sat on the rocker with her embroidery in hand, brooding already, her apology basket already faded from memory apparently. "Benjamin."

"My dear, I have something to tell you, and it won't be easy." Father gripped his bowler hat in his hands.

"After being ripped from my home, I doubt anything that you have to say will surprise me," Mother's words were clipped as she ceased rocking.

"Yes, well, this might." Father launched into explaining the contract Jane had signed. "She will start work as a Harvey Girl at once."

"Benjamin." Mother stabbed the red thread through the material, her voice dangerously even, "You asked me to move here, and I did, but I put my foot down when you ask for the use of my *daughter* as a waitress."

"My dear, you know we must economize," Father replied, coming to stand before her. "And the contract is signed. It is done. If she breaks contract now, she will owe a month of salary, which we cannot afford to pay. Her income will be a boon we cannot pass up."

Jane's jaw dropped. *So, he plans to garner my pay too?* She swallowed back her protest. She would have helped if he had asked anyway, but it would have been nice to be asked.

"So, you are not asking my permission then." Mother shoved to standing, dropping her work to the porch floor. "I should have known. I should have known you had some other motive for insisting she come. You always do. You said it would be good for Jane to get away from New York. She could have stayed with Meg. If she had only used a portion of the funds from the ring, she could have gone to Paris and Italy in the Spring with them and met a nice gentleman. And now, she is to be a waitress? Serving strangers? Unprotected?"

"It's a restaurant, not a tavern." Father rubbed his hand over his eyes. "And there are rules there to protect the ladies."

Mother's bottom lip trembled. "It might as well be a saloon. You are asking our daughter to serve! *Serve*, Benjamin." She waved her hand to Jane, her voice growing louder with every word. "Look at her. She is a lady. She is already working herself to death because you didn't want to spend a few dollars on a maid when you go around handing dollar tips to the hack driver be-cause you want to look rich again. And now, you expect her to earn a wage? To take care of herself?"

Jane glanced down at her broken nails

and resisted the urge to tuck them in her pockets. "We all knew we needed to help out, Mother. And this way, I will see to myself and won't have to take any funds from Father's paycheck. I can earn my own way." *And as for Father's intentions on taking some of my paycheck . . . well, that is a discussion for another day on how much he may take.*

"And she's not just a server. She is a Harvey Girl," Father countered, resting a hand on Mother's arm. "It's a very honorable role in the West."

Mother jerked away, as if scalded. "That's not how our friends will see it. You told me that you were moving us here to give us a chance."

"Mother," Jane grasped her hand. "I don't mind working. In fact, I am looking forward to the adventure." She met her father's gaze. It was obvious that Mother did not know of Austin's offer. If she did, she would no doubt have Jane on the next train out to Marriageville. "With my working there, it will be one less mouth to feed and Theodora can have her own room."

She blinked at Jane. "You mean, you would *live* at the Castañeda?"

"No, of course not." Father snorted.

"Well, thank goodness for small mercies," Mother muttered her favorite phrase of late, pinching the bridge of her nose.

"She will be staying behind it at the Rawlins dormitory."

Jane slapped her hands over her ears at Mother's shriek and ducked inside. Let her father deal with Mother's ire. She needed to gather the few things she had unpacked and begin her new life—like she should be doing with Graham. *No. No self-pity. Too long you have been relying on others for your future. My future begins now. The Lord is my father. With Him on my side, surely this will be a grand adventure worthy of Meg's hopes for me.*

CHAPTER 4

The wind swept through the mountain valley leading to the Sanctuary, the chill air promising snow soon. "'I'm glad you didn't get trampled?'" Wade muttered, shaking his head as he rode ahead of his six brothers and Tanner's herd of twenty Longhorn cattle that they were bringing to their ranch in the Gallinas Mountains. "Brilliant."

"Hey, Wade! Wait up," called his older, half-brother Tanner as he rode up alongside him on his Palomino, Silver. He lifted his Stetson off his blond curls and wiped his forehead with his sleeve. "The boys and I have been talking about you spending some time in town—away from the ranch."

Jackson's horse trotted up alongside Wade, and the sixth Sterling brother gave a conspiratorial grin. "Yeah, it's about time you stop being a hermit and live a little. Now that Tanner's new bride got that fancy lawyer of hers to have that wanted poster removed from your record, there's no need for you to live out in the mountains with just us for company. Corinna has given you a fresh start if you want to take it."

"And while I know we all love the mountain life, we only go into town once a month and we want you to experience Las Vegas," interjected Gray, the fourth Sterling brother.

"We *just* went to town." Wade pointed out. "And now, you want me to go back?"

"Going into town to fetch the cattle from the stockyard does not count," corrected Clint, the fifth Sterling brother. "We went to the stockyard by the station and had to take a small detour because of that overturned wagon on the bridge. That was *not* into town."

Gray leaned on his saddle horn and flicked the brim of his Stetson up, "We think that it is time for you to spread your wings a little bit, big brother."

"Y'all telling him about your plan?" Lawrence shouted from behind. The third Sterling brother kicked his horse to catch up with the pack.

"You all have discussed a plan about me?" Wade snorted. They usually reserved this type of ambush for Tanner.

"Your head was in the clouds. It was easy," Noah, the youngest of the brothers, winked at him. "Probably thinking of that pretty lady you rescued that you refuse to talk about. Experience tells me that the more tight-lipped a brother is over a potential lady friend, the more she is on your mind."

The men chortled as Lawrence halted his horse in the circle of brothers.

"Oh, we have a plan alright." Lawrence grinned as sleet enveloped the group, his breaths turning visible. "I'm planning on going back down the mountain as soon as we return these horses to get you set up."

"Set up? What are you on about?" Wade flipped the collar of his long coat up to block the sleet and reached for his canteen and drained it. He draped the sling over his saddle horn and tugged the top of his leather gloves under the cuff of his coat. "We need to get moving before it gets bad out here. This sleet could turn into a snow storm in a matter of minutes."

"I'm returning to town in the morning because I've got a bounty to hunt, but also to pass on a message to a friend—would you stop fidgeting and just listen? My knee doesn't think it will turn into a blizzard, so calm down." Lawrence frowned. "My friend Mr. Hill owns the stable in town. Well, he hurt his hand while shoeing a horse. He hurt it pretty bad, and he asked me if I knew anybody who would be interested in the job. I told him about you. He knows it's a big ask, considering our ranch is so far from town. I told him I'd ask you."

"I can't—I have my broodmares."

"Which is why I brought in the brothers to my idea before mentioning anything to you," Lawrence patted his horse's withers.

"We all know that they have at least six to eight months before foaling," Tanner continued as he, too, pulled up the collar of his coat as the sleet turned heavier. "So, this is one of the only times you can get away from the ranch for a long period of time and actually enjoy town life. Think about it," Tanner grinned. "You can attend church for the first time in years. You could go to the Harvey House and have chocolate cake freshly served to you that isn't crumbled because we brought it to you on the back of a horse to the edge of town where you were waiting for us for fear of getting caught by the law."

"You can make friends that aren't your brothers," Jackson added.

"You could maybe even court a lady," Noah snorted.

Wade rolled his eyes at them, even though the idea was tempting. "You know I can't up and leave my herd."

"Don't you know us at all?" Noah slapped his hat on his thigh, water droplets splattering from the brim. He mopped the sleet from his face with his questionably clean handkerchief and tugged his hat back into place. "We may all have our different interests, but we can ride and care for horses better than most."

"We will treat them as our own," Gray added. "We know it's hard work, but we feel like we owe you this."

"Because goodness knows that you've given us enough of your horses over the years," Clint interjected, motioning to every man's steed.

Tanner nodded, "If you would have sold us the horses, you would have made a lot of money."

Noah grinned. "And after six months of seeing to your horses' every need, I think that would clear the debt right up."

"We are brothers and don't have debts between us. This is a ranch, and we all do our parts," Wade argued even though the idea of spending time in town sounded awful nice . . . . If he got there soon enough, maybe the pretty girl he rescued might still be there. But he pushed that aside. His brothers were being too selfless. "I may have provided your horses, but that's because my dream has always been to be a horse rancher and that could not have happened without you all. Gray, you are the hunter, you always make sure that we have meat on the table. Clint, you cook it up, and Jackson and Noah, you do all the chores most don't want to do. Tanner, you went out and hunted bounties for years and years to see that the roof stayed over our heads and gave me my start with horses before deciding to raise cattle. Lawrence, you're following in his footsteps and you're setting aside funds for Noah to go to law school. I'd say we are even already."

"I'm only accepting Lawrence's loan because I'm paying him back every penny someday," Noah interjected. "Because, while we are brothers, we don't seek to take advantage of one another."

Tanner slapped Wade on the shoulder. "What we are trying to say is that we *want* you to take this time to get to know yourself away from us. If you can't accept it as a debt owed, then consider it a gift. And hopefully, maybe you will take your time to court a pretty Harvey Girl, or a town girl. But I have to say I think the Harvey Girls might be a better bet, given that the town girls wanna stay in town, and you'll have to come back up to the mountains for your horse ranch. A Harvey Girl may be more open to the idea of living up in the mountains. They're used to hard work and all that."

"Says the completely non-biased man who recently married a former Harvey Girl," snorted Jackson.

"So, you want me to go and take the job as the farrier . . . to work at the town stable?" The months away began to bloom in his imagination. He would miss his brothers, but he could go where he wanted about town. He could attend church and learn from the pastor. *I could meet my future wife.* He swallowed back the sudden lump in his throat at all they were offering him. It sounded—well, it sounded freeing.

"Yeah, you can earn enough money to add to your savings to buy you a new stallion and a couple new broodmares for your herd. You can really increase your business that way. Plus, there is the race on Boxing Day that you always wanted to ride in, but never could," Tanner added. "It's a large purse this year that, if you win, can buy you a horse, and will get the word out about your quality steeds. It's a win-win."

"Why are you trying to get rid of me?" Wade narrowed his eyes at his brothers.

"We're not!" Jackson shouted.

"Man alive, you have a hard time listening." Tanner gritted his teeth. "You are six and twenty years old. We *know* you are lonely. I know you have a dream of your own little family. How are you going to get a family if you don't find yourself a nice girl, settle down, and start building one? We'd love it if you would build your family on the ranch, but you have to decide that for yourself. We are giving you time to go court. Use it."

Tanner did have a point. "Very well, but I'm gonna need some time to set up my horses before I leave."

Tanner nodded. "All right."

Lawrence whooped. "On my way past Las Vegas, I'll tell the stable owner that you will be there in two weeks to take over his stables."

And maybe, just maybe, Wade could find that beauty in turquoise again.

CHAPTER 5

*J*ane wriggled into her new black
uniform, sweat already beading
on her forehead as she worked
the buttons at the back of her gown. If she
kept her arms at an impossible angle behind
her back, she could manage the middle buttons. *How do people do this without a maid?*
She had slept, or at least attempted to sleep,
in her corset to avoid having to lace herself
up without help, and there was no way she
was going to ask her roommate, Pernilla
Margot, for help as she had yet to meet the
Harvey Girl.

When she arrived yesterday, it had been
a whirlwind of meeting the staff, but as

Pernilla had the day off, Jane had only heard tales of the dark-haired beauty's temper. While the rest of the girls might accept her, as Mr. Perkins' niece, Jane feared what Pernilla would have to say upon meeting her. Dolly had discreetly warned her that by getting this job in such an unusual way, Jane was on thin ice with the girls. Jane had to prove that she was willing and able to work hard, and today, she would do just that.

Jane twisted her brown curls into a simple, low coiffure and tied a white bow around the bun as she peeked out of the lace curtains to the street below. With a fresh blanket of snow, the ground glowed in the waning moonlight, offering her soul a sense of peace. She had always loved New York after the first snowfall. Everything was quieter and seemed full of possibilities.

She glanced at her ladies' watch pin. She had thirty minutes until her half past five o'clock shift started, and Miss Dolly had warned her that breakfast would only be available until six o'clock sharp for the entire staff. Sinking onto the bed, she tugged on her most sensible black half boots with the shortest heel she possessed, and tiptoed out of the room, closing the door softly behind her. She hurried down the hall, and out the Rawlins front door, and out across the street to the hotel.

She hugged her arms to her chest as the freezing air stung her exposed cheeks and hands. It seemed silly to shrug on a coat to only dash across the street, but with the fresh powder crunching beneath her boots, she was beginning to rethink her decision. She trotted for the kitchen entrance of the hotel and nearly slipped on the wooden steps. She pushed open the door and was immediately greeted with a burst of warmth and the clang of pots and pans as the kitchen staff were already at work. The smell of freshly brewing coffee and pastries from the hotel's attached bakery enveloped her. She stood beside a coat rack that held several outer garments already.

Miss Dolly hadn't shown her where to go yet, only that she was to report to the kitchen. The staff were all too busy preparing the meals for the day to pay her any mind, the chef shouting out orders in

French, which a man clumsily translated. Seeing that the sous chef was about to add a tablespoon instead of the chef's requested teaspoon of salt to a pot, she hurried across to the man with the spoon. "Excuse me, but the chef said a *teaspoon*, not a tablespoon, sir."

He stared blankly at her, blinking. The head chef turned and gasped at the heaping spoonful about to go into the pot and exclaimed a French word that made her ears burn.

"*Non! Non.*" He ripped the salt away from the pot, spilling the grains upon the floor. He measured it himself and stirred it in. Turning to her, he asked, "*Parlez-vous français?*"

"*Oui.*" She continued to tell him in French that she had been fluent since she was a child.

His expression melted in relief as he smiled at her, mopping his beading forehead with a mottled rag. "Thank goodness, perhaps you can tell him that he over salts *every* dish in this restaurant, as well. I've been trying to tell him, but it is too difficult.

I have only been in this country for a month, and the language barrier is making my food less than perfect."

She conveyed the message with an apologetic smile.

The sous chef's face puffed, his thin mustache making him appear like a boiled lobster. "Well, you can tell him that I've been doing just fine without him since this hotel opened! It's not my fault that I've been oversalting—I've known it but thought that was what he was asking."

"I'm only the messenger, sir, excuse me." Jane nodded to the chefs and hurried to what she assumed would be the servant's hall, nearly sighing with relief at the long table with a breakfast banquet in the center. Six Harvey Girls sat about the long table, some chatting with gentlemen in white uniforms that she guessed were the kitchen staff. She filled her coffee cup and plate, sinking into a seat at the end of the table, observing the conversations flying across the table. Some girls offered her a smile, but others outright scowled at her.

A fair-haired girl joined Jane and smiled.

"Good morning, I'm Vera Ward. You must be the new House Manager's daughter."

"Yes." Jane dabbed the napkin at the corner of her lips, trying to hide the excessive bite she had just taken. "Please, call me Jane."

"Welcome, Jane," Vera kept her voice low. "I must warn you that your roommate has quite the temper and is the niece of the former manager. When she returned from her day off last night after you retired, she was beyond put out with the whole affair and is determined to see you fired if possible." She shivered. "I would not want to get on Pernilla's bad side. That girl is angling for the position of head waitress, and if she somehow achieves it . . ."

"Thank you for the warning." Jane finished her pastry and downed her cup quickly, unsure exactly when Miss Dolly would appear, but she needed this job to work. "I don't intend on giving her a reason to see me fired."

Another girl that Jane had met yesterday joined her side. "Good morning! If you don't remember my name, I'm Jean

May." The brown-haired beauty gave Jane a welcoming smile. "You should try this pastry. It is the best the bakery has." Jean May selected a strawberry tartlet. "The baker makes them especially for us as he knows how fond we are of them, but if you don't claim one quickly, they go in a snap."

"Thank you, Jean May," Jane offered her a smile as she accepted her second pastry and Miss Dolly strode into the room.

"Good morning." Dolly glanced down the table and met Jane's gaze and nodded. "I see you all have been ignoring our latest recruit, except Vera and Jean May. I expected better from you all. We Harvey Girls aren't only supposed to be welcoming to our guests but to each other."

The girls frowned, but all followed Dolly's command and uttered their greetings. Vera squeezed Jane's hand under the table as a dark-haired Harvey Girl appeared in the doorway.

Jane's heart pounded at the familiar color. "Is that—?"

"Pernilla. Better eat quickly before your

appetite is spoiled by Pernilla," Jean May whispered.

Jane stifled a giggle and took a bite of the tartlet, nearly sighing at the perfect balance of flavor. She finished it in three large bites that would have sent her mother into a fainting spell.

"Pernilla. Why, I thought you would have slept until noon after your night shift," Jean May smiled to her, motioning her to the empty seat across from theirs.

Pernilla scowled at Jane. "I would have, but someone was quite loud while getting dressed and I couldn't fall back asleep because I was hungry."

Jane's cheeks heated. "I am so sorry. I tried, but—" She halted her explanation that she had never dressed without a maid or her mother's assistance before. How weak would that make her seem? She was a Harvey Girl now and needed to show that she was strong and independent. "It won't happen again."

"Good." Pernilla sank into the chair across from Jane and reached for the last tartlet and the coffee pot. "So, you decided to become a Harvey Girl. We must be quite the adventure to the little fallen heiress."

Jane blinked. Certainly, people had danced around their loss of fortune, but no one had dared speak with such bluntness to her before. "Yes, it is an adventure, but one that I hope to learn well throughout the coming years."

"Years?" Pernilla scoffed. "I doubt you will last a single week as a Harvey Girl, given you haven't had a lick of training. Our systems are not for the faint of heart and if you happen to wear the last place badge number for two weeks, you will be fired. Just because you are the new House Manager's daughter, you will not be given any special privileges. Goodness knows that I was not granted such as the niece of Mr. Perkins."

"Oh please, you openly defied Dolly about Corinna and saw Corinna get fired by going over her head to Mr. Perkins." Jean May muttered into her cup of coffee, "Special treatments indeed."

Pernilla pursed her lips. "Well, someone had to follow the rules around here. The

Castañeda is a prestigious hotel. Only the best of the best waitresses are placed here and yet, Jane Cady is allowed to work without *any* experience."

Dolly rose from her place at the head of the table. "That is quite enough, Pernilla. Yes, Jane is not trained in our ways, but as the new House Manager declared her fit, we must abide by his decision as he is a personal friend of Fred Harvey. There is to be no more questioning about her abilities. I will train Jane myself." She lifted her finger to Jane, beckoning her. "Jane, if you are finished, we need to begin right away. There is much for you to learn."

CHAPTER 6

*W*ade halted his horse at the edge of town and dismounted. It had been two weeks since he had seen the lady in turquoise. He had been so focused on getting her to safety that he hadn't even taken in the sights of Las Vegas. Everything was so much bigger than he remembered. Of course, the last time he'd passed through town had been over a decade ago. Shouts filled the street, and he whipped around to see what the chaos was. Someone was haggling over the price of a calf in the train's stockyard. Next to them was a pile of furs. *Guess someone came down from the mountain to trade.*

Wade rested his hand on his mare's neck, Raven, grounding himself before he took the first step of his new life into the town of Las Vegas, New Mexico. Freedom smelled different than he thought. It smelled a lot like manure, but that might just be the train's stockyard and unwashed people. But even the stench could not dull the joy of his first trip *alone* into town thanks to his new sister-in-law's lawyer who had finally gotten Wade his freedom after years of hiding in the Gallinas Mountains.

It was up to Wade now where he went, what he saw, and what he did, which was why he relented to his six brothers' encouragement to stay in town for a handful of months while his broodmares awaited their foals. He was a mite nervous about taking a job, but as Wade knew everything about horses, including farriering, it was a fitting position for him, and he'd adjust while he saved enough to increase his herd.

Tanner had done his best when he came into town to trade on Wade's behalf and get the right horse, but it really was nothing like seeing the animal for yourself—running your hand over its flanks and withers and checking its teeth—before purchasing a horse that would become the mother or father of a new generation. A new stallion for Raven was his primary aim for the trip.

She was the fastest horse he had bred yet, which was why he did not plan on selling her. She would be a wonderful broodmare in a few years. It was hard to leave Lone Star up on the ranch, but, he needed to test Raven against the stock of Las Vegas at the Boxing Day Race, something he had been wanting to do for years with his other horses but hadn't dared to enter given the wanted poster with his face on it.

He eyed the Harvey House on the other side of the track. First, he needed to check in at the stable and then he'd get some food. He directed Raven down the main road to the stables, a large wooden building painted a deep green. It boasted of a paddock and a lean-to that served as the farrier workshop, judging from the anvil, fire, and iron horseshoes lining the walls.

He dismounted and led his horse inside.

He squinted as his eyes adjusted to the cool, dark building. "Hello? Mr. Hill?"

"Wade Sterling?" A man poked his head out of the tack room. "Good to see you." He lifted his bandaged hand. "I really appreciate you helping me out of this fix. I've been working with horses for thirty years and always dreamed of running a stable, and I finally convinced the widow Kane to sell me this place when her son, the former sheriff, was put in jail and her daughter-in-law moved to New Orleans with the baby. And then, I look away for one second while dealing with a young stallion and the fool thing steps on my hand." He scoffed. "I tell you, I never felt so idiotic. At least my wife ain't put out about my taking off work to heal. She is using this as an excuse to drag me up the road to the Montezuma for a holiday while I heal and you take over the shop."

"Happy I could help." Wade removed his hat and surveyed the high tin roof. "Great stable you have here."

"Well, let me show you around the place, but from what your brother Lawrence says, you won't have no trouble with the horses because you are some sort of horse whisperer."

Wade grinned. "I don't know about that, but I love them."

"Well, then hopefully they love you back and don't go stompin' on your hand too." Mr. Hill waved Wade on through the stable. The stalls were hewn from rough cut cedar and were slightly faded but appeared sturdy. "We've got fourteen stables in all and with boarding and the coming and going of clients, I converted the small room that was originally here into a tack room because I thought why would I need a room when I got a nice warm bed nearby?" He released a short laugh. "And now that I need a hired hand, I see the wisdom in having a bunk here." He gritted his teeth. "I know I can't offer you a place to stay on site, and it's inconvenient, but your pay includes a room at the Castañeda. I have a deal with Fred Harvey where I keep a few stalls on retainer for any of his guests. Because of our deal, the manager gave me a steep discount on your room. It will be the smallest in the hotel, but it will be a sight more comfortable than sleeping on a cot in the tack room without any facilities at hand. And as for my home, well, I've got four grown daughters that won't be joining my wife and I at the Montezuma, so it's the hotel for you. Can't cover the board though. They've got great meals. Real affordable for you." Mr. Hill ran his good hand over the back of his neck. "I wish I could do more than pay for your stay and the wage, but—"

"It's a fair wage and I can save for another horse." Wade assured Mr. Hill. "It won't take me long to get settled." Wade slapped his saddle bags from his horse's back. He didn't have much in the world beside a few extra pieces of clothing, his worn Bible, and book of poems that Corinna had gifted him. "I can be back in an hour or so after I drop this in my new room at the hotel and have a meal."

Mr. Hill breathed a sigh of relief. "Thank you. You have no idea how hard it is to find good help these days." He nodded to the horse. "You go on now and take your time getting a good meal and take a look about town. There's a sweet shop that just opened a few blocks down the street. It's the opposite way of the hotel, but the owner makes the best pralines. I'll see to your horse and when you get back, I'll be handing over the keys to my hay-filled kingdom to you."

"Thank you kindly." Wade tossed his saddle bags over his shoulder and went to find this sweet shop. Nothing marked a new beginning quite as well as a tasty treat.

It wasn't far from the stables and before he even pushed open the door, the scent of vanilla, sugar, and chocolate greeted him, sending his stomach to rumbling. *Freedom is sweet indeed.* He grinned as the elderly lady behind the counter called her welcome.

Feeling renewed by the samples the proprietor gave him and his small box filled with pralines, fudge, and some cookies, Wade strode down the street to the Castañeda.

He pushed open the door and swept off his Stetson. His hair clung in a ring about his head, and he held his hat to his chest, taking in the handsome lobby with its ornate carvings and large fireplace mantel. He would get to stay in this fine establishment? As a boy, he had only seen one such fine hotel in New York with marble floors and gold leaf moldings. He had been selling his ma's tatted lace trim, and it had taken all of one minute for him to be tossed back out into the streets. He nodded to the clerk behind the desk and approached. "Looking for a room."

The clerk gave him a tightlipped smile. "Yes, sir. For how long?"

How long? Well, until the man's hand healed from being stepped on by that horse. Could be three months, or more. But he had to get up the mountain in six months. Would they make him pay up front for such a sum? Mr. Hill said he had taken care of it. "I believe Mr. Hill has booked a room on my behalf. The name's Wade Sterling."

His eyes widened with recognition as he hurried around the desk. "Ah, yes! Our long-term guest. Mr. Sterling, may I take your bags up to your room for you?"

Wade lifted the saddlebag strap with one finger, grinning. "I believe I can handle it."

"Traveling light." The clerk nodded and

moved behind the desk to lift a key from the row of keys behind him from a hook marked *27.* "You will be on the second floor with a view of the tracks. The bathrooms are shared on each floor. You will have to sign up for your bathing night on the sheet by the door."

A sign-up sheet for bathing? He bathed after he delivered the herd up the mountain. But, with being in town, he'd finally be able to attend church and for that, he didn't want to be smelling like the stalls. Hopefully, Saturday night would be free. "Okay."

The clerk showed him up the stairs, opened the door, and handed him the key. "Have a good stay and if there is anything I can help you with, do not hesitate to ask. The dining room is open at all hours."

"Good. Might go grab me a bite before work."

The clerk motioned to the far corner of the room. "There is fresh water in the basin for washing up. If you do not have a jacket for dining, there is a coat room with guest jackets provided."

Washing up. He glanced at his fingernails with dirt caked under them. He must be a sight. His neck reddened. "Thanks." He nodded, but the clerk had already disappeared out the door.

Wade turned on his boot. The white room was plain, but clean, and everything was of the highest quality. He tested the comforter with his fingertips. He would have trouble falling asleep on that fluffy bed.

He set his saddlebags on the single chair beside the bed and crossed the room, pouring water from the fancy pitcher into the porcelain bowl with painted flowers on the rim and scrubbed his face and neck. Changing into a fresh shirt and slipping into the jacket that Tanner had insisted he bring, Wade raked his fingers through his hair. He glanced out the window to the tracks below and suppressed a shudder at the sight. Lord willing, he would never have to get on a train again. *But today is not the day for dark thoughts.*

To celebrate his newfound freedom, Wade figured he'd get himself a nice piece of chocolate cake from the Harvey House.

He had never had it straight from the dining room. The boys had always brought him back a slightly crushed cake at the edge of town where Wade camped, not daring to show his face in town in case anyone recognized him.

Trotting down the stairs, he passed the clerk's desk and stood at the threshold of the dining room, hat in hand, but at the sight of the ladies buzzing to and fro between tables, he almost spun around on his boot heel right there—save for the promise of that chocolate cake. Was the dessert worth talking to a bunch of women? His brothers would laugh at him for being too nervous to get himself something tasty after living on his younger brother's cooking for over a decade. Wade could ride a bucking bronco, chase a herd of wild horses down the side of a mountain without batting an eye, and take on a bobcat with nothing but a hunting knife. He could face a roomful of pretty women. This was what he'd been waiting for—for the freedom to live. Wade strode forward.

"Good day, sir."

His jaw dropped at the pretty, petite lady before him dressed all in black with her chocolate curls pinned into a bun, her light blue eyes capturing his. "It's you!"

Her full lips blossomed into a becoming smile. "Why, if it isn't my hero. I'm happy to see you returned from the cattle drive."

So, the lady he had rescued wasn't just passing through town, but working in the very hotel he'd be staying?

Her lips were moving.

He jerked back to the present as her lips formed a perfect 'o' as if she were waiting— "Pardon me. What's the question?"

Her smile widened, making her even more blindingly radiant than two seconds before. No wonder Tanner had gotten himself a Harvey Girl for a bride. A beautiful, single woman in a Harvey uniform was just plain bewitching.

"I asked if you would like to sit at the table or lunch counter, sir." She motioned to the counter behind the sea of tables.

He ran his fingers around the circumference of his Stetson. "Where are you working?"

Her cheeks turned a pretty pink, and she nodded toward a cluster of tables in the corner. "I have a free spot or two."

"I'll take that one by the window. And a cup of coffee to boot."

"Perfect." She led him over to the table. "I'll be right back with your coffee, sir. There is a menu beside your plate, unless you already know what you would like?"

Your name to start. He took a seat. He was hungry. His gaze fell on the menu. "I haven't eaten inside this restaurant before."

"There's a lot to choose from, isn't there? I just started working here, but I would recommend the special. It's delightful."

"Well then, I'll order two."

"Two of the same, sir?" She blinked, clearly confused.

So was he, apparently. He couldn't rightly ask her to sit with him when she was working—that was inane.

"Is someone joining you?"

"Don't really know anyone in town to join me," he shrugged.

"You must be quite hungry then," she returned with a smile.

He nodded, hoping to cover his blunder. He couldn't say he was teasing as it wasn't a good joke, and she would think him ridiculous. No. He was committed now. He would eat until his belly burst. And then he would get his chocolate cake to boot. "Yes, with a goodly amount of coffee, and after my meals, I want some chocolate cake, please."

"Of course, sir." She whisked away the tall glass cup from his setting. "I'll get your coffee and place your orders."

He tried to keep his gaze from following her back to the kitchen, but he couldn't help but stare at her pretty hair. It fairly glistened in the afternoon light bursting through the window and made it appear more auburn than chocolate. Her cheeks were as pretty as pink apples and her skin creamy like she hadn't spent a whole lot of time outdoors. Of course, he hadn't been around many women besides his sister-in-law, but if he could hazard a guess, he'd say this lady was as close to perfection as one could get. *Get a hold of yourself, you moonsick cowpoke.*

He cast his gaze about the room,

watching the other ladies work as families dined. How nice would it be to dine with one's family in such a hotel as this? He had never dared to hope that a family would ever be in his future before Corinna had his name cleared from horse thieving—even now, he doubted a woman would want any man with a past like his for a husband. There were too many marks against him. His gut twinged. His marks had been wiped clean by the law and, more importantly, by the Lord Himself.

I sought the Lord, and He heard me, and delivered me from all my fears, the Psalm that he had long taken comfort in, whispered in his heart. It would take some time, but one day, he hoped he could trust that his future was no longer threatened by the law. The Lord had been kind to him and had seen him through tough times.

The lady brought a coffee pot and poured him a cup, smiling sweetly. "Your meal should be ready in a few minutes."

"Thank you." He tried to think of something intelligent to say to keep her longer and perhaps have a name. He scrambled for a topic, anything that wouldn't have her sweeping away. "Uh, nice floors."

Her smile froze in place. "Pardon me?"

"I said, you have nice floors here in the Castañeda Hotel." What was he talking about? Why would he bring up *flooring* in front of an angel? "They would make for good dancing." *Saved it.* "My brother mentioned y'all had a carnival recently to raise money for building a new children's home. And then he also told me about an upcoming dance. As a *single* and newly arrived-to-town fella, it sounds like a good time to get to know the people of Las Vegas." *Full circle and a full sentence.*

"Oh! Yes, in fact, there is a dance that will be hosted here tomorrow on Christmas Eve."

Get her name. Get her name and ask for a dance. "Well then, I will be here." *No, really? You are staying upstairs.*

She smiled and glanced up at the threshold of the dining room. Her cheeks lost all color as her gaze froze on someone. "Oh no."

"Miss?" He rose and grasped her elbow

as she seemed to wobble. She grasped both his arms, swaying. "Miss, are you unwell?"

Her head lolled back and he wrapped his arms about her, keeping her upright. "Miss?" He followed where her gaze had been to find two dandies at the door.

She moaned in his arms as she blinked up at him through her thick lashes before glancing toward the threshold. The Harvey Girl's cheeks went from pale to bright red. She turned to him, eyes wide and wild. "Forgive me."

In a single motion, she threw her arms about Wade's neck and drew him into a kiss that gave him no other option than to splay his hands at her back to balance them as she pressed herself into him, deepening the kiss. There was only him and the woman of his dreams kissing him like the world was ending, her lips parting and moving with his in a fashion that made the dining room fade into nothing.

CHAPTER 7

*H*er world was imploding. What was she doing? Kissing a stranger? Who seemed to be kissing her back now? *And his lips are so soft and full and* —And what was she doing *still* kissing him? She broke it off with a gasp, her cheeks flooding with pure shame. She twisted about and, to her relief, by some miracle, there were no other Harvey Girls present. "I-I am so sorry," she whispered. "I can't believe I did that. I-I—"

Heavy footsteps approached.

His hands stayed at her back, as if he were afraid that she would faint again if he released her. "Why—"

She grasped the man's hand and, keeping her head down, for she didn't dare glance about the room, she darted with him around two tables and through dining room doors that were now vacant. She didn't dare glance to see where Graham Bank and Hyde Austin had gone, but she was certain they would be following shortly. She pulled the cowboy through the lobby to outside to pause under the live oak tree, drawing hungry breaths in a desperate attempt to keep another fainting spell at bay. "What is your name?" She dropped her hold on him and pressed her hands to her scalding cheeks.

"Wade Sterling," he replied, his brows furrowing with obvious confusion over her actions. "And yours?"

"Jane Cady. Please forgive me for what I am about to do."

He chuckled, a slow smile spreading as he crossed his arms and leaned against the rough bark of the tree, all tan and oh so manly. "Why? You going to kiss me again?"

"Maybe." She glanced over her shoulder. "Please, play along?"

His gaze flicked up to Graham and Mr. Austin over her shoulder, his lips pressing into a firm line, as if he sensed that she was terrified of what was about to happen. "They are the ones you're so worked up about? They both are madder than a dog that had its bone taken by its littermate."

"They think that we are seeing one another," she whispered.

"Ah, which they deduced on the fact that you kissed me in the dining room," he stated.

"Yes," Jane admitted, twisting her hands as she craned her neck to look up at him. *Goodness he is broad as an oak.* She glanced over her shoulder at the approaching gentlemen. What would it be like to have such a cowboy as her protector for real? "I know that was extremely inappropriate to kiss you without your permission, even if we were courting, so I apologize once again most profusely. What woman goes around kissing a man she barely knows?"

"Normally, I'd agree with you, but—"

Her heart pounded. "But?"

He grinned down at her. "But, if it's you doing the kissing, I don't mind."

She released her breath. "Then you aren't outraged that I kissed you in my panic?"

He chuckled. "I consider it an honor to come to your aid."

"Thank goodness." She plastered her hands to her cheeks again. "But if Graham knows that I was pretending, he will think me even more pathetic than I truly am."

"No one could ever think that of a lady like yourself."

She snorted. "As a woman who was *jilted* for having her fortune stolen away and lost by her very own father, I think I can fall even farther in Graham's eyes if he thinks this is a farce."

He grabbed her hand in his. "If it makes a difference to you, I don't mind playing along for a few minutes that we are courting."

"Really?" she asked, her voice tinged with hope. "It would truly make a difference. I will pay you back somehow," Jane promised, worrying her bottom lip. *How though?* "Free pie! For a year."

"Not that I need to be enticed to help you and I do love pie, but won't that free pie come out of your pocket money?" He questioned, reaching for her hand as if he really were her beau.

She shrugged. "Well, yes, but I owe you."

"No way. Besides, I don't mind helping you out." He grinned.

Jane dipped her head. "It is a terrible thing to deceive people though."

His gentle touch under her chin brought her gaze up to meet his. "It's a terrible thing to treat others differently just because of a change of fortune that wasn't even your fault. You are poor now, but that doesn't change who *you* are."

She looked up at him. "Not many would dare to say such things to my face."

"I'd rather say the truth to your face, than lie to it. But I don't mind letting them think what they will if it is to help you." He winked.

"Thank you, Wade," she replied softly.

Graham approached them, a toothy grin

in place. "Jane Cady. Imagine finding you here."

At his voice, Jane spun and nearly dropped her hold on Wade at the sight of Graham and Hyde Austin each bearing a bouquet of red roses as thunder rolled. Where did they get the roses? Had they stashed them behind the desk? "G-Graham," she stuttered, suddenly feeling absolutely frigid. "What are you doing here?"

"I could ask you the same question." He removed his top hat, taking a step toward her, but paused as if unsure of what to say. "You're looking, uh," his gaze rolled over her attire, "healthy."

Healthy? Jane ran her free hand over her pristine apron. Certainly, she was not dressed as a fine lady, but had her looks been affected by her long hours of working? "Thank you?"

"It's good to see you. I have to admit it was quite a surprise to see that the rumors were true of your father working here. But I had no idea that you were working as a waitress as well." Graham glanced at his friend, who was still glaring at Wade.

"Why are you here, Graham?" Jane shifted to grasp Wade's arm, fairly clinging to him. He rested his hand atop hers on his arm, warming her heart at his action—even if it was for show.

Graham's brows rose in surprise. "Because your father trusted me with a share in his company as a dowry for you and I wished to return the paperwork in person." Graham lifted his palm, "And before you get your hopes up, no, it isn't worth anything and it isn't why we are here."

"He's here with that paperwork as an excuse to follow me out West when I told him that I was coming to see you," interjected Mr. Austin.

"Oh." Jane pushed aside the girlish fantasy that Graham had come for her despite everything. She was embarrassed that he brought such feelings out of her. After all that he had done to her. *Why does this man affect me so? Why do I continue to allow him to bring out this side of me?* She had learned the hard way not to trust a man who only wanted her for her fortune and good looks. Her gaze landed on Wade, even though they were only pretending to be together, this man seemed to care more about her feelings in their brief moments of conversation than Graham had in their entire time courting. She was glad she kissed Wade, especially since Graham witnessed it. Maybe Graham would learn that his actions had consequences—such as having his former fiancée move on with her life.

Wade's fingers curled around hers for a brief squeeze before he released her and reached out a hand. "I don't believe we have met properly."

"I'd say so," Graham lifted his nose, ignoring Wade's offered hand.

Wade shrugged and turned his hand toward Mr. Austin, who shook it. "I'm Wade Sterling."

"How dare you kiss Miss Cady in the dining room and then run out like some sort of coward?" Graham sneered. "What kind of man kisses a woman who means nothing to him? I'll tell you what kind."

Jane stiffened. Graham had taken a few kisses during their courtship, her *first-kiss* kisses, and those were seared upon her heart. As much as she wished to get rid of that memory, she had considered Graham her first love. Those memories of first love hung on a good bit it seemed, despite her best efforts. She could only hope that one day those whimsical feelings for him would not even be a memory altogether. *What I would give to take those kisses back that I had given to Graham. He didn't deserve them, and my kisses certainly don't belong to him anymore.* "That's not what happened," she corrected Graham, her cheeks already burning.

"And around here, one doesn't throw around the name coward or suggest a man's character is wanting." Wade slipped her hand through his arm once more, like a true gentleman would when shielding his lady from a rogue. "I would suggest you remove that name from your vocabulary unless you are willing to back it with fists."

Mr. Austin scowled at Wade before turning to Jane. "I was told that you were ready to marry me, Miss Cady, which is the real reason that Graham insisted on following me out here. He's never been one to give up something that he wants and just because his mother won't allow him to wed you, he can't stand the thought that I am to marry you here and bring you back to New York as my bride."

"You what?" Jane sputtered. "Did my father say all of that in a telegram?"

Mr. Austin reached into his pocket and withdrew a telegram and handed it to her.

Jane will marry you. Come to Las Vegas to discuss terms and wed straight away. B.C.

Jane held the telegram so that Wade could read it as well. *So, my father would treat me as a bartering chip in his game of life?* Her father's words came back to her that "one gentleman is as good as the next" for her to marry. Well, she did not agree, and she no longer had to abide by his whims and rules.

Wade looked down at Jane, clearly understanding the turmoil roiling in her heart as he rolled back his massive shoulders and rested a hand at the small of her back.

"There has been a mistake. I am courting Miss Cady."

"And yet, I was engaged to her almost a month ago and Hyde received this note days ago." Graham crossed his arms, unbelief in his expression.

"I too am surprised at this turn of events." Mr. Austin shuffled his hat from hand to hand and cleared his throat. "I thought it was a mistake when the driver brought me here and then the clerk showed me to the dining room where you worked, but—" He scanned her white apron and plain black dress again and shook his head with a little laugh, "I'm so confused. Why are you a waitress? Your father made your circumstances seem so ephemeral."

If she hadn't been so mortified at divulging the truth to the two men her father had lied to, she would have laughed at his astonishment. "Well, I'm not exactly just a waitress. I'm a Harvey Girl." She clenched her teeth into what she hoped was a smile. *Father is going to be horrified.*

Graham's brows shot up. "And that's better how?"

Her smile wavered and nearly flinched at Graham's disdain as her confidence sank. Wade lifted the back of her hand to his lips, making her dipping heartbeat patter wildly.

"It is better because Harvey Girls are angels in disguise to the single men of the West. I am lucky she finds me as fascinating as I find her. Harvey Girls receive a proposal daily and yet, Jane agreed to step out with me—a horse rancher from the mountains."

She smiled up at him. Mr. Sterling was so kind to follow through with her wild scheme, especially after her *kissing* him like that. *Ladies do not go around kissing people and yet, he called me an angel and is taking care to see that my heart is not torn out of my chest by my past confronting me.*

"She has only been in the West for a little over two weeks." Graham interjected. "I highly doubt that she could attach herself to —" His lip curled. "To a man like you so quickly."

"Well, he saved me from being trampled our first day here and I suppose life is just so much more vibrant here than in New

York City with its layers upon layers of rules. You know them well, as they were what drove us apart." Jane speared Graham with a look before turning an adoring gaze up to Wade. "Without those unnecessary layers, the true character of a man is more easily discernible, and this man has proven himself worthy of my trust."

"What are you doing here, anyway, if you no longer have an understanding with Miss Cady?" Wade took a step toward Graham in such a show of concern for her that her heart skipped a moment at such a masculine fellow taking her side . . . *But he's just faking his concern.*

"Well, I believe I may have acted too quickly in my termination of our engagement." Graham cleared his throat.

"You mean in your flight from the church where you left me to faint in a heap of tulle in front of the New York Four Hundred?"

"What?" Wade scowled at this, his voice nearing a growl. "He left you at the *altar*?"

"You must not know her as well as you claim if you don't know that I refused to wed her before all," Graham snorted. "It was in all the papers."

"And yet, no woman would likely want that spread about, Bank," Mr. Austin countered. "And we both know that the *only* reason you are here is because I am seeking her hand and, heaven forbid, I have anything that you once wanted but were unable to obtain."

"A woman is not an object." Wade stepped in front of her, towering over her and blocking her from their view. "And I suggest that you let Miss Jane get back to her duties."

"Excuse me?" Graham scowled at him. "Do you know who I am? Who are you to order me about?"

"Nope, and nor do I care to." He reached for Jane's hand. "Shall I escort you to the back, Jane? I'm sure that the head waitress will not put up with two gents disrupting the dining room."

The front door to the hotel banged open and her father stood on the porch, his jaw dropping. "Mr. Bank? Mr. Austin? I was just told of your arrival."

Jane inwardly groaned. Of course, her father would choose this moment to show up.

"Gentlemen, shall we adjourn to the lobby? We can chat in comfort there." He nodded to Jane. "Tell Miss Dolly that you need your break."

"My shift is up and as I have been on my feet for twelve hours, I need a respite." She smiled up at Wade, making her father frown. "See you soon?"

Wade squeezed her hand. "I'll be waiting."

Hoping her father would be too distracted to follow her, Jane spun on her heel and bolted for the stables. Certainly, her father was her boss, but even he could not demand that she sit in the same room as Graham and Mr. Austin. She needed to see Phantom, to run her hands over his mane, to release this boiling anger inside of her through a hard ride over the foothills. Who cared if she had her riding habit or not? She needed to ride, needed to be free. She held herself back from running through town to the stables.

She slowed as she crossed the threshold and approached Phantom's stall, calling out to him. "Phantom, I've missed you. Do you want to go for a ride? It's been ages." She released the latch of the stall door, reaching out a palm to his nose. He tossed his mane in greeting and pressed his soft muzzle into her palm with a snort.

She rested her forehead to his. "Let's get out of here, Phantom. How far do you think we could get?"

CHAPTER 8

$\mathcal{W}$ade watched as Jane wrapped her arms about the horse's neck. He didn't know she boarded her horse at the stable he was managing. Maybe he should step away and let her have her moment? But he needed to speak with her. *And yet, standing in the shadows watching her isn't the best choice either.* Wade didn't want to come across as some creepy cowboy who was obsessed with her, but *she* was the one who kissed *him*. And he supposed that gave him the right to ask for some answers.

Blue perked his head up from the haystack in the nearest stall and released a welcoming howl. Wade strode into the ray of light bursting through the door as Blue yipped and circled his legs, his coon's tail slapping his calves like a whip. He bent and rubbed the back of Blue's ear, smiling as Jane turned. "Miss Jane? I'm sorry to interrupt you, but uh—"

"But you wanted answers, so you followed me?" Her cheeks tinted to the hue of a tomato. "I can't say that I blame you, Mr. Sterling."

Wade flicked up the brim of his hat as he strode to Raven's stall and petted his mare's nose as Blue pranced beside him, his attention never leaving Wade's face, eager for a run. "I am in charge of the stables for the next few months, as well as the farrier and am staying at the Castañeda."

"Oh." She reached for the bridle hanging just outside the stall door. "I should have known when I saw your dog. I thought he looked familiar. He's well trained. He didn't even growl at me."

Wade shook his head and laughed. "Well, he ain't no guard dog, but he's been a constant companion for many years."

Her smile faded. "Please forgive me for

earlier. I don't know what came over me, besides the fact that perhaps I might claim momentary insanity upon seeing my former fiancé stroll into the Castañeda." A tear trailed down her cheek. "I saw the way Graham looked at me. I just couldn't stand for him to see me working and unattached and therefore, in his mind, unhappy and *unfulfilled*. I don't mind working hard, but to be honest, this is all new to me, and I'm not used to it. He caught me at a weak moment, and I swept you into my web of deception. I can only apologize again for my actions." She shook her head. "I'm no better than he is for taking advantage of you. I can't imagine how terrible that must've been for you."

Terrible? That's the best kiss I ever had. Well, I ain't never had the chance to kiss a lady before, but I can't imagine a kiss can get better than that. But he didn't dare voice such a thing, not to a lady who was so obviously uncomfortable with the situation. "I wouldn't say that." He grinned and she ducked her head, focusing on the bit placement.

He pulled the gelding's saddle and

blanket from the wall and, tossing the padding onto the horse's back, settled the saddle atop it. "Nice horse. What's his name?"

"Phantom. Thank you, I've had him since I was a girl."

From the way she moved about the horse, it appeared she was confident, comfortable, and deeply connected with her horse. *A beautiful, kind woman who loves horses and seemed to like kissing me?* His heart swelled with hope that maybe his brothers' scheming to get him a bride might just yield a relationship. "He must be getting up there then."

She giggled as she adjusted the girth. "Most gentlemen wouldn't allude to a lady's age as 'getting up there.' However, I'm not most ladies, not even a fine lady anymore. I used to be. But I'm afraid we can't even afford to keep him for much longer."

"But your father is the manager of the Harvey House, and you are working there too . . ."

"Yes, but our family's income is no longer subsidized by a trust fund, and my mother is used to having a lot more. I would happily give up having new dresses and things just to keep him, but having a horse that does nothing but give me joy with the occasional ride is not worth it to my father to set aside such a large portion from my monthly paycheck."

"Why would he care what you spend your money on? You earned it."

She shrugged. "Father is in charge of payroll. He says that I owe it to the family since I won't marry Mr. Austin and, technically, he purchased Phantom for me when I was five. He takes part of my funds before I even see a dime and plans on selling my horse as soon as he finds a buyer," her voice cracked.

His gut churned. *So, he's stealing from his own daughter and wants to sell the horse too?*

She cleared her throat and pasted on that smile he recognized from the Harvey House—the one that did not quite reach her eyes. "So, I best ride Phantom now while I can."

Wade nodded and moved across the

breezeway to saddle up Raven. "Have you ever been out in the area?"

"No, but I need to ride as hard and fast as I am able. I'm afraid I have a temper. But when I am riding Phantom, something about the wind blowing in my hair takes all my worries and hands them back to the Lord where they belong."

"May I join you?"

She lifted her gaze to see he had already begun saddling up his mount. "Are you going riding too?"

"Raven can use the exercise and, as you can see, Blue is dying to get out of the stables. He is used to running free in the mountains and town life has been an adjustment."

"I can sympathize, but I'm not sure how proper—"

"No need to feel obligated to ride together." He shrugged as if he didn't care one way about it, while his heart fairly ached with the wish to get to know her more. "I offered because you are new to the area. Besides, Graham might be watching, and I'd hate for you to go about unescorted with him about."

"That's a good point." She nodded. "Very well."

He fixed the bridle into place and led the mare out of the stall. "Will you be riding Phantom every day after your shift, given your limited time together?"

"My shifts have been unpredictable as of late with a surge of guests here and there with the arrival of each train, which is why I need to take advantage of the day. I cannot afford to take any time off either." She gripped the reins and guided the gelding out. "We don't have much to our name. Which is why we are all the way out in the West now and far, far from where I was born and raised."

"And is money why that dandy released you from your understanding?" He made quick work of checking the girths on his horse and Phantom.

"Yes. Our wealth was the driving factor behind our union, and as I no longer had it, I understand why our arrangement was not the same as it had been only hours before the ceremony."

He rested his hand on Raven. "Did you love him?"

"Yes," she whispered and then shook her head. "I-I don't know, actually." She grabbed the empty oat bucket in the corner and overturned it, stepping atop it as she gripped the saddle. The bucket tilted and she lurched back. He closed the distance between them in a flash, grasping her by the waist. She gripped his shirt to halt her descent, her cheeks flaming.

"Allow me," he whispered and easily hoisted her up into the side saddle.

"Thank you." She patted Phantom's mane. "I *thought* I loved Graham. But the way he dropped me so quickly, well, it made me question our devotion to one another. Graham had always insisted that he loved me. I knew he thought me pretty. But sometimes pretty and character isn't enough for a man."

"If he didn't consider you a catch when he had the chance, his so-called affection isn't worth the ticket he bought to come out here. Did your ex-fiancé really travel all the way out here because of jealousy of that other dandy?" He swung up into the saddle and led the way out of the stable, Blue at Raven's side.

Jane sighed, following his lead. "If not for a misplaced jealousy and that mention of Father's worthless share, I dare not even think of why. He and my father were in the same circles of business. I don't know why he would come out here to see my father after the ships sank though."

He held his mount back so that they could walk side by side and he could better study her. "Do you think he really regrets his decision?"

She shrugged. "Even if Graham did regret his decision, I don't know his motives. What Mr. Austin said was true. Graham never could be told no when it came to something he wanted."

Wade gripped the reins tight in his fist. The man obviously had no respect for Jane. "He cannot be told no? Do you feel unsafe?" He bit back the need to charge back into the hotel and toss out the dandy.

"While he does make me uncomfortable, given our past, I'm going to have to get used to seeing him for a few days." She glanced at *Rudy's Mercantile* as they rode past. "He's likely staying at the hotel where he can watch me and know how hard I work."

"There's no shame in hard work."

"Oh, I know. But it's also new to me, and he would pity me." Her face hardened. "And if there's one thing that I can't stand, it is a petty man who thinks me not good enough for him anymore when at one time he proclaimed his devotion to me through poetry."

"And so, to escape his pity, you kissed me." He barely kept his grin from appearing. Seems he got the best bargain out of the deal.

Her cheeks went scarlet. "Again, I'm so sorry."

Wade smirked. "I'm not if it helped you."

"I only wish it had been for real," she muttered under her breath. "It would make everything so much easier."

He turned in his saddle to stare at her. Did she honestly find him attractive, or was it merely for using him as a shield? He hadn't been around many women, but the idea of a lady being humiliated by a man who claimed to be a *gentleman* did not sit well with him. He wasn't well versed in how to court a woman, but surely, he could help her with some guidance. "What would you need me to do . . . if it was real?"

She blinked her wide eyes at him. "What?"

"Well, I meant that if we made our courtship *look* real. If we pretended our relationship was real during Bank's and Austin's stay here, would that help you?"

"Yes." She sat up straight in her saddle. "Yes, but I couldn't ask you to do such a thing. What if you meet a nice lady and you are fake courting me?"

He shrugged. "I got some time. Besides, it's only while he's in town, yes?"

She nodded. "Of course. I would never ask you to continue the charade though. I chose to lie in that moment. I don't wish to drag you into my lie as well. As much as it hurts, I'll come clean to him if I have to in order to keep your name clear."

"My brother raised me to be a gentleman. If you are in distress, then it is my honor to help you."

"Thank you, Wade."

"Come on now, I'll show you a little bit of the countryside." He grinned. "I don't know much about the town myself, except for a new sweet shop, but the beautiful Gallinas Mountains have been my home for over a decade." His smile slipped a bit as she cast a glance over her shoulder. "Unless it makes you uncomfortable to spend time alone with me?"

She seemed to shed whatever was in her mind and she sent him a smile. "Wade, I am no longer a fine socialite who needs a chaperone wherever she may go. I am a Harvey Girl. Yes, I still have rules as to when I should return home, but I have more freedom than I have ever had in my life, and I don't intend on giving it up. And I trust you to take care of me. After all, you are my beau for the next few days."

He laughed and directed his mare toward the edge of town, "So, tell me about New York. Surely, your absence has caused heartache in the chests of a score of young men," he commented as they approached the sweet shop where the proprietor was standing with her cart, selling light brown confections with pecans shaped like cookies from her cart.

Jane's eyes lingered on the cart. "Not necessarily a score."

Following the direction of her gaze, Wade asked, "Have you tried a praline yet?" At her shake of the head, he dug into his pocket. "Good evening, Mrs. Boudreaux. May we have two, please?" He handed the woman a few pennies as she petted Blue, the dog's tail thumping the dirt road and lifting a cloud of dust.

"For you, Mr. Sterling, I'll give you two more on the house. You have already spent more in my shop today than most folks do in a month." She smiled at him and bagged four pralines and handed them up to him.

"Thank you, kindly, Mrs. Boudreaux." He tipped his hat to her. "I've got a bit of a sweet tooth, and you can expect me once a week." He nudged the horse forward and balancing one praline between his teeth, he offered Jane the other.

She accepted the confection and took a tiny nibble, her eyes widening at the sweetness melting on her tongue.

"Delicious, isn't it?" Wade grinned, finishing his in one bite.

"Do you know what's in it?" She asked and snapped off another piece, guiding her horse with one hand.

He shrugged as they continued down the road toward the river. "When I was a boy, I used to watch my southern mother whip up a batch in anticipation of them setting. I think she used cream, caramel, pecans and, of course, heaps of sugar. My pa liked her cooking."

"Is that why he married her?" She laughed and popped the morsel into her mouth, dusting off her gloves.

He shifted in his saddle at the question, thinking over his answer.

"Is all food in Las Vegas this delightful?" She continued before he could reply.

"I haven't had time to check out the other establishments, but I imagine that the Harvey House will be hard to beat, but I think between that and the sweet shop, I'll do just fine."

He directed them past a blue chapel into a grove of trees to where a river moved slowly, bending. The gentle breeze stirred her curls, sending them to dance about her face. Pushing her hair back, she tilted her head to block the sun.

"It's so peaceful."

"You seem to enjoy the water. Did you go sailing often in New York during the summers since your father was in the merchant business?"

"Almost never. When I spent the summers at my Newport estate, my friends would go sailing every week, but every week I would find an excuse to stay on the shore, saying that the sand between my toes and the ocean lapping at my ankles was all I needed from the sea. I was too embarrassed to admit how every time I left the dock, I would instantly become ill."

"It's a good thing you don't get sick in the saddle."

"It would be a tragedy, but riding would

be worth getting sick for. Do you ever ride as fast as you can?"

He wheeled Raven around and pointed to the hills. "First one to top of the third foothill wins."

She nudged Phantom with her heels, tearing down the road at a surprising clip for such an old horse. Her form was perfect as the wind rippled through her chocolate locks. Her laughter filled the air and Wade found himself hopelessly drawn to her. His mare could easily outrace her old gelding, but the joy of riding alongside her had awakened something within him—something that was feeling an awful lot like . . . *Love? Who can fall in love in a single moment?* He shook his head. *If I didn't know any better, I'd say I'd hit my head.* He kicked his mount, pulling out ahead of her for a few minutes until he glanced back and saw how far Phantom was from Raven and Blue following on the hills. He pulled back on the reins and allowed her to catch up and slow to walk. She was beaming. "Having fun?"

"That was *exactly* what I needed."

Blue halted beside them, chest heaving and tongue out as he panted.

"Well, I suppose if we are going to be fake dating, I need to know a little bit more about you," Wade began, suddenly wanting to know everything about this lady who had dropped into his life. "Do you think you'll ever go back to New York? Or is being a Harvey Girl just you passing time until something better comes along?"

She worried her bottom lip. "I miss it, but there's nothing left for us there." She shook her head. "What about your family? I know you have brothers. How many?"

Wade shifted in his saddle, a smile spreading across his face. "I am one of seven brothers."

"Seven brothers?" Jane exclaimed. "How on earth did your mother manage all of that? She baked you delightful cookies and raised seven boys?"

Wade grimaced. How did one explain to one's pretend lady that his mother had been a mistress? "It's complicated."

She gave him a small smile. "I'm a good

listener. If you are to be my beau, I would like to know everything I can about you."

He cleared his throat. "First off, yes I have seven brothers, but only Clint and Jackson are my full brothers. My mother was never married to Pa Sterling." He grimaced. "She was his mistress. My full name is Alexander Wade *Franklin*-Sterling. Franklin was her surname."

If she was surprised, her face did not betray her. "I see, but you claim them all as brothers. How did you become close?"

"When the real Mrs. Sterling died, we moved in with Pa Sterling and Tanner, Lawrence, Gray, and Noah. We bonded over our parents' disgrace."

"Oh." She shook her head. "That must have been difficult for you as a child."

He slowly nodded. "No one wanted to befriend the Sterling brothers, but the Lord used it for good. He bonded us closer than any blood ties. And then, my brothers and I were orphaned, and we were put on the orphan train, which is how we got out west."

Her lips parted. "I am so sorry, Wade."

He leaned on the saddle horn. "It was

difficult, but we were not born from loving parents. My brothers though—they were my world, and it was hard to be separated from them. We were taken one by one from the orphan train. It was my older brother, Tanner, who was able to finally bring us all back together."

"You were separated from everyone?"

"Yes, but we knew that no one could take on *seven* brothers. We would have eaten too much." Wade smiled, to lessen the tension, "Some of us ended up in great situations, but in the end, we all preferred to be reunited."

"Were you in a good situation?" She asked as they turned back toward town.

"There was no kindness in that man's heart toward me." He gritted his teeth. He wasn't sure how much he should tell a girl that he was fake courting, but it only felt right to come clean, so she knew exactly what she was getting into with claiming him as a beau. "The man who took me in saw that I was good with horses—great with horses, actually. He knew that I would cost a fortune to replace, so he wouldn't let me go when Tanner found me a year after the orphan train."

"But you said he didn't love you—"

"He loved the money I was making him through horse training. Tanner is not one to take no for an answer when he is in the right. So, he fought Mr. Joe, and the man nearly killed him. The only option I had to distract Mr. Joe from the fight was to steal the man's prize stallion. Tanner took a bullet in our escape, but after we were safely away, I realized the magnitude of what I'd done."

Her lips parted, her horror clear. "Surely, the punishment for horse thieving for a young boy—"

"Is still, in most cases, the same as it is for grown men. My brothers and I couldn't take that chance. A wanted poster in every town is not something you want hanging over your head, so I hid in the mountains, bred the horse I stole, and tried to patch together enough funds to send to Mr. Joe to pay him off. He didn't care for that fact, and he said he needed more because of all the potential siring he had lost out on. I offered more to him again and again, but after three offers, he still refused, and I realized he was never going to let me out from underneath his thumb."

"He was out for revenge." Jane gasped, eyes flashing at the injustice.

"That's what we guessed, so I stayed hidden in the mountains for over a decade. And when Tanner got married last month, his new wife was able to hire her fancy Chicago lawyer, and he has cleared me of all wrongdoing, and all has been made amends."

Jane reached her hand out to him, her eyes full of compassion. "So many years alone . . ."

He allowed his fingers to grasp hers. "I understand if you don't want to continue the ruse of being tied to me after this information. I'm not exactly a catch." He dropped his hold.

"You were a young boy. It *wasn't* your fault, Wade."

He smiled at her. "I'm glad you think so —I doubt many ladies would see it that way."

"If they can't see that you are a cowboy with a heart of gold after spending an hour with you, they don't deserve you, Wade Sterling." She halted her horse in front of the stables and sighed. "I wish we could ride longer, but—"

"There you are!" The bellhop trotted up to her, flapping a note at Jane. "Your father sent me."

Wade gritted his teeth. He hoped he hadn't gotten her in trouble.

"Thank you, Henry." She took the note and broke the seal and sighed, handing Wade the note. His brows rose that she would wish him to read another missive.

Jane, you have this evening off. Return home for dinner. There is much to converse about. Bank and Austin will be in attendance. Wear a pretty gown but bring an apron. We need you to cook the dinner, Father.

"He expects a lot out of you." Wade

frowned, handing it back before dismounting and reaching up to help her dismount. "You know, you could say no."

"And yet, it would only delay the inevitable." She bit her lip as she allowed him to assist her. She stared up at him, her blue eyes sparkling. "However, now that I have you . . . perhaps this isn't such a bad idea. How do you feel about coming to an inferior dinner tonight?"

"Inferior dinner?" He grasped her hand and bowed over it, not daring to kiss her knuckles. "It would be my honor."

She beamed up at him. "I cannot tell you how wonderful it is not to be alone anymore."

CHAPTER 9

Smoke billowed from the oven, sending Jane into a coughing fit as she flapped a checkered cloth above the stove. Yanking open the oven door, she yelped as the slightly damp cloth scalded the tips of her fingers. She dropped the rag as she gripped her hand, swallowing choice words, and inspected the blisters as tears stung her eyes. Remembering Father's advice to only use a dry cloth on hot metal a little too late, she tossed the rag over her shoulder and grabbed a clean cloth from the drawer next to the stove before pulling out the roasted rosemary chicken . . . or what was supposed to be roasted rosemary chicken.

"Oh! Why is it so dark?" She lamented as she picked off the charcoaled pieces, tossing them into the rubbish bin along with bits of burnt rosemary leaves. Seeing as the aesthetics of the uncarved chicken were beyond repair, she decided to slice it before bringing it to the table. She stabbed it with the fork, slicing slowly so as not to tear the meat only to find that the inside of the chicken was still pink . . . not a good pink, but a nauseating, uncooked pink. She moaned as she popped the slices back into the baking pan with the rest of the bird and set it inside the stove to bake.

Determined that it wouldn't burn again, she checked her watch pin. *Twenty minutes should do it.* She turned and stirred the pot of hearty potato and beef stew that Father had made the night before. Her only job was to reheat it, so if all else failed, at least they would have stew if she didn't let it over boil and end up ruining it too. *It doesn't look thick enough.* She tapped her fingers lightly on the counter before snapping her fingers as she remembered that in a novel she read, the heroine had used flour to help thicken it. *Just a dash should do.*

Grabbing the wooden stool, she reached up onto the top shelf for the tin of white flour and stretched onto her toes until she could finally grasp it with her fingertips. She popped open the lid and gasped at the curled lump inside. *A scorpion?* She squealed and dropped the flour tin, sending a spray of flour shooting into the air, along with the rigid and very dead scorpion. Squealing, she darted away, coughing and sputtering the flour from her tongue as she swiped at her curls to lose the flour caught in her ringlets as a knock pounded at the front door.

"They are here already?" She bent down to the copper pot on the stove, examining herself in its distorted reflection. "No, no, no," she muttered as she dusted her cheeks with the large apron she had commandeered from the Harvey House. *I look like I have stepped out of the pages of The Tale of Two Cities with my powdered face and hair.* She tugged her hair from its loose coiffure and tried to rid her hair of French aristocracy by flipping her head over and running her hands through her locks. Pausing in her dusting, she heard the now familiar pop of the stovetop from something boiling over. She snapped up. "Gah!" She grabbed a rag and heaved the heavy pot from the stove and over onto the wooden countertop, praying she hadn't ruined it.

Smoke snaking from the oven door caught her eye and she dove back to the stove, retrieving the black lumps of chicken. "Burnt? Why on earth." She glanced at her watch and groaned. "It hasn't even been ten minutes. How are you burnt?" Ready to sink to the floor in a puddle of petticoats, skirts, and tears, she drew a steadying breath. Why did she even care how the dinner would taste? Austin and Bank were not here for her cooking . . . *But Wade is skipping his meal at the Castañeda.*

At least she had the stovetop food. *Please be okay.* She pulled the lid from the back pot of sautéing green beans and gasped. *How can beans be rock solid one minute and mushy the next?* She picked out a green bean with a fork, blew on it and popped it into her mouth. *At least they aren't burnt.* She shrugged as she leaned on the counter with her palms, head down. *Why didn't Father make the meal himself, or at the very least have the Harvey House cater tonight?* She sighed. She well knew the reason—money. With Mr. Perkins still training Father to take over the position as Hotel Manager, he would never let Father get away with not paying for a whole catered meal.

"Good evening, Miss Cady," came Graham's deep voice from the threshold of the kitchen.

She closed her eyes. *Of course, Father would send them in to fetch me. He'd want to display how I am now a lady in distress and one of them could be a knight with his shining piles of gold.* She tucked her hair behind her ears, turning. "Mr. Bank and Mr. Austin," she curtsied, suppressing giggles over how disastrous she must appear. She brushed at her cheeks for any remaining strands of flour and gave the gentlemen a hopefully calm and collected smile. "Did you both need something?"

"We came to fetch glasses for the pitcher

of water," Mr. Austin explained as he took in the flour covered floor, the sink piled high with dishes, and the open window where a fly ducked under the sash and buzzed inside the kitchen where it would no doubt feast on the charcoal remnants of the chicken.

A smile played at the corner of Graham's lips for half a second before he reached up and covered his mouth, failing at wiping his amusement from his face. "I see you are having a time without servants."

"Ah, yes, um. I'm almost done." She moved from cupboard to cupboard, trying to remember where Father had stowed the glasses. After trying a few cupboards, she managed to locate and retrieve seven clean glasses. "I'm so sorry. I must've forgotten to lay them out."

"From the looks of things, you were a little preoccupied," Mr. Austin replied, allowing his smile to escape.

A flush crept up her neck as she pulled at her collar. *Did it get hotter in here?* "I had a small battle with the flour tin."

"I think it won." His eyes danced as he

reached out to her cheek with a handkerchief and stroked the flour from her cheek
and chin. "There. All signs of the battle have
been erased just in time for dinner."

She gritted out a thank you and stepped
back.

Graham scowled and handed her back
one glass. "I think you over counted."

Wade! While she may not care what these
two thought of her, she did not want Wade
seeing her in such a state. "I didn't. There
will be another guest." She fumbled with her
apron strings, pulling it from her black uniform. "I better freshen up."

"Pardon my asking, but is something
burning?" Graham glanced at the stovetop.

"Wretched greens," she muttered, grit-
ting her teeth. She grabbed her apron for a
rag and yanked the beans from the back of
the stove and set them on the cooling rack
atop the counter. Feeling her cheeks flaming, she pushed back her hair and excused
herself. "I'll be down shortly."

Graham looked about. "You really don't
have servants to cook the meal? This isn't
one of your father's grand ploys?"

"Oh, I am sure it is, but no, we have no servants." She gave a weak laugh. "Excuse me." Without waiting for his reply, she dashed up the stairs to her bedroom, softly closed the door behind her, and covered her face with her hands, mortified over the whole affair. Why was Graham here? He certainly had not come to be kind. Was he really this cruel and mocking when they were courting?

She risked a glance at the mirror and grimaced at the sight of flour still in her accidentally teased hair. She reached for her silver comb and began to brush her hair as quickly as she could, determined to look her best after being caught off guard. Tying her loose curls back with an emerald ribbon, she stepped into her white dinner gown with green trim at the scooped neckline. Reaching into her jewelry box, she removed her maternal great-grandmother's pearl necklace, the one piece she had been allowed to keep as it was an heirloom willed to her alone and had no ties to her parent's fortune. She fastened it about her neck. Pleased with her transformation, she slung her silk embroidered shawl over her arm and returned to the kitchen undetected.

She tasted the stew. Thinking it was rather bland, she sprinkled in a liberal amount of salt and gave it a stir. She ladled the steaming beef stew into the giant porcelain soup tureen, placing the lid atop. She draped a clean rag over it to keep it as hot as possible. Wrapping her shawl about her shoulders, she ducked out the back door to fetch the man who would make this evening not just bearable—but maybe even pleasant.

WADE PULLED at the collar of his dress shirt with his Sunday tie nearly suffocating him. But, when a pretty Harvey Girl in distress asked a cowboy to save her from a dinner honoring her former fiancé, a tie was the least he can do. He tugged on his jacket and hurried down the stairs of the hotel to where Jane stood in the lobby in a beautiful gown of white that really brought out the pink in her cheeks. Her hair was lustrous in the candlelight, and she had let it down with an emerald bow holding some hair back. "Mr. Sterling, thank you so much for doing this for me. Did you eat?"

"Wade," he corrected her and held out his arm, escorting her from the hotel. "And I thought that I shouldn't . . . because we are going to your parents for *dinner*?"

She sighed. "I should have warned you better. I wouldn't get your hopes up. You will likely be starved by the time you return tonight, but if you tell the Harvey House to feed you and put it on my tab—"

He grasped her hand, halting her words. "I'm sure it isn't as bad as you think it is, and I don't know why you keep offering me free food, Jane," He smiled down at her. "I'm just happy to help you as a favor and don't need food to spur me into action."

"Not many people in my circle would do such a colossal favor for nothing."

He shrugged. "Most people haven't been through trials like ours either." He threaded her hand through his arm. "I know what it is like to bear a burden alone and if I can help a lady in distress, the honor is payment enough."

They walked down the boardwalk toward a house on the outskirts of town. The Cady's home was rundown, but a lot bigger than his cabin in the mountains. With a little work, the townhouse could be quite elegant once again.

She paused on the steps, tugging his arm and drawing his gaze down to her. "Are you ready for this, Wade? There are going to be a lot of questions and judgements. The only one who will be remotely kind is Theodora. Honestly, she's been the only one who is conscious of any comments regarding my jilting and will be happy that I'm moving forward with my life with another outside of our circle. This is your last chance to run. I can take telling them the truth. It will be hard, but—"

"No. For you, I'll be willing to be uncomfortable."

She smiled up at him. "Wade, you are so kind, especially after I threw myself at you when you already rescued me from those cows."

"Texas Longhorns," he corrected with a chuckle. "Being rescued from a cow and from a Texas Longhorn is a big difference and can change my level of heroism." He winked. *And kind?* No, he had ulterior motives for going on with this lie. It was a safety net that allowed him to court her while he discovered the kind of man she wanted and then, he would do whatever he could to make this farce a reality.

"Miss Cady?" Graham called from the porch. "We wondered where you had gone."

Wade grimaced. He was losing his edge in allowing Austin and Bank to open the door without noticing, but then, he had never been so distracted in his life before meeting Jane Cady. But, judging from her blush, it seemed she didn't notice them either. Was she that distraught in her anticipation of the evening, or did he distract her too?

"I mentioned our other guest. Well, here he is!" Jane motioned Wade up the steps and into the house.

Mrs. Cady swept into the hall, dressed in an elegant marigold-colored silk gown that made him self-consciously adjust his tie and run his hand down the front of his jacket.

He hadn't even had a chance to get the wrinkles out of it yet. *Good thing I wore my Sunday best.* "And you must be Mrs. Cady," Wade lifted his Stetson and bowed. "It's lovely to meet you."

Mrs. Cady's gaze roved over Wade, confusion clouding her gaze. "Did you have a delivery, sir? If so, it will be at the back door."

"Mother, this my new beau." Jane smiled up at Wade and held out her hands to him. "May I take your hat?"

He handed it to her, feeling rather undressed without it.

Mrs. Cady's smile froze. "A new . . . beau?"

Wade bent into a bow. "Nice to meet you, ma'am."

Mrs. Cady gave him a smile that barely lifted her lips, much less reached her eyes.

A little girl with brown hair raced down the stairs, stopping in front of Wade. "You're a cowboy."

Wade grinned. "I am. And who might you be, little lady?"

She stuck out her hand to him. "Theodora. Call me Theo."

"And may I ask how you met?" Mrs. Cady grabbed Theo's arm and gently tugged her away from Wade.

"He actually saved my life," Jane replied, casting a glance at Wade.

Mrs. Cady released a tittering laugh as she fluttered her lace trimmed handkerchief and pressed it to her forehead. "Oh Jane, how you exaggerate. When were you ever in danger?"

"It was the morning of our arrival." Jane gave him such a trusting, small smile that his chest expanded with pride that he was there for her then and now. "I was about to be trampled by a herd of Texas Longhorns, and he plucked me right out of danger into his saddle."

Theo's jaw dropped. "You mean to tell me that you were almost trampled and then saved by a handsome cowboy and didn't tell me?"

"Into his saddle?" Mrs. Cady gaped at her daughter.

Wade grasped Jane's hand in his. "I am thankful I was able to get to her in time."

"It was providence that we met." She squeezed his hand.

He certainly thought so.

"And what brought you to the Harvey House?" Mrs. Cady flapped the handkerchief wildly about again.

"I am staying for the next few months, maybe longer. I am taking over for the stable owner as farrier, while he heals from a hand injury."

Mrs. Cady frowned and threaded her arm through Jane's, tugging her away from Wade and toward the parlor.

"What is a farrier?" Theo asked, her freckled nose wrinkling.

"He specializes in horse health, dear," interjected Mr. Cady as the group joined them in the parlor.

Mrs. Cady perched on the settee, carefully avoiding the spring, as Theo sat beside her, jouncing Mrs. Cady as she did so. Jane moved to stand by one of the long windows instead of taking the single rocking chair that was their only other piece of furniture in the room.

"Wade—Mr. Sterling— is a horse rancher," Jane supplied. "His mare, Raven, is one of the finest horses I have ever seen. He bred, raised, and trained her himself, so I trust the quality of the rest of his horses will be something to behold and worth their weight in gold."

"You don't say? That is high praise indeed coming from you, Jane," Mr. Cady's brows rose with interest as he took a seat in the rocker. "If my daughter could only care about one thing in the world, it would be her horses. So, with such a high-quality mare, I must ask if you are entering in the horse race on Boxing Day then?"

"Yes, sir, that's the plan. I want to get the word out about my fine horses. I'll be riding Raven." Wade stuffed his hands in his pockets, joined Jane, and rocked back on the heels of his Lucchese boots. "I'm keeping Raven, though. I plan to make her a broodmare in a few years."

"And yet, you want to race to get the word out about . . . future foals?" Graham scoffed as he leaned against the fireplace mantel, where the flames licked a cedar log. "Not much of a business plan if you ask me."

Wade shrugged. "It wouldn't be much of a plan if that was my aim. But it isn't. I have a handful of three-year-olds ready to go, a couple of two-year-olds, and three yearlings that I am working with now. I also have a couple foals arriving in the coming months that I plan to train and sell."

Jane's smile broadened. "What an industry you have."

Graham snorted. "A handful of horses to sell? I wouldn't leave my armchair for such a paltry sum that they would bring."

Austin sent him a scowl. "Then you would miss out on many opportunities, Graham."

Wade grinned. "Well, that's the difference between us, isn't it, Graham? Those horses mean the world to me, and I don't care how long it takes to build my ranch but build it, I will—one finished horse at a time. And it all starts with Boxing Day."

"Boxing Day? What is that?" Theo frowned.

Wade turned to Theodora. "Well, from what my brothers told me, many years ago there was an English dude, Mr. Edwards, that settled in Las Vegas, and he was really into his country's holiday called Boxing Day. He turned it into a race because Las Vegas was basically Dodge City before it reformed. Fred Harvey's house did a lot for this town. But some of the townsmen here still have a taste for gambling that they indulge in once a year. Anyway, for the Boxing Day Race, all the best horses in the area ride for a purse," Wade explained. "And I aim to get that purse to purchase myself a few new broodmares for my herd."

"Well, you can't argue with that logic," Father laughed. "I am a man of passion myself and well understand the drive to better my station. Good for you, Mr. Sterling."

Mrs. Cady paled at this. She cleared her throat. "So, Graham and Mr. Austin, I have to admit that I am quite curious as to what brought you all the way to Las Vegas?" She beamed at Jane, as if waiting to hear the men gush their praises over her beauty.

"I came because of Austin's inane idea

that he wishes to wed Miss Cady." Graham frowned.

Mrs. Cady gaped and clasped her hands to her chest as she rose and turned to Mr. Austin as if he had sprouted wings and a halo. "You wish to wed my Jane?"

"My, it appears that Mr. Cady makes all the decisions in this family without consulting a single one of its members," Mr. Austin muttered with a side-eye at Mr. Cady. He smiled to Mrs. Cady and Jane. "Yes, that is my intention with this trip." He bowed. "I wish to pay court to Miss Cady and leave with her as my bride."

"Which is absolutely ridiculous," Graham protested.

Wade reached a hand to Jane. She slipped beside him, clutching his arm. He could feel her trembling and it set his teeth on edge that these men were causing her such discomfort.

"And why do you care, Graham?" Mr. Austin interjected. "You were the one that rejected her."

Graham grimaced as he pushed off the mantel and looked apologetically to Jane. "I might have been a bit hasty. Your grand-parents—"

Jane's jaw dropped, along with her voice, "You came all the way out here because you think my maternal grandparents will bail out my father?"

"I'm sorry for your wasted trip, Graham." Mr. Cady slapped him on the arm. "Unfortunately, they will not be helping us. They feel as if my wife's dowry was enough, even though we married over two decades ago, and I've never asked for a penny more," Mr. Cady frowned. "So, I suggest that you grant us all some grace and peace by step-ping aside and allowing Mr. Austin and my daughter to have a bit of happiness."

Graham shrugged away from his touch. "Step aside? I seem to recall you tearing up when Jane and I first became engaged, saying that you were proud to call me a son-in-law. What happened to this family's devotion?"

"I have a suggestion, perhaps don't *jilt* their beloved daughter," Mr. Austin growled. "Do not be petulant, Graham. Our friendship does have its limits."

"I shouldn't have to beg for her hand after what Mr. Cady has done."

Austin frowned. "And yet, I'm thinking you should after your tossing aside Jane."

"And I understand that no man wishes to admit to his family that he is a failure, but sometimes, a man must swallow his pride for the sake of his family," he narrowed his eyes at Mr. Cady. "Yes, I jilted Jane, but I'm here now, offering to save her from the life Mr. Cady has thrust her into. I don't know what Mr. Cady was thinking, making you work as a shop girl."

"I didn't see you offering to help, Mr. Bank." Theo scoffed, earning her mother's whispered correction.

Jane gripped her hands before her skirts. "My father did what he thought was best and I'm not a shop girl—I'm a Harvey Girl. My circumstances have changed and yes, I have changed, but I'm still Jane Cady, a gentleman's daughter whether I stay cooped up in this ratty old parlor or work a twelve-hour shift at the hotel."

"Of course. I did not mean to insinuate that you are not still a lady. Only that it is not seemly for you to work so hard when you should be my wife."

Jane gave him a wobbly smile. "I might have agreed with you once, but I have no intention of leaving my new job for you."

Graham stiffened and Austin sent him a victorious smirk.

How dare they discuss her like this? She should be treated with respect, no matter what she does, or whose daughter she is. Wade clenched his fists. *She doesn't need you to fight her battles, Wade. She only needs you as a shield for now.* He drew a breath and leaned toward her, whispering, "It smells delightful."

Her strained smile softened as she directed it at him. "Thank you, but you've been warned and I'm not entirely certain it won't make everyone violently ill."

He chuckled and felt everyone's eyes on them, but he made a show of escorting Jane to a chair in the dining room where the table was set in the Harvey House's finest linen and china. He held the chair for her.

"Thank you, I need to fetch the soup first," she whispered and darted off to the kitchen and returned with a tureen, setting it on the table.

"Did you forget the chicken, dear?" Mrs. Cady asked, tilting her head slightly toward the kitchen.

Jane's eyes widened. "Chicken? Um, I decided not to bring it out." She settled into the chair and smiled up at Wade. "Thank you."

"Any particular reason why?" Mrs. Cady gave a little laugh as if to disguise her confusion as Mr. Cady began dishing out scoops of soup. "I thought it was our main course?"

Theo shuddered as she plopped into her chair. "I caught sight of it, and it does not look like chicken anymore. Trust me, it will make you lose your appetite and, judging from the rest of the dishes I saw, that might be a good thing." Theo grabbed a roll from the plate of baked goods.

I suppose the Cadys don't do grace. He bowed his head and whispered a prayer before picking up his spoon, noticing that Jane did the same.

"Jane?" Mrs. Cady prompted.

"It didn't quite come out as I had hoped, but the rolls are safe as they are the day-old rolls from the hotel." Jane dipped her spoon into the stew and took a mouthful. Jane and Mrs. Cady gagged at the same time, Jane dropping her spoon.

Curious, Wade tested it and fought back a coughing fit as Mr. Cady gulped down his glass of water, sending Theo into a fit of giggles. Mr. Austin and Graham pushed their bowls of soup away from them.

Jane stared down at her bowl. "I don't know what happened. I didn't even add flour like I was planning. I just reheated it and added a little salt because it tasted bland to me."

"How much salt?" Mrs. Cady coughed, reaching for her glass of water as Mr. Cady poured himself a second glass.

"Well, I figured since I use a dash in my own bowl, I'd better at least put in a quarter cup for the whole pot," she mumbled.

"A quarter cup?" Wade choked his laughter into his napkin.

Mrs. Cady stood, removing the bowls from the gentlemen as she motioned for

Jane to follow suit. "I'm afraid we will be dining on bread."

"And green beans," Jane muttered, her cheeks flaming. "Soggy green beans," she added in a low voice so that only Wade would hear.

The meal went a lot faster than it should have due to the lack of fare, but by looking at Jane, Wade couldn't imagine her appearing any more content at a feast than she did over her simple plate of bread and butter with a side of mushy greens.

"Mr. Sterling?" Mrs. Cady called, her eyes wide as if expecting a response.

"Sorry." Wade straightened. "I didn't hear your question, ma'am."

"I was saying that it is getting rather late, and I believe there is a dance marathon on Christmas Eve tomorrow, so Jane needs some time tonight," Mrs. Cady repeated, barely keeping the note of exasperation from her voice. "Jane, would you show him to the door?"

Jane moved to scoot back her chair, but Wade shot to his feet and assisted her.

"Thank you," she muttered and led him

to the front door. She pulled her silk shawl tight about her shoulders and leaned toward him and whispered, "I am so sorry she was so rude." She shut the door and stood on the porch, wrapping her arms about her waist, shivering. "You can see the whole town from this vantage point. It's quite pretty in the night with the stars shining upon the tin roofs." Jane rubbed her arms for warmth. She glanced back to the house. "I need to get back to the dormitory. If they are going to say it is too late for you, then it is time I get back before curfew, but I don't necessarily wish to go back inside for my cloak in my upstairs closet, or they will have me doing dishes long after my curfew and most likely have Mr. Austin asking to be my first partner for the Christmas Eve Dance Marathon."

"Then let us make our escape." He slipped off his dinner jacket and draped it over her silk covered shoulders. It practically swallowed her tiny frame.

"Oh! You don't have to," Jane protested as she tried to hand it back.

He laughed and wrapped her inside it

again and helped her down the steps. "It's no trouble. And I'd like to thank you for the fine dinner," Wade grinned as they strode down the dirt road with only the moonlight guiding them. "It was unlike any dinner party I've ever attended. Quite lovely. Though, I must admit, I've never attended a dinner party before."

Her mouth slacked before she burst into laughter. "Thank you, Wade, but the only edible thing that stayed on the table that I made were the greens, and they were far from lovely."

"I happen to think they were superb green beans," Wade grinned. "And compared to some of the fare I've had to endure at my brother's hand, your meal was far superior."

She giggled as she slid her hand about his arm as if it were the most natural thing in the world. He hoped she could not hear the pounding of his heart.

"You must have had some horrible meals to call mine 'superior.'"

"Okay, I may have exaggerated." A spot of yellow shone in the darkness. He bent and plucked a late blooming desert marigold from the side of the road and offered it to her.

Smiling, she tucked it into her curls. "Thank you."

"Not to change the subject, but there is a dance tomorrow."

She glanced up at him through her lashes. "Wade, I know it is a lot, but—"

"Will you allow me to have the first dance? It's for charity, after all, and I happen to have a vested interest in the children's home being built, being an orphan myself. It does my heart good to see the townsfolk build a home for children even before there is a need in the area."

"It is a noble cause. Preacher Martin and his bride felt called to build it and the town agreed." She smiled up at him and paused in front of the dormitory. "Thank you again for tonight. The Christmas Eve Dance Marathon will start promptly at seven o'clock and I look forward to hearing more about your childhood and well, everything about you."

A tapping at the glass drew her attention to Miss Dolly in the parlor window. She gave a dramatic scowl and held up two fingers.

She laughed. "I best go inside before I am locked out of the dormitory. Miss Trent, the House Mother, has been away visiting her family almost since the moment I became a Harvey Girl and Miss Dolly takes her duties quite seriously."

"Well, we don't want to get you in trouble." Wade bowed over her hand. "Thank you for the lovely evening, Jane. I look forward to dancing with you tomorrow."

At her smile cast over her shoulder, Wade swelled with hope that she trusted him.

CHAPTER 10

*J*ane tiptoed about her room, not wishing to wake her roommate. She still had not had any more conversations with Pernilla besides a few grunts in the hallway as they changed shifts. Pernilla was livid about the outing of her uncle, Mr. Perkins, and was using it to justify ignoring Jane.

Jane's gaze fell on Meg's floral dictionary on her side table. She flipped through it until she found the "M" section. Gliding her finger down the page, she read the meaning behind the marigold Wade had given her. *Sacred affection.* Her smile spread and she bit her lip. It was silly to read into Wade's spontaneous offering, but she couldn't help but press the book to her heart after dreaming of Wade coming courting with a bouquet of the desert blooms clutched in his fist for her.

Setting the book down, she grabbed her apron and snuck down the stairs and out the door, drawing in fresh breaths of the crisp morning air. *I mustn't let myself daydream, but if I have to dream, what a wonderful man to dream about.* She had long since given up Graham, but his condescension chipped away at her heart. *What good am I? I was trained to be a gentleman's wife and now—* She glanced down at her blistered thumbs from holding all the teapots. *Now, all I'm good for is work . . . so what right have I to dream of a life with Wade?*

She pushed open the kitchen door and helped herself to breakfast, knowing the minute her feet touched the dining room floor, she would not stop until her shift ended. She would have some time to recover after her shift and then the dance would begin, and she had no intention of missing the first bit of fun to be had since her wedding day was ruined.

Jane sat down with her cup of coffee when Dolly joined her. "Good to have you, Miss Jane. I was afraid you were going to miss curfew last night."

"I was five minutes early and I was inside before your two-minute warning was up."

Miss Dolly nodded. "Yes, but it is disappointing that you would not take advantage of rest while you could, given that today is for the new children's home final fundraising. Every dance you complete, a quarter is given to the home."

"A . . . quarter?" She blinked. *So little?* If she had her funds, she could have given—*but you don't. You only have time now.*

Dolly nodded. "Generous yes, but given there are sixteen of us waitresses dancing, along with another twenty, or so, ladies from town joining the fundraiser, we should easily raise over two hundred dollars by midnight. It will be quite difficult for you to be on your feet for so long, but that's why we called it a marathon—because it will be exhausting and therefore, competitive."

"Merry Christmas Eve!" Jean May sang out as she sat beside Jane. "If you miss a single dance, you forfeit your ability to continue dancing for the rest of the night and will no longer be eligible to win the Mistletoe Maiden crown and prize."

"What's the prize?"

"A *five-dollar* gift certificate to *Rudy's Mercantile.*" Dolly clasped her hands together. "The owner's mail-order bride, Angelique, came up with the additional prize as a way of giving back to the community by incentivizing the dancers to stay the longest on the dancefloor. Goodness knows that anyone would love to win such an amount."

"That is more than a week's pay!"

"I know," Dolly smiled. "You will have some fierce competition. I, for one, have no intention of stopping until the bitter end."

"And if there are more than one pair of dancers left?" Jane questioned.

"Then the girl with the most donations in her reticule will win," Jean May answered around her pancake. "You really should have found out the rules sooner and therefore, made the prudent decision to retire early last night like the rest of us who were not on the night shift."

"I wasn't planning on staying out late, my father pulled me into making dinner for a spontaneous dinner party—"

"*You* can cook?" Pernilla's brows rose as she sank into the seat across from her.

"When did you wake up?" Jean May pushed a cup of coffee to Pernilla.

Pernilla glared over her cup. "About when Jane here started getting dressed."

"I'm so sorry. I try to dress quietly, I really do," Jane grimaced. Seeing Pernilla's scowl planting itself on her forehead and burrowing deeper, Jane changed tactics. "But, no, I cook about as well as a dog in a rubbish bin."

Pernilla snorted into her coffee cup. "That must have been some dinner then."

Jane shook her head. "It was memorable for all the wrong reasons. But, despite my late evening, I am ready to work hard and dance the night away." Jane smiled, pushing enthusiasm into her words and expression. She desperately needed a new pair of practical half boots—ones that did not pinch her toes or make her back ache because of the stylish heel. And for the first time in her life, she couldn't see to a clothing need with her family's money.

Miss Dolly nodded. "Let's get started with the decorations as soon as we finish with the breakfast rush, shall we?"

Jane glanced longingly at her pastry, but as she was still trying to earn her place here, she gulped her coffee and rose to do Miss Dolly's bidding. It wasn't long into the breakfast service until Jane felt a trail of sweat trickle down her back, and it did not stop for as soon as the guests left, they began preparations for tonight's dance marathon and worked around any returning guests.

It seemed Dolly was determined to decorate every inch of the dining room, wishing to make the Christmas Eve Dance Marathon a smashing success and, with her determination, the decorating was taking longer than Jane had thought. After being on her feet for half the day and hauling boiling kettles of water for the coffee urns and steaming pots of hot tea, her head swirled, and her balance became uneven. But, as the hour drew closer to the marathon, the dining room filled once more.

She collected the penny tip from a table of a spoiled and judgmental family of six and turned the corner into the clean dishes storage area. Jane leaned against the wall, taking a deep breath as she pulled her high collar away from her sticky neck to let in a wisp of air. *Why did I cinch my corset so tight? I can hardly breathe.* She pushed her palms down against her hipbones and tried to take a full breath, but she couldn't seem to get enough air. *If I am this hot in December, how in the world am I going to survive the scorching summers here?*

Pernilla bustled into the area and frowned. "What are you doing just standing there? Someone in your station just left and you're convalescing like a grand lady when Dolly pulled me in to work a few hours before my half-shift starts."

"I'll get right on that." With a jagged breath, she saw through the potted palm fronds another couple entered the dining room, foretelling an early death for her if her shift didn't end soon.

As Miss Dolly was busy serving her own tables, Jane fanned herself with her hand and dabbed away the moisture on her upper lip before she plastered on a welcoming smile and seated the couple by the window. Jean May caught her attention from behind the lunch counter and pointed to the front door. She swallowed back a groan and turned to greet the next guest.

"Wade!" Her smile turned genuine, and she almost sighed with relief at the friendly face after the family who had treated her poorly. "How lovely to see you before the dance tonight. Are you eating?" She turned, worrying her bottom lip. "I think there should be a spot opening soon. Even the counter is filled, and it has fifty-one seats. Seems everyone came into town for the Christmas Eve dance tonight."

"I can wait." Wade's eyes widened at the sight of the Christmas décor of red and green streamers along with the stunning evergreen arrangements that adorned the dining room that it appeared to have been decorated overnight to the lunch crowd. "Festive. This wasn't up when I left."

"Thank you. We've been working all morning to help transform the space." Jane craned her neck, searching for an open table as a group of ladies vacated their table in the corner by the window. "But didn't you have breakfast? You would have seen us working, but I didn't see you and I would have noticed."

Wade placed a palm on his stomach. "I slept in and needed to get to the stable and didn't even have time to stop until now for a late lunch."

"Why, it's almost four o'clock. And given that you had such a lovely dinner of bread last night, you are no doubt starving now. If you wait just a moment, I'll prepare your table." Jane stripped the linen, replaced it, and set the table in a matter of three minutes, returning to his side with a menu in hand. "So sorry for the delay. Right this way, please," she gestured for him to follow her to the small round table and withdrew her notepad out of her apron pocket. The pencil shook in her hand. She pressed the tip to the paper to disguise her unsteady hands.

Wade gently grasped her elbow and whispered, "Jane, you seem flustered. Please don't feel like you must rush to take my order. Can't you take a short break and allow another to handle the orders for now?"

"With you having not eaten since lunch yesterday?" She gave a slight shake of the head even as her heart dipped at his intimate use of her name in public. "And please, don't make a fuss over me. I don't want the others to think I can't handle myself." Her cheeks tinted red. "My shift will be over in a quarter of an hour, and I can't afford to stop now. I'm already the worst on the team." She gestured to her badge, number sixteen. "Please have a seat before people notice," she whispered, for if he pressed her anymore, she might burst into tears of exhaustion over his thoughtfulness.

He pressed his lips together as if against his protest and reluctantly sat. "I'll have the Earl Grey, please." He handed her his menu, his concerned eyes not leaving her flushed face. "And the fried chicken with a baked potato and chocolate cake."

"I'll have that right out for you," she assured him, flipping the teacup and turning the handle in the correct direction for the drink girl to fill, which was herself, but rules had to be followed, and headed for the kitchen when she was hailed by a couple for a dessert and refill of Darjeeling.

Shouting her orders into the kitchen, Jane grabbed the pot of fresh Darjeeling and the pot of Earl Grey, filling the couple's teacups before filling Wade's, only giving him a smile before she whirled back to the kitchen to fetch the couple's dessert order.

Her father certainly was not considerate with keeping her up so late before an early morning and the dance marathon being tonight. *What was he thinking? He knows about this dance?* She straightened as realization dawned. *He's trying to break me—to get me to marry Mr. Austin. Well, I won't do it. I can do this. I can.* Jane delivered Wade his meal and flitted from table to table, not giving into her exhaustion, pressing forward in the hope that her shift would be over soon. However, as the minutes ticked far beyond her shift and Miss Dolly had yet to dismiss her given the influx of guests, Jane's hands began to shake. The guests kept coming, so she kept smiling and serving.

Returning with a refill for Wade's tea, she felt Wade's gaze on her trembling hands as she filled his cup. "Here you are, Mr. Sterling."

"Oh, could I have a fresh pot of Rosehip tea as well?" A lady beside Wade's table asked as she spread the lemon curd over her vanilla scone.

Jane gave her a tired smile and nodded. "Absolutely, ma'am."

Without a word, Wade rose and took her by the hand.

"Wade! I mean, Mr. Sterling," she hissed. "What are you about?"

He led her out into the dining room to the storage room and pulled her inside.

"Wade, you can't—" She gasped at his hands on her waist as he lifted her atop an overturned barrel. "What do you think you are doing?"

He took the pot of Earl Grey from her and set it on the storage shelf. "You cannot burn the candle at both ends like this. Where is your relief? Your father should be seeing to your health." He growled. "I'll fetch him myself if I need to and let him see what his carelessness with his daughter's time is reaping."

She sighed, leaning her head against the wall. "I have no idea where Father is, but even if I did, you couldn't tell him that."

"Then allow me to speak with Miss Dolly." Wade ran his fingers through his hair. "You're working yourself too hard. Why, your cheeks are redder than a pickled pig's foot!"

"What a picturesque compliment," she muttered, her lips pressing into a determined line as she clutched her hands together, massaging her aching palms.

"I'm sorry, but it's true. You need to stop, or you could get really sick." He grasped her hands and gently rubbed them. "I've seen it happen before, and I won't stand by and watch you work yourself into an early grave because you want to prove you are a hard worker. Jane, you work twice as fast as most of those girls in there, but in your haste, I've seen mistakes, which is why you are number sixteen." He nodded to her badge.

"Wade," her gaze flashed to meet his, hurt that he would say such a thing.

"I'm only telling you this because speed isn't everything. Slow down a little and you won't go spilling tea, or getting orders mixed up. Focus on each task, instead of being the fastest, and then, you'll see your badge number improve."

Her bottom lip trembled as she struggled to keep her tears at bay, not caring if having her hand in his was inappropriate—she was in a storage closet, so appropriate had ridden away into the sunset. "But I have to do this."

He nodded. "And you can. I am only saying to slow down."

He rubbed her palm, and as he massaged, she felt her defenses crumble. "Thank you for speaking the truth instead of what is nice."

Wade smiled. "Thank you for taking my words . . . I am used to speaking straight with my brothers, but with a pretty lady like you, I'm in uncharted territory. But, if you like honesty, I'm upset with your father. This is your father's place of work too. If he deems it unnecessary to help you on your biggest day yet, I think it is well within your rights to ask for a break."

She tugged her hands out of his, needing the clarity that space would bring. "It's not about rights. It's about money. Besides, it's an all-hands kind of day for us waitresses. Everyone is tired."

He sighed, as if realizing that no amount of urging would change her mind. "I worry about you." He reached up and gently brushed her hair from her cheek.

Her hands grew clammy and, while her upbringing as a socialite had trained her to be composed in every situation, she wondered why she was having such a difficult time breathing in such close proximity with this handsome cowboy. *Does this mean he's interested in me more than a friend?*

She felt her resolve to stay unattached melt away as hope rose to the surface of her heart that there was a good man who saw her—who cared for her—despite her change in fortune. Wade had nothing to gain from his friendship with her and yet, he stayed. He stayed while Graham went flying out of those church doors. What would it be like to be loved by a man like Wade Sterling—one who was as strong and pure in heart as his surname.

Maybe . . . maybe there is a chance for happiness here. I didn't dare dream that such a man would ever want to marry me when I'm penniless, but Wade doesn't seem to care about that. Her fingers brushed his hand, clasping them at her cheek. She leaned into his palm for only a moment. She broke the connection and hopped off the barrel. "You are too kind to me, Wade. I only need to remember to drink more water, or I won't be much good to anyone in a fainting spell."

"You feel faint too? You need to stop," he pleaded, taking her elbow to steady her if needed. "Heatstroke is very common in Las Vegas and just because it's December doesn't mean you can't get it from working."

"I must be a sight to have you so worried." She ran her fingers over her apron and patted back her hair, ensuring that it hadn't loosed itself from her braided, low coiffure. It was a little ostentatious for a waitress, but she didn't like the way a bun made her seem so stern. She giggled. "I mean, what really worries a mountain man? Snow? Mountain lions?"

He leaned toward her, his voice low, "There are only a few things that worry me, and you, Miss Jane Cady, are one of them."

She ached to plant a kiss on his cheek and her breath caught at the frightening impulse. "Thank you. You rescued me and prevented a potentially very embarrassing fainting spell in front of the whole town."

"I will always be here to rescue you," he whispered.

Her heart pounded at his words, and before she did anything rash, she grabbed the tea pot and dashed out of the closet. She hurried behind the preparation station.

"There you are. I noticed you were looking particularly red." Dolly approached her and handed her a glass of water. "Drink this. I'm so sorry. I realize the hour is far beyond your shift, but with the train arriving, I must ask you to stay another half hour. Do you think you can manage?"

"Of course, thank you." Jane finished her glass of water. After taking a break in the closet, she no longer was in danger of fainting. She took Wade's advice and slowed down and he was right. It made the room not spin and her head cleared. All through the dining room, she felt Wade's gaze burning into her shoulders and it brought her a surge of strength, knowing that he cared for her.

When the last large group had departed, she gathered the table linens and turned to find Wade rising from his table and offering her a wave. She smiled from behind the pile of dirty linens and nodded to him. She dumped the linens in a basket in the back corner of the kitchen where they would be sent down the line to be laundered when Father appeared in the back door.

Of course, he would appear when the hardest work is over. She forced her tone to remain calm. "Where have you been?"

"With your mother. We had a late dinner after all and we needed our rest. It is my day off today, but I wanted to come in a couple hours before the dance began."

Jane's jaw dropped. *Has he always been this selfish and self-centered?* "And yet you had me prepare dinner for a late night that you forced me to attend when you knew I'd be working all day before the dance?" Her voice cracked as she rubbed her forehead, wanting to release her frustration with a scream.

Father's eyes widened with feigned innocence. "Did I?"

"Never mind. The day is over and I'm only exhausted." She straightened her shoulders. "One quick nap and I'll be ready for the Christmas Eve dance."

CHAPTER 11

ade gripped the corsage of a single crimson poinsettia flower that he purchased from *Rudy's Mercantile* and tugged at his tie as he strode to the Harvey House with his six brothers and sister-in-law behind him. Corinna squealed and dashed across the room to embrace a petite red-haired lady who was standing next to former Texas Ranger Reid. The lady whole heartedly hugged Corinna back and released a squeal of her own as they clasped hands and began whispering and giggling away.

Tanner slapped him on the shoulder. "I'm proud of you."

Wade's brows rose. "Why? For putting on a tie?"

"No, for actually living your life and using your time in Las Vegas well, given you've only been in town two days and already have a lady that you are bringing flowers to at a *dance* no less. Corinna told me that you've been courting a Harvey Girl?"

Wade's jaw dropped. "How did she find out that?" He'd have to correct his brother, given their courtship was a farce, but he wanted to see if he could change that before he needed to confess to the charade. He would just take care not to make the farce a bald-faced lie. "There's a lot more to the story than that."

Tanner shrugged. "She was chatting with Miss Dolly Matthews outside just now and apparently, there are no secrets between sisters. So, where is she?" Tanner gestured to the clusters of women about the room.

"She's uh," Wade twisted to look about the room. "Not here yet?"

Corinna and the red-haired lady burst into peals of laughter.

Tanner grinned at his quiet wife's exuberance. "And while I want to hear more of the story, I best follow my wife before she tells Mrs. Lorna Reid all our family secrets, including how she saved me from a snake. Reid will never let me forget it if he finds out."

Wade turned to his brothers, Lawrence, Gray, Clint, Jackson, and Noah, who all appeared frozen on the spot at the sight of so many beautiful, single women and the mounds of perfect food. He grinned, thankful that he at least had gotten his awe out while seated at a private table and didn't look like a freshly caught largemouth bass dangling from the line with his mouth agape.

"Maybe I should get me a job in town too," Gray, the family hunter, whispered to Lawrence. "Seems we didn't consider that while Wade is our hermit, we haven't exactly been courting either. And he's only been here two days and already got himself a girl. If the hermit can get a girl so quickly, I could be married by next week if only I spent more time in town."

"You could just join the family business of being a bounty hunter now that Tanner has retired and turned to cattle ranching, I could use help and there is plenty of time for flirting and courting in the down time." Lawrence grinned at a nearby Harvey Girl, a Miss Jean May from what Wade recalled.

"Yes, but Tanner never courted no woman while on the trail," Noah interjected.

"I'm not Tanner and besides, he *caught* himself a bride through being a bounty hunter and fell in love while she was his prisoner." He shrugged. "The Lord works in mysterious ways, and I wouldn't mind Him picking me out a bride too."

"Flirting, huh?" Noah hitched up his pants and tugged his jacket. "Guess I could take a swing at it. Maybe I'll catch a bride myself."

"You are barely old enough to stay up this late, Noah. You shouldn't be thinking of marrying yet," Jackson snorted.

"And yet, you are barely older than me and I see you got your sights on that pretty young lady over yonder," Noah argued. "Do you even know her name?"

"No, but I'm going to."

Their conversation faded as soon as Wade beheld a vision in blue silk drift into the dining room as couples already swarmed the room, a buzz of eagerness to begin the dance marathon permeating the air.

Jane turned about as if searching. *Is she looking for me?*

Wade slipped away from his brothers and wove about to reach her side and grasped her hand through the crowd, drawing her to his side. "You are absolutely stunning." He bowed and presented her with the corsage.

"Oh, what a stunning flower. What is it called?" She smiled up at him as she pinned it beneath her left shoulder.

"Poinsettia. The lady who owns the mercantile was selling them."

"You are too thoughtful. And you look quite handsome." Her gaze settled on his shoulders, darting back to his face.

"What?" He brushed at his coat and turned for her. "Do I have anything on my coat? I dressed at the stable, but I don't want my brothers to have any more ammunition to add to uh, this situation."

"It's really nothing." Jane scanned the back of his coat. "But, you have a little dust mark on your shoulder blade and a piece of hay."

"Hay? And here I was trying to impress you." He unsuccessfully swiped at the smudge on his back.

She giggled. "You already have, Wade, and no bit of hay marring your clothing could change that." Jane stayed his hand. "Let me," she whispered and in three swift rubs with her handkerchief, she smiled again. "All gone."

"Ladies and gentlemen," Mr. Cady's gaze found Wade, his lips pursing at Jane's hand on Wade's back.

Wade held the man's gaze. *I am doing nothing wrong. Unlike Mr. Cady, who is practically forcing his daughter to wed a man she doesn't wish to marry.*

Mr. Cady looked away and cleared his

throat. "Tonight, we have the honor of hosting the final benefit for the construction of the children's home. To join a lady on the dancefloor, every gentleman will pay a quarter per dance with the lady of his choice. While a gentleman might wish to pay a dollar to secure four dances, only one quarter, or a donation of any *greater* amount, at a single time is permitted and is good for only one dance. There will be a three-minute break between songs and only a handful of ten-minute intermissions. Each lady must dance every dance this evening in order to stay in the running, but she may not dance two dances in a row with the same gentleman. At midnight, the final lady on the dancefloor with the most funds in her reticule will be crowned the Mistletoe Maiden and the Harvey House will match the dollar amount the Mistletoe Maiden has earned on behalf of the new children's home. For this evening, both gentlemen *and* ladies may request dances." Mr. Cady laughed. "It can't be deemed improper when it is for such a worthy cause."

The ladies about the dancefloor giggled

in delight, some batting their eyes at their desired partners. From the corner of his eye, Wade spotted Eliza Brady, one of the elite town girls that he had met in passing while working in the stables. She rested her gaze on Wade and smiled at him, crossing the room toward him. Wade's heart hammered and he averted his gaze. Maybe Miss Brady didn't see him see her heading his way? He cleared his throat and leaned toward the petite Miss Cady. "Jane, I believe I have the first dance?" He dug into his pocket and lifted out a quarter.

"I would be honored, Wade." She opened her reticule, and he dropped the coin inside as the fiddlers struck a lively tune and the room teemed with eager couples, and she pulled him onto the dancefloor.

"There is only one slight problem," Wade gritted his teeth as the realization hit him. "I have only practiced one or two dances with Corinna before heading to town."

Jane smiled up at him. "Lucky for you, I'm a wonderful dancer. If you don't mind me leading you a bit, I can help."

"Mind? Never." *The last time you led, there was a kiss involved.*

Jane was sweet in trying to direct him without being bossy and whispered more than a few words of encouragement and when the dance was over, he at once missed having her in his arms, especially with that stinkin' rule about no dancing with the same partner twice in a row.

"Oh dear," Jane murmured.

"What?" Wade scanned the area and spotted that coyote, Graham Bank, heading their way. "You want to break the rules?"

"I would be disqualified." She sighed. "I suppose I have to get a dance with him out of the way eventually, but," she grinned up at him, "perhaps we can break the rules without anyone noticing." She placed her hand in his.

A trill of laughter made his ear itch.

"Now, I know Miss Jane here isn't going to bend the rules already by accepting another dance from the bachelor of the evening," Miss Brady swayed her hips as she approached them.

He nearly glanced over his shoulder

looking for this elite bachelor, but her eyes were fixed on him.

"Mr. Sterling, would you do me the honor? We have a children's home to build after all."

Jane released his hand and gave her an apologetic smile. "So sorry, Miss Brady. Of course, he is free to dance."

Wade bowed over her hand and led the woman onto the dancefloor. "I should warn you, I am not light of foot. Pretty sure Miss Jane Cady will have bruises on her toes."

Miss Brady grimaced at the mention of Jane but recovered quickly with a brilliant smile. "Oh, Mr. Sterling, the town is simply buzzing over your horse. My father said you entered her in the Boxing Day Race, yes?"

He blinked, he had been attempting not to step on her, but conversing *and* dancing? Impossible. "Race?"

"Yes." Her smile faltered. "You entered?"

"Oh! Yes. The prize money would be beneficial to my business. I am a horse rancher."

"That is what my father was saying. You

met him yesterday while you were hitching the buggy, but that was before I walked up to join you."

He nodded. Being new to the town, it had been a whirlwind of meeting people, but it would have been impossible not to remember Eliza's brilliant smiles at him.

He stepped on her toes, and she bit back a gasp. "Sorry. I told you, I'm awful."

She giggled as she curtsied at the end of the dance. "I'd be more than happy to give you some lessons. In Las Vegas, we always have a dance planned, especially since the Harvey House opened. Would Sunday evenings work for you? Not tomorrow, of course, being that it is Christmas morning and all, but perhaps next week?"

"Next week?"

"It's a date then," Eliza crooned up at him and spun away to join a cluster of giggling ladies.

Tanner approached him and crossed his arms. "What just happened?"

"Not rightly sure." Wade scratched behind his ear. "I nearly broke her foot, so she offered me dancing lessons and the next thing I know, she thinks I'm coming next week."

Tanner nodded to a familiar woman with chocolate colored hair, hurrying toward the powder room. "Well, I think your poinsettia princess overheard."

CHAPTER 12

*J*ane pressed her hand to her stomach in the corner of the powder room during the ten-minute intermission, trying to still her annoyance over the town girls swarming Wade. She had thought that the ladies in the Four Hundred could be aggressive with a bachelor, but that was nothing compared to how the women had reacted to Wade Sterling. *But we hardly know each other. Why am I being so possessive after only being together, well not actually a couple, but with him for two days?* Her gaze rested on the thoughtful poinsettia corsage. She couldn't wait to return to her dormitory to find out its secret meaning.

She had noticed she wasn't the only lady wearing the red star flower tonight, but with the sweetness he had presented the flower, it made her feel so unique and special—something Graham had done not too long ago, but this feeling was so different than what she felt for Graham. Wade made her heart skip.

"I think he will ask to come courting," a lady Jane thought was named Eliza whispered to the blonde in the powder room. "Especially since he needs dance lessons."

"Oh? Has Mr. Sterling shown any interest in more?" Asked the blonde as she pinched her cheeks.

"He will after dancing with me and, when he does, my father will be asking to purchase Mr. Sterling's stallion that sired that impressive mare." Eliza coaxed a curl into place on her forehead. "His mare, Raven, has been the talk of horse country, especially with the Boxing Day Race in two days. Everyone is wondering where the horse came from and who Wade Sterling is, but my father doesn't care about his past as long as he can get the stallion that sired her to sire foals for us that he can sell to his buyers in Kentucky. Lucky for my father, I don't mind the sacrifice of marrying a handsome horse breeder to improve Father's business."

It seemed that even in the West, ladies' hands were bartered for the betterment of the family's estate.

"Honestly, Darla, I was shocked that those *waitress* girls were hanging all over Wade Sterling. No matter how pretty they are, they are working girls and have no business trying to take a suitor away from us—ladies who are established in town." Eliza adjusted her neckline and turned in the looking glass to view the back of her gown.

"I'm certain he is only being kind, which speaks well to his character to show any sort of concern for their feelings," Darla slid her gaze toward Jane.

They not only don't care that they are overheard, but they wish *to be heard by me. Do they think they can scare me off from him?* Jane almost laughed as she fixed the flowers in her coiffure.

"He really is kind, but more importantly, handsome," Eliza giggled.

"And he possesses the prize racehorse that your father wants and with your father's fortune, how long do you think it will take for Wade Sterling to come calling on you, Eliza?"

"After what I have planned for him during our next dance, including a mention of the amount of my dowry, Mr. Sterling will be knocking on my father's door tomorrow evening, Christmas or not. No doubt. Mr. Sterling wants to build his herd and the amount my future husband will be offered will make him an instant millionaire."

A millionaire? Jane's heart sank. She ducked her head and exited the powder room to stand along the wall to await the music. *Wade is only that much further out of my reach now. What was I doing entertaining the thought of even the slightest possibility of a future with him?*

She spotted her mother arriving late. Theo was not behind her. Her little sister likely had been told she was too young to attend a dance. She sighed. Time to greet Mother and face the inevitable argument for her to accept Mr. Austin's hand.

"There you are," Wade grinned, lifting a glass of punch and handing it to her. "Can't have you fainting . . . though, I have to admit I wouldn't mind catching you."

Her cheeks bloomed. "My hero." She straightened. Would he think her too forward? Feeling eyes upon her, she glanced up to find Pernilla and a cluster of town girls staring at her so hard that one could almost call it a glare. Jane blushed, unused to such censor. In New York, as the daughter of the prosperous Mr. Cady, she was held in high regard, but until recently, she hadn't realized how many people might have only been kind to her due to her wealthy position in society and not because they liked her. She angled her body away from Pernilla, intending to engage Wade in conversation. "Do you have an interest in—"

"Excuse me, may I have this dance?" Mr. Austin lifted a silver dollar in the air as the music began again.

She smiled apologetically to Wade and

handed him back the punch. "Certainly, Mr. Austin." She opened the reticule as he dropped the heavy coin inside.

Mr. Austin drew her into his arms for the waltz, sweeping her about the room in perfect time, bringing back memories of her time of ballrooms and beaus.

"I hope you have given thought to my offer?" Mr. Austin glided with her about the room. "I know we don't know each other well, but Graham spoke so highly of you from your courting days that I feel like I know you. I wish for a wife with character such as yourself—a character that has been proven time and time again with the hardships that you faced with such grace and dignity."

"Thank you, sir." Her heart warmed at his praise. Mr. Austin was certainly kind. It wasn't his fault that she didn't feel any sort of spark toward the man, or that her father had spoken too soon and sent him on a wild goose chase to New Mexico. "Graham spoke highly of you as well, but that was back when he was in business with my father. He would not agree that my character was improved by our fall."

"Hmm, well, it was your father's *remarkable* business style which ran him into the ground—not by any fault of your own."

Jane dropped her gaze, desperately grasping for a polite reply to dissipate the discomfiture of his statement. While it might have been true, it was far from polite to discuss her father's failings. "From what I understand," she lifted her eyes to Mr. Austin, "it was more from a series of unfortunate occurrences with storms than my father's ability to manage his business. However, we were very blessed that lives were not lost in the tragedy."

Mr. Austin clicked his tongue. "A tragedy which could have been avoided all together if he hadn't sent those ships out when he understood storms were known to brew. Every merchant knows to avoid those waters during hurricane season, but he had diamond ships sailing as well as merchant ships. Such hubris to have one's entire fleet of merchant vessels in the waters at such a risky time. However," Mr. Austin met Jane's mortified gaze, "I greatly admire the strength of his daughter who so willingly gave up a life of luxury out of honor and to serve her family."

She bit her lip, uncertain how to respond to such hard truth that ended in a compliment.

He furrowed his brows. "But I see I have offended you in my attempt to compliment you."

"It's fine. Really. One would think I'd be hardened to such realities now, but it is still difficult to hear of the risks my father took to increase our wealth, only to lose it all."

He shook his head. "No, it's not fine that I inadvertently insulted your family. It was inexcusable. What I meant was that you do not have to continue to work so hard—not when there is a better solution that will not only bring you back to your rightful place in society but also aid your family as well."

"Mr. Austin. I've tried to tell you, and my father, but no one seems to be inclined to listen. I am courting Wade Sterling and am not free." Oh, how she wished it were true— to be courted in earnest by such an honorable man would make all the shame and exhaustion worth it.

"In my opinion, you are not taken until there is a ring on your finger." Mr. Austin grinned down at her. "While you may refuse my suit now, I have something that your Mr. Sterling does not."

"And what, pray tell, is that?"

"Money. I can make your family's dream come true with a simple transfer."

She stiffened in his arms, aching for the next song so she could escape the ballroom for a few moments. Even though she wished to end this night, she couldn't leave—not when the children's house depended on the Harvey House to raise money and the night was young. The music mercifully cascaded to a close and she curtsied, abandoning Mr. Austin on the dancefloor, fleeing for the door for fresh air for the blessed three minutes between songs.

Fingers dug into her arm, halting her. "Jane. I can only put up with so much," Father whispered, loosening his hold on her. "You cannot treat Mr. Austin this way. Go back and apologize."

"I danced with him. It's no longer his turn."

His lips pursed. "You will accept his hand, or things will prove hard for you at the hotel."

She lifted her chin. "I have two and a half minutes until the next song begins, excuse me." She rushed around the corner of the porch, leaning on the arched colonnade.

"You aren't leaving already, are you?" Wade called from behind her, jogging to her side. "The next dance is about to start, and I finally got away from the ladies of Las Vegas."

"Just taking a break. I'm afraid I have lost my taste for veiled threats tonight." Her chin trembled.

His expression hardened. "Someone threatened you?" He clenched his fists. "Was it Graham or that Austin?"

She shook her head, shivering as she lifted her gaze to the starry sky. "My Father. Mr. Austin was the perfect gentleman while promising me the world if I marry him."

He shrugged out of his jacket and

wrapped it about her shoulders. "And you do not wish for the world?"

She gazed up at him—at this man that she hardly knew, but one that had begun to steal into her every thought. "I do not."

He nodded. "I have to admit, I was a little worried he would try to use his funds to turn your head."

"He is trying, but I know the truth behind marriages brought about by gold and my head is solidly fixed ahead." She laughed. "But I don't think that pockets, or reticules, full of gold would turn your head." She dipped her gaze.

"Ah, you overheard Miss Eliza?" He shook his head. "I'd like to clear any doubt. I did not agree to call on her." He grasped her hand. "Even if you only need me for a farce, I would never act so."

"There are few men like you, Wade Sterling, and I'm proud to call myself your friend."

He nodded and leaned his hand on the brick colonnade above her head, closing the distance between them, "But, you see, that's the problem."

"Problem?" Her breath caught. *Does he want to be rid of me after tonight?* She dismissed the thought instantly. *Wade isn't that superficial.*

"Yes. Even though we have only known each other for a short while . . . I want us to be more than friends." He reached out, stroking away the tears she hadn't realized fell. "You have become very dear to me."

She felt her heart drop. *Tell him not to care for you. You heard the town girls. If he falls in love with you, he will forfeit his future. Do you really want him to end up like you? Penniless? Exhausted?* But his countenance was so hopeful and his heart so kind. How could she lie and tell him that she only thought of him as a friend? Especially after that earth shattering kiss that broke all the rules— both in courtship and timing.

She knew it should be too soon to fall for another man after her jilting, but just after days as this man acting as her beau, she was beginning to suspect that what she had felt for Graham had been nothing compared to what *could* be with Wade. How could she feel so connected to Wade despite the amount of time knowing him? If she were honest with herself, she had dwelled on that rescue many times since then. Her mouth spoke as if against her will. "And you to me."

"Then come back inside and allow me the next dance? And afterwards, I'd really like to introduce you to my family before they go back up the mountain and then, maybe we can talk more about what this is between us."

She handed him back his jacket and after he shrugged it on, she slid her hand through his arm. Jane loved the sound of "us." But the idea of his family wanting to meet her had her stomach knotting. "They are here?" Jane rubbed her lips with her fingertips, sorely tempted to bite her nails and stopped just short of gnawing on them. "Oh? Not to sound rude, but why would they want to meet me? With this being a fake courtship that really is only benefitting me."

"My brothers have been asking for an introduction with the lady I bought a corsage for when I've never shown any interest in courting before now." Wade grinned as he guided her around the perimeter of the dancefloor and, finding an opening, he pulled her onto the dancefloor. Pulling out a quarter, he dropped it into her reticule and swept her into his arms. "I've held them off all evening by not pointing you out. Corinna was smug in saying the poinsettia would give you away, but with there being at least six other ladies wearing them tonight, Corinna is about to do something drastic to get me to confess to your identity."

Jane laughed, trying to distract herself from his invitation. *His brothers and sister-in-law wish to meet me? How much has he told them about us?* "Very well. We shall meet them at the next break."

His attempts to dance made her heart light. He was not as fluid as Mr. Austin, but the enthusiasm with which he swung her about made her laugh like she hadn't in years. All too soon, the song ended.

He stopped in front of a group of men that were all as tall and broad as him and, in the middle of the group, was a petite blonde woman with sparkling eyes. Jane nodded to the gentlemen and smiled at the lady. "Good evening, you must be Mrs. Sterling," Jane guessed.

"Call me Corinna, please." The petite lady smiled at her. "And you must be the mystery woman that we have heard so much about. I'm glad Wade brought you to us. I was about to ask every woman with a corsage if they were seeing Wade."

"Corinna, boys, this is Miss Jane Cady," Wade supplied.

The man she recognized as Lawrence, who had been spending so much time at the lunch counter during Jean May's shift, stepped forward and bowed over her hand. "He's quite taken with you."

Her cheeks flushed with pleasure and she dared to glance at her pretend beau. "Wade has spoken of me?"

"Oh no," Lawrence replied. "He hasn't mentioned a word. He seems like he's almost afraid for us to get to know you. However, I get all the good news from Miss Jean May. But she was a good sport and wouldn't give up the identity of the Harvey Girl who caught his eye."

Corinna clapped her hands. "And I certainly approve of him picking a Harvey Girl." She smiled at Jane. "You see, I was a Harvey Girl not too long ago, myself. Well, that's before I was fired, that is."

"Fired?" Jane gasped. She hadn't heard anything about that . . . except that Pernilla had gotten a girl fired. Had it been Corinna?

Corinna waved her hand dismissively. "I probably would've fired me too for not telling the whole truth like I did when I started. It couldn't be helped, but it all turned out right in the end and I even made another friend out of mess that was my life," she said, laughing. "Not that you need to know any of that just yet, especially when the dancing is about to begin again." She tucked her hand through Jane's arm. "Now, meeting Sterling men can be quite intimidating, especially if you're a petite woman like myself, which you are." She motioned to the first gentleman. "The oldest is Tanner, my husband. Then you have Wade, then there is Lawrence, Gray, Clint, Jackson, and Noah," she went down the line, pointing to all the brothers. Half of them had brown hair, and the other half had blond, but all possessed the broad shoulders and kind eyes of Wade.

She dipped into a curtsy as the music began to play again. "It is a pleasure."

"I would like to be the first to get to know our future sister-in-law," Noah piped up, holding up his half dollar in the air. "I know I can only dance once per donation, but I think you should remember that I am the youngest and the most *generous* of the group."

Jane laughed and accepted the coin, proceeding to dance with him and the rest of the brothers while fielding questions and trying her best not to lie about their situation. She cycled through all of the brothers and at last turned to find herself face-to-face with Graham Bank.

He held up a folded bill between two fingers. "May I have this dance, Jane?"

"I don't think we should dance." She took a step back, glancing about for another partner. *Where is Wade?*

"It's for the children." Graham reminded her. He unfolded his wallet and withdrew more bills. "I'd say twenty dollars should be enough to entice you, wouldn't you agree? And maybe even get you that little Mistletoe Maiden crown."

Jane bit her lip. She wished she could say no. She wished she could say that amount was too much, and it was bordering on scandalous. However, it *was* for the children. How could she say no when that amount could do so much for them? The home was almost ready to be built. This was the last fundraiser. Perhaps this donation could secure a water closet for the children. She would be selfish to refuse. She sighed and accepted the cash, tucking it into her reticule and allowed Graham to lead her onto the dancefloor for a waltz. In the corner of her eye, she found Eliza with Wade again and Dolly with her arm threaded through Mr. Austin's as they took their places.

Graham bowed to Jane. "We've been through a lot, Jane. There is no need to scowl so fiercely at me as if we are no longer even friends."

"Friends?" Jane gaped at him. Had he

always been this delusional? "You discarded me on our wedding day, Graham. That is more than just a lot. That is nearing unforgivable, but I am attempting to really and truly forgive you so that my heart is free and not caught in the brambles of bitterness because those thorns will only draw my blood, my hurt and I won't heal unless I choose to forgive." She squeezed her eyes shut. "No, I do forgive you, but that doesn't mean I will forget your actions. I do not trust you anymore, Graham."

Graham grimaced. "I don't blame you for your mistrust, but surely a marriage contract would bind up the wounds I inflicted. We can start afresh. I acted in haste and now, I repent most heartily."

Jane forced herself to pause to keep her anger from coloring her tone. "I'm glad you realize what you did is wrong, but I cannot marry you. Please don't make this harder than it already is for me by continuing to be here in the town where we have chosen to start over. It makes it impossible to forget the past with you here."

Graham gave her a smile. "At least I know it is hard on you."

She jerked back. "You want this to be difficult on me? I thought you were a gentleman, Graham."

He laughed, twirling them around a stumbling Wade and an impatient Eliza. "That's not what I meant. What I meant was that I might have a chance to win you back if this is hurting you. If I stay long enough, you will return to New York, not with Austin, but with me."

She shook her head. "Graham, I don't think you understand the situation. I can never go back to New York, not with my family being poor. And I know you well enough to know that you can never live life without money, especially when no money will be added through a marriage. You're too much of a businessman not to see the transaction involved."

She pressed her lips against the less flattering things. She also knew him to be spoiled and selfish, which Austin had confirmed. She would not fall prey to this man again, especially not when there was such a wonderful man across the ballroom. Wade may not have the funds Austin and Graham had at their disposal, but he was a man of character, and she was beginning to see how much more a man's character was worth than the money in his bank account.

At long last, the painful dance ended, but Graham did not release her hand. "Can you please talk with me out on the veranda? There are a few things I need to tell you."

Jane pulled her hand from his and folded them in front of her skirts. "Mr. Bank, I thank you for the donation that you've made on behalf of the children, but I'm afraid this is where we must part ways tonight. Please do not ask me to dance again." She turned around and smiled at the first cowboy she spotted. "Care for a dance?"

Jane tried not to think about Graham and his cattiness as she danced. She needed to put that behind her. A couple twirled directly behind her, and she could overhear Pernilla with her shrill voice talking to the man she was dancing with.

"Mr. Austin, I know she is beautiful and all, but one can't help but question why she is so taken up with Wade Sterling and he with her so quickly," Pernilla said. "I know you came down here to see if you could win her hand. However, I feel like it is my duty to tell you that it was a shocking thing to see them kissing in the dining room."

Jane's cheeks flared. So, there had been somebody who witnessed her kiss. She couldn't help but glance over at Dolly. If Pernilla had seen that kiss, there was no way that she hadn't told Dolly. And why hadn't Dolly corrected her? Unless Pernilla was thinking about holding this over her head. Or was she holding out just for the right moment to take Jane down?

Mr. Austin must have said something, and Pernilla laughed.

"Why, of course, I'm talking about that," she said. "Why else would she leap into a relationship with a man she hardly knows? And why would that second fellow be here seeking her hand so hard? No, my guess is that she is with child, and she wants to wed quickly. Though, I don't know why she doesn't just accept Graham right away if he's the father of her child."

Jane stumbled in the cowboy's arms. How dare Pernilla cast such disparagement against her very character? She whirled around to correct Pernilla but kept her hand in the cowboy's, her feet still moving in perfect time, for she did not wish to be disqualified from the dance. But Mr. Austin beat her to it.

"Miss Pernilla, there are ladies in the New York Four Hundred who have been cast out of society for saying less than you have insinuated tonight. You need to hold your tongue. I have not known Miss Jane Cady for very long myself, but I do know her by reputation. She is a diamond of the first water, one of the most highly sought-after women in all of New York society before her fall from the elite Knickerbocker standing. She's still a Knickerbocker. She is just a poor one. I would suggest you do not disparage the woman I am attempting to win as my wife." He bowed and ended the dance, Pernilla's jaw dropping as he left her on the dancefloor.

"Miss Pernilla, you are now disqualified from the dance marathon. Please bring your reticule over to the table, and we will count out your earnings," Father called out.

Pernilla's cheeks burned as she glared at Jane. Jane lifted her chin. Pernilla deserved to be thrown out. Jane finished the dance with the cowboy and thanked him with a smile. She hurried over to Dolly's side. "Miss Dolly, I wanted to address something before it got to your attention."

Miss Dolly held up her hand. "Stop right there and say no more. I heard Pernilla telling her lies to anybody who would listen. However, everyone here knows your character. I know we haven't worked for very long together—not even a month, in fact—but I feel as if I know you very well. And I have no doubt that what she says is false. I can't imagine you kissing Mr. Wade Sterling in front of the whole dining room for all to see."

Jane's cheeks flamed. "Well, while what she says about Mr. Graham Bank is completely false, I did in fact kiss Wade."

Instead of the anger that she expected, Dolly's eyes flashed with mirth. "Well, seeing as I didn't *catch* you kissing the man,

I will let you off with a warning, but I would love to hear more about this kiss and why."

Jane's smile blossomed. "Thank you, now I better get back to dancing before I am disqualified too."

The evening was a blur of dancing and by the end of it, Jane's feet ached so much that she almost gave up, save for the thought of the children's home.

At last, the final dance was called and still ten couples remained on the dance-floor. Wade bowed before her. "May I have the final dance, my lady?"

She smiled up at him as he dropped a half dollar into her reticule. "Thank goodness, I need someone trustworthy who can catch me when I faint from exhaustion."

His brows furrowed as concern lit his gaze. "I can do that."

She rested heavily on his arms, praying she would not topple over, but Wade's arms never wavered and before she knew it, the dance was over and the final count of the funds was called for.

The girls dropped their reticules at the judges table and within minutes, all funds had been counted and Father stood atop a chair, clinking a fork to a glass. "Ladies and gentlemen. I am proud to announce that the Christmas Eve Marathon Dance has broken the record for the highest fund raiser. We have collected two hundred and twenty dollars. With the Harvey House matching the sum, it brings the total to four hundred and forty dollars."

The room burst into applause.

"Which means, from what Preacher Martin has told me, the remaining proceeds will go to clothing and feeding the children for a year!"

The crowd cheered even louder, some of the men releasing whistles.

"And now, for the naming of the Mistletoe Maiden," Father called out over the crowd as he accepted the red and green ribbon crown from Mrs. Martin. "This young lady brought in over seventy-five dollars. Congratulations, Miss Eliza Brady!"

CHAPTER 13

The scent of coffee pulled her from her slumber. She stretched her arms above her head. The Harvey Girls had the morning off, so Pernilla had stayed with her family in town last night and for the first time, she could stir without fear of Pernilla putting a toad in her coffee. Though, she had a feeling that Jean May had to be teasing Jane about what happened to Corinna involving a score of toads. Jean May was certain Pernilla was the culprit, but as no one had caught her, Pernilla's job was safe.

Her gaze landed on the corsage that she attempted to save by setting the stem in a glass of water when she returned last night and looked up the flower's meaning. She stroked the broad green leaf. Wade indeed brought *good cheer* wherever he went. Did he consider her to bring *merriment* to his days as well? She shook her head over her silliness, but it would make for a good letter to Meg.

At the sounds of the dormitory rousing, Jane dressed quickly in a simple gown of crimson and tied her hair back with an emerald ribbon to join her Harvey Sisters in the parlor. She gasped at the sight that greeted her. A small fir tree stood in the corner of the room, dressed in ribbons and lit candles and beneath its graceful boughs were a handful of wrapped presents.

Dolly smiled and waved Jane over to where she stood before a roaring fire and a tea service. Dolly must have risen before dawn to prepare all this. "Merry Christmas, Jane. Join us for coffee and pastries."

Jean May lifted her full coffee cup to Jane from the wingback chair where she was curled up in a thick blanket with a plate of tartlets on her lap. "Jane! Merry Christmas."

"Merry Christmas, ladies," Jane poured herself a cup. "Dolly, did you do all this?"

Dolly smiled. "Normally, Miss Trent does this, but with her away visiting her mother for Christmas, I thought I'd carry on the tradition." She lowered her voice. "Most of us girls can't take the time to travel home, and this is all the Christmas they will have."

Jane wrapped her hands about her steaming cup. "It's perfectly charming, Dolly."

"And there is a present under the tree with your name on it." Dolly pointed to a brown papered medium sized package.

Jane's heart skipped and she knelt at the foot of the tree, mindful of the candles as she retrieved it, glancing at the card attached.

Jane, you are a true Harvey Girl at heart.

Your Harvey Sister, Dolly.

She carefully pulled the pretty blue ribbon and unwrapped the brown paper, tugging off the lid to find low-heeled half boots. She gasped and lifted them out, tears springing as she turned to Dolly. "You bought me shoes."

Dolly shrugged. "I noticed you were limping and figured that you might need a simple pair, so I snuck into your room and took your highest heel and brought them to the mercantile and then general store until I found a pair in stock that would suit."

Jane rose and threw her arms about Dolly. "Thank you."

Dolly's cheeks pinked. "I'm happy you like them."

Jane slipped on her new half boots and enjoyed the company of her Harvey Sisters until the clock on the mantel sounded seven o'clock. With a sigh, she bid the ladies farewell and slipped on her woolen cloak and grabbed the little basket with Wade's gift tucked inside.

"Don't forget to return by seven o'clock if you want to join us for singing Christmas carols about town. We meet at the church!" Dolly called after her.

"I'll be there," Jane called over her shoulder as she closed the dormitory door. Before heading to her parent's home, she stopped at the bakery attached to the Harvey House to fetch a basket of pastries for her family and a carrot for Phantom from the kitchen.

The crisp air nipped at her cheeks as she swung the basket on her arm. She paused in front of the stable. Would he be inside? Or still asleep at the Castañeda? She would love to see Phantom . . . but she had really brought the carrot for him as an excuse to see Wade.

She pushed open the stable door, the warmth enveloping her along with the sweet scent of fresh hay and the nickering of horses. She strode to Phantom's stall, rubbing his nose as she offered him the carrot. The sound of a stall door opening brought a smile to her lips.

"Jane."

She turned at his voice, her cheeks already pinking. "Wade, merry Christmas."

She reached into her basket and withdrew the folded silk scarf. "It's not much, but I thought you could wear it during the race."

He unfurled the emerald scarf with its ornate gold embroidery of roses. "A knight sporting his lady's colors." He grasped her hand. "And I have a present for you as well." He reached into his back pocket and withdrew a paper, handing it to her.

She smiled as she unfolded it, tears filling her gaze for the second time this morning. "Y-you bought Phantom?"

"I know you can't afford to care for him, so my gift to you is that I will care for him all his days and you may visit and ride him whenever you wish." He ran his thumb over her hand. "You could even ride him in the Boxing Day Race if you'd like. He's got a lot to offer, even at his age."

"Oh!" She threw her arms about his neck, clinging to him as the fear of Phantom being taken from her ebbed from her bones. "I was so afraid that Father would sell him to someone far away and I'd never see him again. Wade, you are so thoughtful."

"Jane," he whispered into her hair. "I need to talk with you about—"

"Jane Cady. There you are. I went to the dormitory to escort you for your parents. We are having Christmas breakfast soon. I figured you would be visiting your horse." Graham frowned at Wade and Jane embracing.

Jane slipped from his arms and squeezed Wade's hand. "We *will* be finishing this conversation."

"Now would be preferable, but I'll wait. I'd wait forever for you, Jane Cady." He kissed the top of her hand, as Graham coughed.

Jane smiled over her shoulder to Wade, her heart soaring. *Wade saved Phantom for me, and he wants to court me. Wade thinks I'm special for only myself and not just money.*

Graham offered her his arm. "Shall we?"

She handed Graham her basket instead of her hand and tucked her hand into her fur muff. "Thank you."

Graham gripped the basket at his side. "My dearest Jane, there is something that I must confess."

She glanced sideways at him. "Oh?"

"I know it has only been three weeks since you left, but New York is empty without you. Parties have all but lost their lure and operas only serve to remind me of my heart's absence as the singers' longing melodies of unrequited love finally hold meaning for me. While I once mocked the heroes for their passion, I now understand what it means to be separated from the woman you love."

Love? No, you never loved me—and I can see that now. And given how quickly I was able to put you out of my mind when I kissed Wade, I never really loved you either. "Graham, while I appreciate your sentiment—"

"I must continue before we reach your parents' home. Austin would certainly object and attempt to change your mind. My darling, please end my torture and come home. If you need more time before accepting my hand in marriage, I implore you to stay with your grandparents, so we can at least be close before the wedding, for I want none but you, no matter what my mother says."

Her eyes widened at his confession. "And you came to this conclusion *after* you decided to humiliate me?"

"Yes, but consider what a step up in society it would be for you since your calamity."

"Step up?" She whirled on him. "Just because I work for a living now does not make me beneath you."

He set down the basket and grinned. "I was speaking that it was a step up from your horse rancher beau. I am flattered that you would take the charade so far in order to make me jealous."

Her cheeks flamed. It may have started as a farce only three days ago, but those three days with Wade had changed everything. How could she go back to such a gray life when Wade brought such vibrant light? "No, Graham."

He blinked. "What?"

"No. I will not marry you."

His neck and ears burned scarlet. "You would stand me up after I came all this way to speak with you? Even though I had to practically beg my mother not to disinherit me?"

"If you really loved me, you would have married me weeks ago when you had the chance and proved to me your devotion. But you did not. And not to be cruel, but I know for a fact that I did not love you—I only loved the idea of you." She sucked her cheeks in, trying to contain her frustration. "I don't mean to be harsh, but I don't belong to that world anymore and you mustn't pretend that I do." She moved to grab the basket from him.

His hand shot out and enclosed her wrist, pinching her skin with his grip. "You will *not* humiliate me like this."

"Graham, let go." She gasped in pain. "You are hurting me."

His fingers tightened. "You *do* mean to be harsh. You mean to exact your revenge. Well, I won't stand for it. Your father will make you marry me when he hears how much I am willing to give him for you."

"I am not an object, Graham." She glared up at him. "Now, release me before—"

"You loved me once. You can love me

again." Graham tugged her against him, his hands splaying over her back, the basket tumbling to the ground. "Perhaps a kiss will remind you?"

She drew a breath to scream, but Graham was wrenched back and Wade shoved him to the ground. "Are you really that pathetic that you have to buy a woman's affections? And *force* her to kiss you? Let me tell you, love can't be bought. Touch her again and I'll show you how a real man deals with your type. Now, get up and go buy yourself a ticket East before I forget that it is Christmas Sunday."

Graham scrambled back on his hands. "Do you have any idea who I am?"

"I know *exactly* who you are, and Miss Cady deserves better than a scorpion like you." He clenched his fists.

Jane rested her hand on Wade.

He turned to her, the fight in his eyes softening at her gaze. "Did he hurt you?"

She shook her head even as she rubbed her wrist. "Thank you, Wade. I've got it from here."

Wade stepped to the side and nodded,

but he held his body loose, ready to fight if necessary.

"Graham Bank, do not come back to Las Vegas in pursuit of me. I am not interested." She threaded her hand through Wade's arm. "As you can see, I am perfectly content where I am."

"How? Our families have never been content." Graham rose and dusted off his pant legs.

"Losing the family fortune is the best thing that has ever happened to me." She glanced at Wade, a shyness stealing over her. "It led me to a man who has completely captivated me. Now, if you don't mind, Mr. Bank, I will bid you farewell—hopefully forever."

Graham opened his mouth, a protest on his lips, but at Wade's glare he snapped his mouth shut. "This isn't over, Jane," Graham warned.

Wade narrowed his gaze at him and something akin to a growl passed his lips, sending Graham scrambling back and tripping over his own feet to avoid the large Sterling man, shouting over his shoulder,

"You'll be hearing from my lawyer for your gross misconduct."

Wade stiffened at the threat but shrugged it off. "I've done nothing wrong and, if given a second chance, I'd do more than shove you away from Jane. Besides, I have a great lawyer of my own now."

Graham scowled at him but continued down the street to the train station.

Jane sighed and lifted the basket lid. A few of the pastries were smushed, but they would still taste divine.

"Sad, desperate galoot." Wade shook his head. "Can I walk you home?"

"It's early and I doubt I will encounter any other uncouth gentlemen. Besides, the animals need you, yes?"

He nodded but glanced toward Graham's retreating figure. "But, if you need me, they can wait."

"I'm fine, thank you, Wade. You scared him off." She smiled up to him. "See you tomorrow for the race."

"I'll be the one with the emerald scarf tied to my arm." He squeezed her hand and waved farewell. "And then, we will have that talk?"

"Yes." Jane gathered her skirts and hurried up the hill to the edge of town to the cottage. Jane pushed open the door to her family's home. She didn't feel like it was her home anymore. It never really had been as she hadn't even slept one night under the roof. But seeing the little juniper tree, that Theo had no doubt cut down, in the corner of the parlor with cloth-covered presents beneath the leaves, fond memories of her childhood surfaced. This Christmas would be nothing like those of yore, but it was already proving to be one of the best.

She knelt and tucked the three presents she purchased with her remaining funds under the tree. She knew her mother would enjoy having some fresh handkerchiefs trimmed in lace. She sewed them herself. Theo would like her new book on bugs. Her father had been running low on his favorite tobacco, she had noticed while in his office at the Harvey House, so she had ordered some from Rudy's Mercantile. It wasn't the most extravagant of Christmases, but it would do nicely and prove to be thoughtful too.

She listened, but nobody stirred upstairs, and she realized that not even the scent of coffee filled the air. Thankfully, she knew how to make a good cup of coffee now that she was a Harvey Girl. Between the coffee and her pastries, they would have a lovely Christmas morning. She tiptoed to the kitchen and made quick work of stoking the embers in the stove and pushed the kettle into place.

Creaking on the stairs alerted her that someone had risen. "Merry Christmas!" She sang over her shoulder while she reached for the tin of coffee grounds on the counter.

"And a merry Christmas to you too, my dear Jane."

She stiffened at the male voice and turned with the tin clutched to her chest. "Mr. Austin? I-I thought you were staying at the hotel."

"I was, but last night, your father and I got to talking and I ended up staying the night in the room that would have been yours." He grimaced. "They had poor Theo moved into their room before I even knew what was happening. I thought it was a guest room, only to discover the jars of bugs that could only belong to one young lady."

"Can I get you some coffee? It should be ready in about ten minutes. I just put the water on to boil."

He reached for the tin and placed it on the counter. "I didn't come to Las Vegas for coffee. Though I am quite pleased that you know how to brew a superior cup, given your time as a Harvey Girl. However, I hope that your time as a waitress has come to an end."

Her stomach twisted in her gut. "I am not free to accept your hand, Mr. Austin."

"I believe you are. I don't believe for one moment that you and this cowboy are going to go the distance. You and I are from the same stock. We are Knickerbockers."

"My father is actually parvenu," she corrected him.

He chuckled. "Yes, but your mother is a Knickerbocker. Your grandparents are Knickerbockers. It is in our blood. Not everyone understands us, but everyone *ac-*

cepts us as part of the New York Four Hundred. Come back with me. Claim your rightful place in society as a matron."

She reclaimed the tin of coffee and opened it, the burst of grounds nearly scattering out of the tin. "Mr. Austin, you know I cannot."

"You can. If you marry me, you will have surpassed even the wealth of the Bank family. Graham is not worthy of you. He only followed me out here because you were something that he could not have. He's always been selfish and spoiled. His mother never did him any favors by giving him everything he ever wanted, including you, at first. When she took you away from him, he went along with it at first, given that she could've taken away all his money too. But he worked her down like he always does, like a petulant child wanting a pet."

"I am no pet, Mr. Austin." She measured out the coffee, deciding on a strong brew.

"And I know that. I knew during your courtship to my friend that you were a special lady. And I also hoped secretly that you would not work out with Graham so that I might have a chance with you."

She slowly turned. "You did?"

He grasped her hand in his. "Please, just consider my offer of marriage. I did not come out here with the intention of going back home alone."

"I'm certain Pernilla will have you in an instant."

He chuckled. "Yes, but she is not you. I know that you are an independent young woman now, and I wholeheartedly hope that you will give this proposal consideration apart from your father."

She looked up at him, setting aside the coffee grounds. "Apart from my father?"

"Yes, I know I went about it the wrong way with trying to secure your hand, but I am old-fashioned in that sense." He shrugged. "And I thought that I would ask your father for permission first, for permission to seek *courtship*. I had not expected him to write back saying that you *would* marry me. It gave me great hope, and I thought perhaps that you would be more open to the idea than you are."

"He overstepped."

"Absolutely. He was reaching for the chance at returning to his old life." He frowned. "And I don't want you to think that I am like that. I would never foist upon you anything you did not wish. I have chosen to pursue you, yes, but I will leave when I am convinced that we do not belong together."

"Mr. Austin, would it persuade you that *I* am convinced?"

"Hyde," he gently corrected her. "Please, call me Hyde. And you have not given us a chance yet. I believe we belong together because we are so similar. You and this cowboy are not. You're from two different worlds. You cannot possibly think that you could be a frontier woman, or a mountain man's wife. You are built for a life of crystal, gold, and diamonds. I can give you those. I will give you the world if you will let me."

"Hyde—" *I don't want the world. I just want to be happy. I don't think that I can be happy being the woman I once was.* But as she glanced up at Austin, she realized she had been silent for too long as a slow smile spread on his face.

"Thank you for your consideration," he bowed. "I realize it is Christmas morning, and I do not wish to intrude upon your family until I am part of the family. I will take a rain check on that coffee and I will make myself scarce." He kissed her hand. "I hope that you will answer favorably to me, Miss Jane Cady. I would hate to think that you would tell me no just because your father wants you to say yes."

IT WAS a quiet Christmas for Wade. While he and his brothers weren't extravagant in their gifts, he enjoyed the camaraderie of laughing with them as they roasted whatever game they shot on the open fire. He enjoyed their Christmas horseback trek together as they beat the bounds of the ranch every year on Christmas Day. He hoped they were doing well and that Tanner and Corinna were enjoying their first Christmas as a newlywed couple. He would see them soon enough and as he had only seen them yesterday, they, of course, couldn't stay for the Boxing Day race since they came to the Christmas Eve fundraiser instead.

There had been a steady flow of customers this morning as people came in to take their horses and buggies out to see their kinfolk across the Las Vegas countryside and back into town. He was thankful it was nearing quitting time. He glanced at his watch and sighed. The sun set so early in the winter that his stomach misinterpreted the nightfall as dinner time. He still had a half hour before he could close for the evening and sit down with Corinna's book in the lobby of the Castañeda.

Singing caught on the wind, and he peeked out of the doors to see carolers were already singing and going door to door. He would like to enjoy some of the festivities and then maybe see if Jane was working the lunch counter. He heard that a few girls would be working the lunch counter on Christmas evening. All the Harvey Girls had been given off the morning of Christmas, so he was certain the counter would be crowded with hungry, single cowboys awaiting their first decent meal of the day.

He sighed and grabbed up the curry comb and set to working over Raven, getting her ready for her big race in the morning.

"Good evening and merry Christmas, Mr. Sterling," came a bright, feminine voice from the threshold. "I was hoping to have you ready the buggy."

He looked up from brushing Raven. Miss Brady leaned against the door, dressed in a scarlet cloak that accented her dark hair and wore the crown of green and gold ribbons from the Mistletoe Maiden contest.

"Miss Brady, Merry Christmas to you too. Isn't it rather late for an evening drive, especially alone?"

She approached the stall door and smiled up at him. "Well, I was hoping that I might run into a knight in shining Stetson who might escort me to go see my relatives. They didn't come in for the dance last night and will be happy to know that I won the Mistletoe Maiden."

"That's, uh, nice. People like to hear

good news." Was she positioning herself for him to offer to escort her? He didn't like the idea of allowing her to drive freely across Las Vegas at night without an escort, but that really wasn't his responsibility, nor his position to correct her. "Are you certain your father would appreciate you driving alone? I don't mean to give advice where it isn't wanted, but with your father boarding the horses here, I don't want him to get upset with me for hitching your horse when you don't have an escort to keep you safe. Las Vegas is reformed, but we still have a saloon."

Miss Brady's trilling laugh filled the barn and made Raven snort and stomp. "You're so kind to think after my welfare, Mr. Sterling."

"I care about all my customers and the town folk. Good neighbors look out for one another."

The carolers were growing louder, and she swayed with the music.

"They certainly do. And that reminds me of my own promise to help you."

He swallowed. "H-help me?"

She giggled. "Well, it is Sunday, and you did promise that you would come take a dance lesson with me on a Sunday."

"I did?" His eyes widened as she circled him like raccoon searching a henhouse for weak points. "I don't think—"

She laughed again. "As if you could forget, Mr. Sterling. Come, let's do our first lesson now. We already have the music. We shouldn't waste such a divine blessing, should we? And you know that you cannot say no to the Mistletoe Maiden."

Wade gritted his teeth. He didn't like the idea of dancing with another woman, especially at night and unchaperoned, and with one who was not Jane.

She reached for his hands, tugging him out of the stall. How could he reject her without hurting her feelings and having her run off to her father and hurt Mr. Hill's business by Mr. Brady pulling out all of his horses from the stables? The man rented six of the eighteen stalls.

Before he could decide what to do, she had her right arm resting atop his and her left hand drawing his to rest on her back.

"Now, let's dance." She pulled him, and his feet moved of their own accord to keep him from stumbling over backwards. The carolers were coming nearer and nearer, and he turned his head to look as they passed the stable, and his eyes met Jane's. Her mouth dropped and her expression of hurt was undeniable.

"I think that dancing will have to wait." He extricated himself from Miss Brady's arms.

"Eliza?" Mr. Brady called from the doorway, grinning at seeing them so close.

Wade practically leapt to the other end of the breezeway.

"I wanted to wish you well in the race tomorrow." Mr. Brady slapped Wade's shoulder and gave it a squeeze. "It will be a true testament to your horsemanship. If you do well in the race tomorrow, I'm sure that we can do business together. Now, if you wouldn't mind getting our horses ready, my daughter and I must take a drive to visit my mother. She only lives a mile outside of town, but I don't fancy a walk in this chill."

Wade turned his gaze to Eliza, and she shrugged.

"You never asked if my father was coming." She smiled up at him. She lowered her voice. "It's a shame he came so soon because you know what else mistletoe is good for?"

He jerked back, his neck burning as she laughed. Was she trying to entrap him? He shrugged it off. He didn't like that thought, but he didn't want to accuse a woman of doing something she wasn't doing. So, he set to work to get the horses ready, hoping that Jane had not misread the situation and saw Mr. Brady approaching the stables.

CHAPTER 14

This was it. This was the reason why Wade came into town—to showcase his horse and his skills as a trainer. He wasn't planning on selling Raven, of course, she was too special, but surely this would garner attention of the townsfolk that Raven was his masterpiece, bred, raised, and trained. Today was about getting the word out that his brothers' ranch, the *Sanctuary*, was open for business.

Wade glanced down at the pretty silk scarf tied on his bicep. He had wanted to ask Jane to make their courtship real yesterday before they were interrupted by Graham, but after the little shoving match, it didn't really seem like the right moment. However, he didn't want Jane to think that just because Graham was out of the picture, *he* wanted to be out of the picture. And then, of course, there was Miss Brady.

"Yoohoo, Wade," cried out Eliza Brady . . . still wearing that crown.

He gritted his teeth, biting back a groan as he accidentally made eye contact with her.

She lifted her handkerchief, waving, and then it slipped from her fingers, floating and tumbling into the middle of the road. She gasped.

Seemed like a mighty big waste to drop a perfectly good handkerchief in the middle of the road, not to mention it was needlessly cluttering the street. He nudged Raven forward, hopped off the saddle, and bent, scooping it up, handing it back to her, sending the town girls about her twittering and giggling like a flock of cow birds as he swung back into the saddle with ease.

"You are too kind, Wade." She smiled up at him. "It is such a shame that you never came to town before now. But try to win because I will be presenting the gold . . . and maybe even more to the winner."

Not knowing what to say, he tipped his hat and turned his horse with a muffled, "Excuse me, miss."

Wade looked across the street and saw Jane standing beside Miss Dolly, one of the few Harvey Girls that dared to befriend her. He tipped his Stetson to her and directed Raven to stand before her. "Miss Jane, I appreciate you coming out to support me today."

She smiled up at him. "I'm happy to be here for you. Besides, I love horses, and if Phantom wasn't so old, I'd be racing him with you. But I wouldn't want to take the spotlight away from Raven." She reached toward his horse with her hand, allowing the mare to smell her before rubbing Raven's muzzle.

Miss Dolly smiled. "And after what Jane told me what you did for her, I hope you win, Mr. Sterling. Just be sure to keep your horse out of my dining room." She shook her head and laughed. "Your brother's horse, Silver, seems to have a liking for fine dining."

Wade grinned. Tanner had told him the tale, which he didn't doubt, given Silver came like a dog when whistled for. "I'll be sure to keep her out, Miss Dolly."

"Everyone is going to want one of your horses after today, Wade." Jane beamed up at him. "People are already talking about your mare. I overheard several people during the dance and even while serving the townsfolk. People are *buzzing* about this beautiful horse and who bred it."

"I hope you gave them a good word about me?" Wade winked at her.

"I might have given them a *few* good words about you," Jane returned, her eyes sparkling with conspiratorial mirth as Miss Dolly shook her head, laughing softly.

"Everyone up to the starting line," shouted Mr. Edwards, the Englishman who had begun the Boxing Day Race tradition over a decade ago.

Wade grinned at Jane and sent her another wink as he pulled his horse into line. A rider nudged his stallion between them.

Austin. "I didn't know you brought a horse with you, Austin."

"I didn't. I bought this magnificent beast on Christmas Eve during the dance based on description alone from Mr. Edwards. He says Charleston here has won the race two years in a row and would be a sure bet. And if there is anything I don't do, it is take a bet that I cannot win." He met Wade's eye, leaning forward in his English saddle with ease to rub the stallion's mane. "I know that our Jane is fond of horses. I figured this would make a great present for her."

His eyes narrowed with Austin's challenge. *He means to give her a horse. While it is a superior horse to Phantom, the stallion does not possess Jane's heart.*

"If I win against your mare, I'd say that makes this stallion even more valuable to Jane. Besides, I intend to give her the money from the race when I win."

"You are confident, I'll give you that, but I doubt she would accept your charity," Wade snorted. "She hasn't yet, why would she start now?"

"Well, I proposed to her last night."

"That is nothing new." Wade pressed his lips into a firm line.

Austin shrugged. "She still hasn't given me an answer. So, that's progress."

Now that *is* new. Wade was well aware that Austin wanted to marry her. He also knew that her father had all but pushed Austin toward her more times than she cared to mention. But to be formally proposed to and not respond? Was Jane actually considering the man? *I suppose now that Graham is out of the picture for good, and our arrangement is nearly up, there's nothing stopping her from accepting him.* An urgency pressed on his chest. He needed to speak with Jane. He glanced over his shoulder as Raven danced underfoot.

She was deep in conversation with a lady from town.

He shifted back into the saddle. He couldn't get distracted—not now, not when this meant so much. If he won, he could expand his business and have something to offer the former heiress. He didn't have much in the world, but whatever he had, he wanted to share with Jane. That much, he was sure.

During their short time together, he had come to know her quite well and he did not want to live without her—if she would have him. The uncertainty of their fake courtship was maddening. Sure, he had seen her every day in the building where she worked. He had her horse in his stable and saw her every evening after her shift when she visited Phantom. But was that enough time for her to feel anything for him? He shook his head. He never thought he'd be the one to fall prey to love at first sight, given he hadn't believed in it until it happened to him.

"On your mark," shouted Mr. Edwards, his gun pointed to the sky. "Get set—" the bullet split the air and Raven shot into motion. Her feet ate the ground in confident, eager strides as she broke away from the pack of horses. A glance under his arm revealed Austin right behind him, but Wade could tell that Austin was not connected with his horse, not like him and Raven. Raven knew Wade's every command before he seemed to even give it with his legs, his arms, or his voice. She knew him. She'd known him since birth. Maybe even before that if horses could hear in the womb.

When he was a boy, his mother told him that his little brother could hear him in the womb. Maybe it was the same thing with horses. That was another strike against him. But, Jane didn't seem to be like a lot of people. She didn't judge him based on his parentage. But her family would. He braced himself as Raven leapt over the log placed in the road. He heard a shout behind him, but he didn't dare glance back. A rider must not have made it over.

When he cleared the round in the bend, the pounding of a horse's hooves beside him neared closer and closer. Austin could ride a horse. The man's English saddle was lighter and surely gave his horse a bit of an edge. But Raven did not need an edge. She was just getting started. "Let's go, Raven!"

"DO YOU SEE HIM?" Dolly squinted near the finish line, shielding her eyes from the sun.

Jane hopped to see over the heads of the crowd. "I see a cloud of dust, but I can't see the horses yet, much less the riders."

"Austin is going to make me a mint," Father interjected from behind.

Jane swiveled to her father. "You placed a *bet?*"

"Why do you think this Boxing Day Race is such a tradition in a place that was nearly as bad as Dodge City?" Father snorted. "Of course, I placed a bet." He patted her arm. "Nothing like the old days, I assure you."

She clenched her fists. How could he gamble? Certainly, it was an acceptable vice with the Four Hundred gentlemen, but Father no longer had that connection, nor the funds. *Don't think about him and his choices. Focus on Wade.* The riders approached and she saw the black beauty that was no doubt Raven. Austin's mount was closing in on the mare.

Jane lifted her handkerchief, cheering with the crowd, her heart pounding at the sight of Wade at his most comfortable—

atop a horse, riding as if he had been born in the saddle. Few men could look so graceful, while still being so utterly manly and handsome. If only their courtship was for real. Her cheer caught in her throat. With Graham leaving, and Mr. Austin soon after, there was no one left to pretend for.

Raven surged ahead and crossed the finish line three lengths before Austin. The crowd erupted, her father visibly slumping, his cheeks pale as he stumbled away into the crowd, disappearing from her view.

Wade swept his leg over the saddle before Raven pranced to a halt, the crowd pressing near him, men shouting offers to buy his horse, but Wade pushed past the crowd and found Jane, grinning.

"You did it!" She laughed, impulsively wrapping her hands about his neck to tug him into an embrace, their lips brushing.

He drew back a breath, his gaze never leaving hers as he slowly leaned in. She should move away, but—her gaze landed on his mouth, and she lifted her chin, allowing his full lips to claim her own. Bursts of fireworks dotted her vision as she closed her eyes and leaned into Wade, eager for his touch, for his affection, for this man to be hers for real.

She broke away, her cheeks burning as she caught Hyde staring at them with a sad smile from atop his mount.

Hyde approached them, dismounting and fisting the reins. "I know when I am beat. I'll be honest, I didn't think you actually cared for the cowboy until now, but I was raised in a home with parents that loved each other, and I know true love when I see it." He bowed and handed the reins to Jane. "Congratulations on finding what so many seek. Consider this my wedding present."

"Wedding present?" She gasped, glancing up to Wade. The charade had gone too far if people were expecting a ring from this kiss. Her cheeks burned.

"Yes. And please, make sure your father doesn't get his hands on the stallion." He sighed. "He would sell anything you own if he could. This horse is for your future with Wade, and I would consider it a boon to bless you both with him and know that even though I could not provide the life I wished for you, I can, in some small measure, affect it." He bent and kissed her hand. "Have a beautiful life, Jane. If anyone in our group deserves it, it is you." He held out his hand to Wade. "Take care of Jane."

Wade clasped it. "I intend to."

"Mr. Sterling!" Mr. Edwards clasped him on the shoulder. "Time for the award ceremony. The purse will be presented by our very own Mistletoe Maiden."

She glanced up at the platform where Eliza was waving at Wade . . . and blowing him a kiss.

CHAPTER 15

Someone grabbed the reins of Raven and guided them to a platform that the town had constructed for the event with festive green and gold buntings draping the side where Mr. Edwards presented him a small gold cup.

Eliza beamed at him. She had on the crown again and clasped the small purse of gold over her heart. "I knew you could do it."

He nodded. "Thank you." Her lips puckered, but before she could get any ideas, he held out his hand, and she dropped the purse into his palm. He stepped back at once.

Her expression faltered but she lifted her hands with the crowd and cheered for Wade.

He grinned, lifting his Stetson in the air and searching the crowd for Jane, but he didn't see her or Charleston again with the flood of congratulations pouring in from all sides.

Raven needed a good scrubbing down and oats for her effort today and while he appreciated the clamor for his attention, his horse's needs came before any more celebrating. He waved to the crowd and made sure the purse of winnings was tucked inside his buttoned-up vest. He guided Raven to the stables and glanced backward to see a crowd of about fifteen men following behind him. His heart pounded. Surely in a town like this, they weren't going to rob him of his winnings in front of everybody?

"Mr. Sterling, do you have a moment?" A man in a flat crown planter's hat called to him. "We'd like to discuss your stock availability, and I'm afraid that my friend here is insisting that he will get the best that you have. However, I am insisting that *I* will get the best you have for I have more funds than he."

"I'm certain I have a satisfactory horse for each of you." Wade grinned and waved them inside the stable, and spotted Charleston already cared for in the stall, munching away on some oats. He smiled. Jane had been here. She was likely long gone to the Harvey House by now. He unsaddled his horse and grabbed the curry comb. He worked on Raven as the men asked him how he got into the horse business.

"I've been raising and training horses since I was a boy, well over ten years now, and Raven was one of the first foals that I bred and kept for myself. I have a stallion that is the prized sire for most of my herd. I have about six broodmares foaling in the summer months. I also have a handful of yearlings and finished mares ready for sale. Now, I can sell the foals and yearlings at different levels. I can offer them green-broke, or fully broke, and also have them training to race like Raven here. It really just depends on what you want."

A man shoved to the front of the crowd. "Well, I don't know if we'll have time to wait for all that now. If you've got those foals arriving, I want my name to be the first on the list to purchase one."

"No, mine!" cried another man from behind him. "I will give you two hundred dollars for that foal right now."

"Three hundred!"

"Four hundred."

Wade's jaw dropped as the numbers rose to an astronomical high. The foals weren't even born yet, and he didn't even know their condition, or if they were male or female, yet these people were going senseless over his horses. Wade grinned as the men placed their bids. He set aside the curry comb and took the bids down until, at last, all that remained was a finished prized mare that was being bid over between two gentlemen. The numbers thrown made Wade almost dizzy until one gentleman turned red in the face and struck at the shorter man, knocking him into a pile of fresh manure.

"This is what it's going to be like, huh?" The short man charged, and a full-blown fight broke out as the men formed a ring around the two so-called gentlemen who were fisting it out in his stable.

"What's going on over here!" cried the sheriff as he pushed his way through the crowd.

"Sheriff Maverick, don't mind us." The men in the dirt stopped brawling and dusted off their jackets. "It's merely a dis-agreement between two friends."

Maverick's brows rose at this. "A mere disagreement, huh? I would hate to see what would happen to a fellow that wasn't your friend, and you really had an argument with. Y'all stop fighting now, or I'll have to put you in the jail cell for disturbing the peace." He nodded to Wade. "I haven't met you yet, but you're Lawrence's brother, right?"

Wade nodded and extended his hand. "Nice to officially meet you, Sheriff Maver-ick. I've heard a lot about you over the years. Well, that was before you were made sheriff but seems that you and my brother Lawrence had a good friendship up in the mountains."

Sheriff Maverick nodded. "I would have liked to get to know you as well, but hearing the full story from Lawrence, I understand why I never met you when I met the rest of the family. It's good to finally have that put behind you, and you can live your life." He leaned toward Wade and lowered his voice, "Are *all* these men here bidding on your horses?"

Wade let out a disbelieving laugh. "Yes, they are. I can hardly believe it."

He slapped him on the back. "Looks like you are having a mighty fine time off the ranch. Well, I'll let you get back to it, but no more fights, you hear?"

Wade nodded. "Thank you, Sheriff."

With the sheriff's departure, the men took a more organized approach, and Wade took down names and amounts pledged as well as those on the waiting list.

Wade had never expected so much pa-perwork to come with selling his horses after winning the race. He didn't leave the stalls for the rest of the day, working steadily on the contracts on the wooden table in the farrier's shop. Not for the first time that day, he wished Noah was here to help him. The aspiring lawyer would be quite welcome with his advice right about now.

In plain and simple language, Wade drew up what he thought was a decent contract for the men who had bid the highest on the horses. A deposit of twenty-five percent would be needed at signing and the remainder of the payment would be required upon delivery. If they were unable to pay, then the next man on the waiting list would receive the option to purchase and the original buyer would forfeit his deposit.

As for his yearlings and finished horses, those were a bit more straightforward since they were ready to come down the mountain. All he had to do was go back up and fetch them, if he got someone to watch the stables. Or he could send Lawrence up with a message to his brothers. A shadow fell over his paperwork, and he looked behind him to find Mr. Brady standing in the threshold.

"Hello there, Mr. Sterling," Brady nodded to him and moved toward Raven's stall. "I see you have had a lot of offers for your stock and heard that you rejected multiple offers for Raven. I almost didn't come down here, but I thought perhaps you were just waiting for the right number."

Wade stood up. "No, sir. Raven is not for sale. I plan on breeding her in a few years. She will be the mother of a new generation of horses, and since she's won this championship, all of her foals will be worth a small fortune. I'd be mighty foolish to give her up now."

Mr. Brady took the end of his mustache and rubbed it between his fingers, drawing it into a curled point. "Every man has a price. I have been trying to purchase Charleston for years from Edwards. It seems Mr. Austin offered him the right price. I simply need to wait to find out yours," Brady smiled. "If you will not sell me Raven, how about you allow me to purchase her sire?"

Wade shook his head. "I can't do that. That is the cornerstone of my herd."

"How about a sire contract?"

Wade shrugged. "I really hate to disappoint a potential customer, but I have to protect the cornerstones of my business. Can't have my stallion breeding with other horses and diluting the potential price."

Mr. Brady laughed. "You're much more of a businessman than I gave you credit for." He slapped him on the shoulder. "Well, I know you probably already have a waiting list as long as my arm by now, but I would love to do business with you. How about we have dinner tonight?"

Wade grimaced. "I have meal meetings set up for the next three days for buyers to sign contracts. The only day I have free next is Thursday evening."

Mr. Brady nodded. "Very well, how about an early dinner at the Castañeda on the third night and discuss some options?"

Wade wasn't sure what kind of options he could suggest, given the entire stock that was available was already spoken for. However, he didn't want to be rude. Wade nodded. "Not sure what I can do for you, but I'd be happy to meet with you."

"As I said, every man has a price. I need only to think about which one yours is. I have a lot of good mares for sale myself. Maybe we can work out a deal. Have a good night, Wade."

CHAPTER 16

*I*t had been three days since Jane had spoken to Wade for more than a few minutes while taking his breakfast and lunch orders, for which he always had company. Apparently, everyone wanted an appointment with him to discuss his horses and to reserve any future foals. She understood why, but it was unsettling how much she missed him. She had never missed Graham this much. *His time fake courting me is over . . . but I know it wasn't all for show. He returned our kiss. He did.* But so much time had passed since their Christmas morning conversation. *Is he avoiding me?*

"Table for three and I prefer a seat by the

window," Eliza Brady swept into the dining room as if she owned it, not waiting to be seated.

Nodding, Jane disposed of her tray in the back and quickly followed them to the round table nearest to the window. "Would you ladies like a taste of the tea of the day? It's a black tea—"

"Give us a moment to get settled, would you?" Eliza Brady snapped, brows arched.

As Jane turned away, she heard Eliza's low laugh as she muttered to her friends, "That's the poor girl who tried to land a *Sterling.* Can you believe it, Hannah?"

"*Her?*" Hannah laughed. "I don't know why you even bothered being worried about such a creature. Did you see her hands?"

Jane's gaze fell on her red, chapped fingers before she tucked them into her apron pockets. *It's true. I've ruined them with work.* She headed toward the lunch counter, but was halted by a nearby guest asking for advice on the best places to see in the area.

"I wasn't worried," Eliza snorted. "More annoyed by her presence than anything.

Wade can't seem to think straight when she's around, but for the past three days, he's been completely devoted to me, so I think he's gotten over his little charity case."

Jane stiffened. Was he really moving on without her? She pressed her hand to her stomach. Was that what he wanted to talk about? She mumbled a few places of interest to the guest, needing to flee.

Hannah scoffed. "I can't believe he was jeopardizing a possible match with *you*. But you couldn't have thought him serious in his attentions to the girl, especially with a fortune tied to your name?"

"Of course not," Eliza gave her little trilling laugh. "I mean, you saw her. Pretty, but not so pretty as to lure a man into losing a fortune when I could only enhance his wealth and opportunities. Speaking of the girl, where is she? I want to order." She turned, the smirk in place revealing that she well knew Jane was right behind them.

"And lastly, you should take a mule ride in the Gallinas Mountains during your stay at the Montezuma." Taking a deep breath,

Jane waited a moment to collect herself before returning for their order.

"I thought this place was supposed to have excellent service," Eliza muttered under her breath. "We will have a plate of scones with the lemon curd, clotted cream, and strawberry jam," Eliza calculatingly closed her menu. Looking to the two girls with a smile playing at her lips, she added, "And I think a large pot of *Wade's* favorite tea, Earl Grey. I must get used to drinking it more with all his visits to the house."

Jane refused to give Eliza the reaction she so obviously desired and replied, "Certainly. We have two types of scones for today. Our standard vanilla and a lovely cinnamon scone."

"Do half of each," Eliza handed back the menu. "Make sure that the scones are a *light* golden brown. I noticed last time that one of them was too dark for my liking. I don't want to break a tooth before Wade comes to dinner tonight." Her gaze met Jane's in triumph.

"We certainly wouldn't want that," Jane forced herself to let out a little laugh. *But it might actually improve your personality through a little lesson in humility,* but when her gaze fell on where Eliza's hand rested on her collar, her jaw dropped. "Where did you get those pearls?"

Eliza's smile flashed gleefully as she ran her fingers over the beautiful ivory beads. "My father gave them to me a few days ago —on Boxing Day actually. Gorgeous, aren't they? He mentioned they are worth a good bit as they are an antique."

She would recognize her great-grandmother's pearl necklace anywhere. She had left it in Mother's jewelry box for safe keeping. How—? Her nails dug into her palms. *Father. His gambling must have been more significant than he let on.*

Eliza stroked them. "Weren't you supposed to fetch us some tea, girl?"

Reeling, Jane swept into the kitchen, and with the staff's quick assistance, she assembled the plates in a matter of minutes while the large pot of tea steeped.

With a racing heart, she set the scones in front of each lady, returning with the steaming pot of tea while the second friend gushed to Hannah, "I completely expect to be throwing an engagement party for dear Eliza next week. Mrs. Brady fairly announced it herself by the way she went on and on about how perfect Wade was for Eliza and how he knows it's a union set in the stars for his business. Now that he is free from distractions, Mrs. Brady said he will likely be ready to propose and settle down the way a breeder of his standing deserves."

Thumping the pot down on the table, Jane spun on her heel and managed to get herself behind the storage room door before her tears spilled over. *He's courting her.* She sobbed, fumbling for a handkerchief. *Wade didn't even come to see me to let me know* — She twisted her hands, willing her sobs to abate. *Stop. You were the one who brought this on yourself. Now, get yourself together and get to work to save your job before Eliza takes that away from you as well.* Blowing her nose into her handkerchief, she jumped at the sight of Eliza standing in the open door.

"I know everything," Eliza whispered.

"What do you mean?" Jane asked, raising

her chin and tucking the used handkerchief into her pocket as if that would hide the evidence of her hurt.

"Don't play dumb with me. I wore these pearls as a warning. If you dare try to come between Wade and me, I will crush your family by calling in the debt your father owes mine," she hissed into Jane's ear as she grabbed her by the forearm. "We will take everything from you, and you and your family will be thrown out into an alley."

Jane's shoulders shook from suppressing her anger. "Why are you doing this? How can you be so . . . so hateful?"

"Because Wade is *mine*. He always has been from the moment he came into town, and he always will be mine." She dug her nails into Jane's arm and shoved her back. "Keep away, Miss Cady, or you will live to regret it more than you've ever regretted anything in your sad little life."

Jane lifted her chin. "Maybe I don't care about wealth."

Eliza rolled her eyes, dismissing her declaration as folly. "If you care one whit about him, you will stay away from him." Without another glance, Eliza flung back her yellow skirts and marched through the door.

Throughout the day, customers trickled in, and she didn't have a chance to stop and consider all of Eliza's warning, but at about half past four o'clock, the dining room quickly began to fill until there was only one large table left. After taking orders from several tables, Jane bustled into the kitchen as she checked her seating chart that Miss Dolly had created to help Jane remember who ordered what to prevent mistakes. Just when she finished giving the orders to the chef, she returned to the dining hall to find Eliza Brady draped on Wade's arm alongside Mr. and Mrs. Brady.

Why is she back so soon? Did Eliza appear at the restaurant earlier just to issue her warning? She forced herself not to stiffen at Eliza's deviousness. *Hopefully, she will be kinder to me than last time, given Wade is here.* She swallowed and refrained from patting down her hair and greeted them. "How wonderful to see you so soon, Eliza. It will be the four of you for an early dinner?"

"Of course," Eliza replied, her expression bored. "Do you see anyone else here?"

Mrs. Brady snorted.

Wade's brow rose at her tone, but he gave Jane a reassuring smile. "Good afternoon, Miss Cady. I hope you are well?"

Jane hid her hurt at his obviously being on an outing with his new beau's family. "Quite well, thank you. Please, follow me." Jane retrieved four menus and led them to the last large table in the middle of the room.

Mrs. Brady sighed, her lips pursed. "If you don't have enough room to fit your patrons comfortably, you really should consider removing a table or getting a larger dining area to accommodate everyone."

Jane glanced at the distance between the tables. While it seemed every bit as acceptable as a fine restaurant in New York, she quickly replied, "I'm sorry if you're uncomfortable, Mrs. Brady. If you'd prefer to wait for a table in the corner—?"

"Mrs. Brady and I do not *wait* for tables." Mr. Brady snatched the menus from Jane's hands and held the back of the seat for his wife.

"I should say not," Mrs. Brady added under her breath as she took her seat.

Wade rotated as if to speak to Jane, but Eliza had already turned her cheerful attention to Wade to gush over his new suit. "I knew that if you went to my father's tailor, you would never want to go to another."

"Well, given I only had one that was made for my brother, I needed something for church and the tailor already had one in stock that he fitted for me." Wade cleared his throat and extricated his arm from Eliza.

"Well, it's too early for dinner and too late for lunch. What desserts would you recommend? And with what tea?" Mrs. Brady's stony eyes captured Jane's gaze.

"Chocolate cake and for the paired tea, Pai Mu Tan, which is also known as White Peony. It goes well with both scones and sweets," Jane replied rapidly, thankful she had memorized the description cards.

"Pai Mu Tan?" Mrs. Brady's brows rose as she closed her menu and handed it to her.

"If I don't like it, I want another pot free of charge."

Eliza plunked down her menu and without looking at Jane, murmured, "Wade and I shall have the usual tea."

Wade frowned at this, but kept his mouth shut.

"Certainly." She picked up the menus and tucked them under her arm and listed her head toward Mr. Brady. "And for you, sir?"

"What do you have that is an Indian tea?" He asked, his eyes dancing as if he knew he was testing her knowledge.

"Assam is excellent. It is grown in north-eastern India and has a rich, malty flavor. It goes quite well with the tea sandwiches."

"Hmm," Mr. Brady nodded, visibly impressed. "I'll take it but be sure to bring heavy cream. I only have tea with heavy cream."

"Certainly, sir," she replied before turning to Wade, already knowing his answer. "And for you, sir?"

"I already ordered for us," Eliza narrowed her gaze at Jane.

Jane chose to ignore her. "Still Earl Grey?"

"You know me too well." He smiled up at her, causing Eliza to stiffen and increase her attempts to garner his attention as she lightly brushed his hand with hers and began a new stream of compliments to distract him from Jane.

"I'll have those teas out right away and give the chef your order," she replied to the table, although no one was listening to her, not even Wade, as Eliza was laughing loudly enough for the table next to theirs to turn their heads. Spinning on her heel for the kitchen, she nearly collided into Jean May. "Oh!"

"Sorry," Jean May whispered, her eyes bright and cheeks flushed.

Jane twisted to see the cause of Jean May's flushed demeanor and caught the leering gaze of two men from the corner table that Jean May was fleeing. She quickly looked away and following Jean May into the kitchen, she gently grabbed her by the sleeve and asked, "Are those men giving you trouble?"

"I didn't know what to do." Jean May blushed to her hairline. "They made a comment . . . about how they'd leave a large tip for me if I went out with them tonight. I was so taken aback I didn't know what to do but hide in the kitchen with Vera until I had a chance to gather my thoughts."

Jane's eyes grew wide as she plunked her fists onto her slender hips. "How dare they. I'll take care of it. You just give these orders to Vera." She shoved her pad into Jean May's hands and darted back through the kitchen door toward the table. Her eyes narrowed with determination as she approached the offenders. "Excuse me."

The two men's gazes roved up and down her body, causing her to cross her arms over her chest while she glared at them. "Why, hello there," the man with the auburn beard greeted her with a yellowed grin.

"I would ask that you would be respectful to the staff or vacate the premises," she tried to say in a strong, confident voice, but it came out rather squeaky. Furrowing her brow, she attempted to appear aloof by lifting her chin.

"Bill and I were only being friendly to the girl," the other broad-shouldered man countered. "She should be flattered that we want to see her after work and treat her to a drink." His gaze rested on her hands. "You could join us if it's an invitation you are wanting?"

She dropped her hands to her sides, clenching them into tight fists as she drew a deep breath to keep from slapping him across his smug, portly face. "We are not that kind of establishment. If you think you can consider your words to be flattery, then you two are not gentlemen and I'd like you to leave," she replied in a low voice so as not to disturb the other customers. When they didn't move, she added, "At once. You are no longer welcome in my establishment. Pay your bill and don't bother coming back for you won't be given a table."

The men grinned up at her. "Make us."

Jane inhaled sharply at their defiance. *Why did I insist that Miss Dolly take the day off? She would have them out on their heads by now.* Pressing her lips into a firm line, she grabbed the coffee cups by their handles and lifted the plate of chocolate cake from their table, intending on dumping it in the kitchen's rubbish bin.

"Hey! We weren't done yet." Bill's voice rose to a bellow the further she brought the food, making Jane cringe as the tables turned to see the cause of the outburst.

Wade strode across the room and laid a hand on each of their shoulders. "Yes, I believe you were. Listen to the lady, leave your money and be on your way before I do something that *you* might regret."

The men sized up Wade's height, broad shoulders, and muscled chest that even his suit couldn't hide. They grumbled, threw down some cash and left, tugging on their hats as they glared at Jane in passing.

Mortified, Jane couldn't face the dining room of gaping mouthed guests and dashed into the kitchen.

"You look a little sick," William the wash boy commented from the sink, his arms submerged in soapsuds up to his elbows while he carefully scrubbed a china plate.

"Do I?" She splashed cool water on her

cheeks as Jean May filled the two pots for Wade's table.

"I can't believe you just did that for me," Jean May whispered as she handed her the large pot of Pai Mu Tan and the smaller pot of Assam. "You actually had them thrown out."

"Aww, I miss everything back here," William grumbled and reached for a half-eaten chocolate dipped sugar cookie left-over on the plate Vera had just brought back and popped it into his mouth. "What happened?"

Jane pressed a hand to her mouth, fighting a gag. "Me either," she murmured to Jean May, deciding not to reprimand William for eating off other people's plates. "Jean May? Can you reset those horrible men's table while I take the tea?"

"Certainly." She nodded and turned to fetch clean linens from the storage room with Jane following closely behind, bal-ancing the fresh pots of tea. "Did you see how Wade came to your rescue, Jane? I thought he was going to throw them out on their ears."

"I did too and I'm afraid that it may have displeased his table." Jane bit her lip to keeping her smile from spreading.

Jean May peeked out the doorway at the Brady table. "I'd say it's a safe bet. Good luck."

"Thanks." Jane swallowed back her nerves, held her head high, and marched over to Wade's table with the pots in hand. "So sorry about that." She gave a nervous giggle and set the pots of tea in front of the ladies, pouring the correct brew into each of their cups. "Quite the show."

"I thought I was about to experience my first saloon fight," Eliza smiled as Mrs. Brady laughed.

"Me too." Jane's mouth went dry as she removed the used dish from Mrs. Brady's place and thought how she must remember to thank Jean May for bringing the table something sweet to keep them content until the staff finished with their food.

Wade caught Jane's eye and whispered, "You okay?"

She nodded. *I will be once Eliza and her family are gone, and you tell me that you aren't officially back on the marriage market . . . unless you are back on the market.* She gave a quick nod and having all the cups filled, she took the pots back to her workstation to await for when they would need refills.

Returning within the minute with another pot and a plate of chocolate cake, she reached by Eliza's right shoulder to pour Wade's cup from his left side, but Eliza turned and bumped into Jane. She jerked back the pot to keep from spilling hot tea on Wade' lap and instead, sloshed it over her own hands, scalding her. Tears sprang into her eyes, and she bit her lip to keep from crying out in pain.

"Oh! I'm so sorry," Eliza exclaimed, her lips parted with feigned horror as she placed a delicate, porcelain hand over her heart.

"Please don't distress yourself," Jane managed to grit out. *She's not sorry at all.* She swallowed and whispered, "It's my fault." *No, it's not. Quiet! What does Mother say about how to deal with snotty socialites? Smirk and bear it.* Jane laughed to disguise her pain. "Please, let the tea be on the house as an apology for my clumsiness disrupting your teatime. Jean May will bring you a new pot of Earl Grey, Mr. Sterling, while I freshen myself up."

Feeling badly for Jean May, but not so badly that she serve in a soiled apron while Eliza laughed at her, she smiled brightly to keep Wade from rushing to her aid in front of his table of guests a second time. Excusing herself, she rushed out the back door to the Rawlins dormitory and up the stairwell to the hall and threw open her door. She collapsed into her bed without even bothering to kick off her shoes.

Light footsteps sounded in the hall. "Are you unwell?" Dolly poked her head inside, her book tucked under her arm. "You dashed up the stairs so quickly that you didn't even hear me call to you from the parlor."

Blinking, Jane rolled herself into a sitting position and rubbed her eyes, grimacing when she accidentally used her injured hand. She hissed and curled her lips inward as her hand blazed in agony.

"Let me see." Dolly gently took Jane's hand in her own to examine it.

Jane inhaled sharply as Dolly accidentally touched the blistering skin.

"I have some lavender lotion that I can rub on it to help with the pain," Dolly murmured as she crossed the hall and returned with it in a moment. "Whenever I burn myself on the iron doing my bangs—"

"You do your bangs? But they look so natural."

"Thank you, it took a while for me to figure out how to do them correctly, so I used to use this on my burns, so it should work on your hand."

Jane dipped a finger into the pot of lotion and dabbed it onto her left hand, exhaling at the instant coolness, and filled Dolly in on the events.

Dolly gasped at Eliza's parting words. "I don't know why you let Eliza treat you that way. In New York, I know you would've *never* let a girl like her speak to you like that and even if she dared, you would've just given her the cut direct. Just do the same with her."

"You know why," Jane laughed softly. "In New York, I had money and status with my mother's name and wealth, but here," her shoulders sagged, "no one knows anything about me except that I *was* rich and now am 'reduced' to working." She fit the lid back on the porcelain pot and handed it to Dolly, "Thank you. But you know what the strange thing is? I am enjoying life *more* working than I was attending tea parties, and balls, and weddings. I'm working to put clothes on my back, and food in my belly, and on my family's table, but I *like* it!"

Dolly patted her arm. "I'm not the least bit surprised you enjoy it. Like many of the girls who come to the Harvey House, you only needed the opportunity to soar. However, you really have shocked me as to how well you've adapted to this life after the extremely unusual way you came to sign the contract. But you aren't the first girl to do so. Belle Parish was a mail-order bride turned Harvey Girl. Miss Trent took mercy on her and took her under her wing. And then, Sophia, came from Charleston without any training." Dolly shook her head. "I was rather a tyrant to them both, but I've written to Sophia and spoken with Belle, and they graciously forgave me for how I treated them."

Jane shook her head. "You? I can't imagine *you* as a tyrant. Were you as bad as Pernilla?"

"Nearly." Dolly's cheeks burned. "I'm afraid I was allowing my past fears and ambitions to get in the way of the Harvey Girl sisterhood. The Lord chastised me and well, I've been trying to rest on Him for my provision instead of myself and it has made my heart lighter and easier to let my guards down."

Jean May burst into the room, sinking on the edge of the bed as she picked up her skirts and massaged her calf, breathing heavily. "I shouldn't have run over here, but Wade Sterling was *most* anxious about you after you didn't return." Jean May slipped off her shoes and stockings, stretching her toes.

"Oh?" Jane rose and pulled back the lace curtain, taking comfort in the flicker of the lanterns being lit about the town as the winter sun sank behind the Gallinas Mountains. It grew dark so early here.

"His table didn't seem pleased at all with his inquiries either," Jean May added with a snort. "I simply told them that your shift had ended, which it did."

Jane let the curtain fall and retrieved her silver hairbrush on the vanity. "Thank you for taking over their table for me. Was Eliza wretched?"

"Dolly, do you remember Gemma Robins from when we first opened?"

"Yes..." Dolly's eyes went wide. "She was that bad?"

"Let's just say that Eliza's treatment makes Gemma seem like a saint."

"I don't know who this Gemma Robins is, but I can believe it." Jane gave a soft laugh and ran the brush through her hair.

"Well, I don't care one whit what Eliza says, and you shouldn't either," Jean May retorted, wrapping her arms around her legs as she tucked her knees under her chin.

"But she is right. I have no money, and my family depends on me to meet the gap."

"But what about *your* needs. Don't you

want to be loved and cared for by a husband one day and have cute little babies?"

"Yes," Dolly whispered.

The girls turned to the head waitress. "*You* wish to marry?"

She gave them a smile. "Even a girl with ambitions such as mine, yes, I long for a happily ever after too." She patted Jane's hand. "And your happily ever after is in reach. Are you going to let Eliza win, or have a slightly awkward conversation with Wade to clear up any miscommunication between you and perhaps have all your dreams come true?"

CHAPTER 17

"Why don't you walk Eliza home?" Mr. Brady suggested as they stood on the Castañeda porch as an owl hooted nearby. "My wife and I need to pop in to see a friend a few blocks down."

Wade gritted his teeth. The dining experience with them had been nearly unbearable. What had been a promised dessert and tea turned into a two-hour long dinner. *Is this what business is like? Kissing the rings of kings and hoping that they bestow upon you, a mere mortal trying to earn an honest wage, their favor? Or in this case, striking a deal with Mr. Brady for his mare that doesn't require jeopardizing my business.*

This was not what he imagined it would be like when he got into business being a horse breeder. He only saw the love of the horse, he didn't ever see this side given that Tanner had sold and bought horses for him. *Seems I owe Tanner an apology for being rather judgy about the quality of horseflesh he bought me and the price he obtained for the horses he sold.* He sighed.

"Yes, sir," He agreed, even as his fingers itched to tug on his Stetson and bolt after Jane and explain why he was dining with the family. It had been far too long since he had been able to talk with her.

Miss Eliza hung on his arm as they strolled out of the Castañeda, taking the street behind it, which ran directly in front of the Rawlins building.

She paused on the boardwalk and leaned into him, lifting her eyes to him and blinked her long lashes at him. "Oh, Wade, it is so wonderful that you have taken the time to dine with my parents to get to know them better. It means the world to me."

What is she on about? "Yes, well, Miss Brady—"

"Eliza. I know we've only just met, but I feel like we have known each other for years. We have so much in common."

His brows rose. He doubted the girl ever set foot on the mountainside. "Such as?"

Those long lashes dipped again, and she gave him a flirtatious smile. "Horses. We both love them, so there's a kindred spirit level right there."

There is kindred spirit, and then there is a crazed she-wolf. He knew which category Eliza fell under. Something in the bushes next to them rattled. Eliza screamed and wrapped her arms about Wade's neck, hauling herself into his arms. Wade instinctively wrapped his hands about her as she pressed her cheek to his. Nothing leapt out at them, and he narrowed his eyes to the bush. *Eliza wouldn't have planted one of her friends behind there would she?* He glanced up to the Rawlins building and saw the lace curtains of a bedroom flutter. His heart hammered. *Jane.* She had told him once that she had lace curtains in her window and she always kept it open before bed. He dropped Eliza and she tumbled to her backside.

"Mr. Sterling! What are you about?"

He gritted his teeth and jerked her to her feet. "I'm so sorry, Miss Brady. Thank you for the lovely evening. I really must see to some business that came up unexpectedly. Let's get you to your house." He grabbed her hand and fairly trotted down the street, dropping her at the fence line that belonged to her parents. He pushed open the gate, drew her through it, and closed it. "Have a good night, Miss Eliza." She called after him, but he was already running for the dormitory. This had to end. He had to speak to Jane. He had been distracted and pulled aside more times than he could count before he could speak to Jane. There was nothing more important than her right now, or ever.

He paused at the dormitory door. It was locked for sure. And he didn't really wish to raise a ruckus by hammering on the door. He looked down the windows and found the only one open with a lace curtain. Taking the chance that it was hers, he picked up a pebble and tossed it through the window. Jane poked her head through the curtains and his heart leapt at the sight of her tear-stained face. "Jane? Come down, please."

She shook her head. "Miss Dolly has the key."

"Please? I really need to speak with you alone."

She sighed. "If I fetch her, she will play chaperone."

"What I have to say really doesn't need an audience. Can you go to the side window? There's at least a trellis there."

"You want me to climb out of the window?" Jane's brows shot up.

"I'll catch you if you fall, but we have put off talking long enough, and there are things that are left unsaid. And if they are left unsaid for any longer, my gut will start to boil, and I'll die."

Jane wrinkled her nose. "That is utterly ridiculous."

"Why don't you come down and tell me how ridiculous it is then?"

She glanced back over her shoulder. "Give me a moment."

Wade shifted from foot to foot as he

waited for what felt like ten minutes, but the front door of the dormitory opened and Jane slipped outside.

Dolly stood at the doorway and crossed her arms. "As the highest-ranking Harvey Girl, I am giving Jane *special* permission to be out alone with you unchaperoned. See to it that you guard her and bring her back, or have her escorted back by her father."

He nodded. "Thank you, Miss Dolly. I'll take care of her." He reached out his hand to Jane.

She blushed, crossing her arms as she stepped away from him, frowning.

No, that won't do. He reached out his hand once more. "Walk with me."

Her frown deepened for a moment before she sighed and slowly, grasped his fingertips. Relief instantly shot up his arm, as if her touch was healing him. "I've been trying to talk with you for days, but I kept getting pulled away. It's been a whirlwind of meetings, which was what that thing was in the dining room. But business proposals are something I've never handled before and then I had to work out schedules of when horses could be delivered and at what stages the owner wished to purchase the horses. But that's not important now. What's important is talking with you."

"You didn't seem to be trying too hard in the dining room with Miss Eliza."

He grimaced. "Mr. Brady said he would only talk business with the whole family. Pretty sure he wants Miss Eliza to marry me so he can have access to Raven even though I said I wouldn't sell her."

"So, you aren't courting Eliza Brady?" She dipped her head and pulled away from him to play with her cuff. "I suppose there is no need to keep up our charade anymore with my suitors leaving."

"No. I was trying to buy Mr. Brady's mare." He reached into his pocket and retrieved the silk scarf, tying it above his arm. "I only wear colors for one girl, if she will allow me to make this courtship a real thing."

Her eyes widened, the corners of her lips slowly curving upward. "You want to make this for real?"

He clasped her hand in his, rubbing his

finger over her hand. "Since day one. I've always known you were special, and I would be honored if you would be mine."

She lifted her hand to rest on his chest as she gazed up at him. "I knew you were special too."

His heart exploded in his chest. She wanted him too? "Is that a yes?"

Her fingers grazed his jaw. "Yes, Mr. Sterling, please come calling."

"Yes, ma'am. Your wish is my command." He bent, leaned his forehead to hers, and breathed her in. "Now, I reckon we should test to see how our fake kisses stand up to our real ones."

She giggled, rose on her tip toes, and kissed him on the cheek. "How does that feel?"

His hands grasped her waist, keeping her on tiptoe. "Real." He slowly, gently pressed a kiss to her cheek, brushing the corner of her lips. "I could get used to courting, Miss Cady."

Her fingers lifted to touch the spot where he kissed her back, her eyes sparkling in the moonlight. "Yes, I could as well."

Bawdy laughter sounded down the street as the saloon music grew.

He frowned. "We better get you back inside." He pulled her into his arms once more, savoring the feel of her. "Miss Dolly will be ready to hear everything."

"Not yet." She shook her head, a shy smile appearing. "I'd like to keep this away from the Harvey Girls and between us for a little while—to savor the news before sharing with her in the morning. Besides, I should probably tell my family that you aren't going anywhere first. I owe my father that much."

He grinned. "Growing up with a houseful of boys, I know how good it feels to have a fine secret that is just your own." He nodded toward the hotel. "Is your father working late?"

She nodded. "I'll tell him now and then get him to escort me into the dormitory."

Taking her tiny hand in his, Wade strolled with her toward the hotel. Her feet dragged as much as his—as if she too didn't want this moment to end.

He bent and kissed her hand. "Then, I will bid you farewell, my sweetheart." He loved watching her cheeks pink under his words.

"Until tomorrow, my beau."

JANE WAVED to the desk clerk, but he had his chin propped up in his hand and soft snores sounded. She scooted past him into the hall, pausing at the two deep voices speaking low. Thinking she heard her father's voice, she peeked around the corner to see her father with a middle-aged gentleman enter his office. *Mr. Brady?* Great-Grandmother's pearls flashed to mind.

"I'm sorry, Mr. Brady. It won't happen again," Father raked his hand through his thinning hair. "I'm struggling to make ends meet this month. My wife doesn't seem to understand the meaning of the word *economize.*"

"You promised me up and down that I

could trust you enough to loan you the three thousand dollars for the horse race. I warned you about Wade Sterling's horse and yet, you were still sure that the former champion would win. Despite my warnings, I thought you were reliable with you being from the New York Four Hundred, but I should have looked to the past to determine your word."

Father straightened his shoulders. "Look. I know I've let you down with not repaying you right away, and only offering my daughter's pearls as collateral, but with your daughter courting Wade, the horse is basically yours, which is worth far more than a few thousand dollars. We could almost call it even—"

"You better believe that you are going to make it up to me and you know how? With interest." He growled.

"Now, Mr. Brady. Let's be reasonable. Perhaps a payment plan?"

"Don't patronize me." The man growled. "I am a businessman, as you yourself once were, and you know I need to protect myself from a bad investment."

"But bad investments can prove lucrative when the party is desperate." Her father yelped.

"Very well, I will agree to a payment plan, but I'm raising the interest and your monthly payment and if you have a problem with that *very* reasonable solution, I'll bring you to court and take away every penny you have left. Understand?" Footsteps approached the office threshold.

She threw herself into the broom closet, not daring to close the door for fear of the squeaking hinges.

They passed her hiding spot as Father pressed an envelope into the man's hands. "I know it doesn't make up for the amount, but this jewel does cover most of it. Maybe you'll hold onto this as my gesture of goodwill."

The man tore it open and peered inside. Scowling, he nodded. "I'll put it toward your debt, but this doesn't change anything. I'm still raising your rate and if you do not pay, say goodbye to your right knee."

"I won't let you down." Father released a nervous laugh. "I just need more time."

The reply was too muffled for Jane to hear. She pressed her hand to her mouth, shocked that her father would gamble so much. She peeked through the crack to see if Father had returned to his office and, seeing as he had disappeared into the hotel, she hurried inside and retrieved his private accounting book. Within a few pages, she realized that the money from her time working at the Harvey House was already long gone and so was his salary. The family was bleeding money and, if they didn't pay, her father could lose his knee. She pressed her palms against her hot cheeks. *We have to figure out a way to make money soon or that man will take any chance of a decent future away from us.*

Hearing her father's shuffling gait, she stayed with the book open before her. Her father had too many secrets. It was time he let her into his secret world.

Father jolted in the doorframe, a cup of coffee sloshing onto his hand. "Jane! What are you doing down here at such an hour?"

"What is going on with Mr. Brady?"

He paled, gripping his cup until his

knuckles turned white. "What do you know about Mr. Brady?"

"Not much, except that Eliza was wearing *my* pearls this afternoon." She planted her hands at her waist. "And just now, I overheard your rather heated argument regarding what sounded like a gambling debt. What is going on, Father?"

Removing his spectacles, he rubbed his eyes and sighed. "Jane, I know what you think you heard, but you have to trust me with the business side of things." He polished his lenses and returned them to the bridge of his nose. "You never did have much aptitude for numbers and showed little to no interest in my investments before now."

"False. I've always inquired, but it was you who shut me out," Jane dared to voice the truth, wincing at his reddening face, but pushed forward as she paced the small room. "This was not another investment. It was gambling, Father. Do not treat me like a child, please."

"Oh really? I'm not sure you could handle it. Well, I suppose now that you are so grown up and an *independent* woman, you feel entitled to know." He narrowed his eyes at her as he sank into his leather wingback chair behind the desk. "Very well. While I had enough funds for the rent, I didn't quite have enough to fill the place with furniture, china, goods and fix the kitchen. Your mother has not ceased complaining that she doesn't have a decent place to sit. I had to have help. I took the Boxing Day Race as an opportunity to supplement the income after I exhausted the advances I could receive on my wages . . . and yours."

"Advances?" She pinched the bridge of her nose. "Father, I make $18.50 a month. You make far more than that. I know what it takes to live now, and you should have had enough, especially since you told me you'd garnish ten dollars out of my wages from my very first paycheck and every paycheck afterwards."

"It was ten dollars. It is nothing to your mother."

"But it is nearly sixty percent of my wages."

"Well, I needed it all this month. What

do you want from me, Jane?" He threw his hands up in the air and bolted out of his chair, pacing the cramped room. "Do you want me to admit that I am a failure? Because I can't. I won't."

"Of course not. I'm just trying to understand how I can better help you," she returned, stepping toward him to calm him, but he shrugged her off.

"You want to help me? As if you could. I don't want to discuss this with you right now," he growled, snatching the book from the table and out of her reach. "Besides, what do you know about keeping books?"

"We have to talk about it sometime," a frown knit her brows together. "How else can I learn and help you with the family's finances if you won't even tell me how far behind payments we are."

"I bought us some time."

"I heard. With what jewel?" Jane crossed her arms.

He avoided her gaze, "Just with some, uh, collateral. He gave me two weeks to provide my first payment, but if I can't pay him on time, we are going to lose everything . . . again." He sank back into his chair and buried his face in his palms.

She straightened her shoulders. "No. We won't. This time we aren't relying on good weather for our fortune to be saved. We have our health, and, with a lot of work, we will get through—"

"Yes, we will, because you will be marrying Austin if it's the last thing that I do. I've already sent him the telegram."

CHAPTER 18

*A*t last, her shift had ended and Jane knew it was time to bring her mother into the circle of lies that her father had attempted to swear Jane into secrecy. With the sunset came the rattle of the vendor's street carts as they rolled down away from Thursday's market day. Jane pulled her cloak tight and hurried past. She huffed as she climbed the little hill to her parent's home. She took the steps carefully as Father had yet to fix them and paused at the sight of an envelope stuffed into the corner of the door.

She tore it open and found a significant bill from Rudy's Mercantile. *What on earth did Mother buy?* She moaned, burying her face in her hands. "I can't take it anymore," she muttered under her breath when she heard muffled voices coming from around back. Stepping around the yard, she saw her father and a brawny man waving a piece of paper in the air as his voice rose.

"This isn't a charity. My wife and I work ourselves to death to make sure your precious clothes are laundered and arrive on time, but if you can't even afford to pay your laundry bill, you can't afford to keep us washing your fine clothes." The giant man bellowed.

Jane paled and clutched her reticule to her chest. She only had two dollars left after all the Christmas gifts. She only hoped it was enough. "Good morning, sir. I am his daughter. How much is your bill?"

The man shoved the paper under her nose, and she fairly gasped at the amount. *Father definitely did not record this in his ledger.* "I'm guessing you are billing us for multiple weeks of service?" She reached into her purse and retrieved the two dollars in cash and change, handing it to him.

"Yes, and I don't appreciate having to come down here to get my fair wages for a job well done." He glanced at the coins. "You are short."

"It is all that I have until I'm paid next. I work at the Harvey House and promise I will see you are paid the remainder along with a tip for your troubles. I am afraid I must release you from your services until we are able to pay you in full every month without an embarrassing ordeal in the streets."

He tugged down on the brim of his cap. "Thank you, miss." To her father, he merely nodded as he muttered under his breath, "At least someone around here understands how a business is run."

Father grasped her by the elbow and heaved her through the back door. "How could you embarrass me like that, Jane?"

Jane's cheeks flared. "Embarrass you? I used the last of my money to pay him. Can you explain to me why we don't have enough to pay the launderers? You didn't even reserve a small amount for your living expenses? How could you have let things get this bad?" She lifted the itemized bill from the mercantile. "And it seems Mother hasn't lost her taste for shopping either."

"I can't talk about this right now," Father mumbled and headed for the road.

She waved the bill in the air. "Please, Father. Let me help you come up with a plan."

"The plan is Austin." He didn't stop.

"He won't come. He knows I am with Wade. Father, please," she called after him. "I can help. Where are you going?"

"To get some fresh air," he yelled, slamming his hat on his head.

Then I guess it is up to me to talk with Mother. Jane's heart squeezed with suppressed anger that she was the one who had to tell Mother that any spending had to stop. This was not her place. She pushed open the door to find Mother in her favorite rocking chair in the parlor, embroidering a silk shawl in the light of the kerosene lamp. They hardly spent much time together these days. She shouldn't have to speak with her about this. She swallowed. *Lord, give me strength.* "Mother, we need to speak about something rather delicate. Is Theo about?"

"She's playing with a school friend," Mother mumbled, absorbed in her embroidery.

She sank onto the ratty settee, avoiding the spring that was poking through the cushion. "I'm afraid that I'm going to need you to halt your shopping." She braced herself.

"Excuse me?" Mother dropped her sewing into her lap. "Not that it is your business, dear, but your father told me that I could spend fifty dollars and to put it on credit and that he would take care of it later. He also gave me ten dollars to take Theo about town and buy her a toy as well as a nice meal at the Plaza."

Jane wrung her hands in her lap. "Father must have given you the money intended for our bills."

Mother paled. "What? But he told me all was well. He said to go shopping."

Did Mother spend far more than just one vendor's wages? Oh no. "How much did you spend? Was it more than just this one shop?

Shall I expect more bills to appear on our counter?" She passed the paper.

"I just spent the ten dollars." Mother pursed her lips as she set aside the bill. "This was not me."

Father lied, again?

Mother's lips trembled. "I knew he was acting too much like his jolly old self." She grasped Jane's hand. "But cannot we allow him such a small pleasure at least? We've been uprooted from my beautiful mansion and brought where we have no friends and placed in this tiny little house. I bear my troubles in silence, and then you have the gall to ask me how much your father spent on a shopping trip that would pale in comparison to what you spent daily in New York!"

"I realize that, and I apologize for bringing up such an untoward topic, but we aren't in New York anymore," Jane whispered, rising to place a hand on Mother's shoulder and knelt beside her. "We must retrench. You must economize."

Tears pooled in Mother's eyes. "Jane, you don't know how hard this has been for me, or how much I've sacrificed already. I'm so afraid—"

"You will *not* speak to your mother about the finances." Father glared at her from the doorway. "How dare you distress her thus, Jane? I have it handled."

Mother lifted her hand, staying his wrath. "It is well that I understand now, Benjamin."

Jane drew a deep breath. "I apologize for my forwardness, but I fear that if you do not curb your spending, Father, you all will be out on the streets."

Father narrowed his brows at her as if to make her feel ashamed as he knelt and wrapped his arm around Mother. "I appreciate your concern, but it isn't your place to tell us how to spend the money made at the Harvey House."

She wanted to scream, but instead, she decided to go and scrub the pots that Theo couldn't get to the night before. After warming a pot of water on the stove, she poured it onto the hardened dough in the mixing bowl and got to scrubbing. Elbow deep in suds, she allowed her tears to flow freely. *Lord, show me what to do. I cannot control my father's spending, but I cannot allow my family to be out on the streets either.*

She finished the dishes, cleaned the kitchen and swept the lower level, pausing at the parlor, but her family had apparently long since retired or left. Setting aside the broom, she turned up the wick of the lamp and opened the window, drinking in the fresh, sweet air. *Lord, why is this happening? Why did we have to lose everything? And now, we might lose it all again?* Her tears came so fast that she hiccupped. *I can't do this.* At first, it had been easy to be brave, to be the daughter who would sacrifice it all for her family. "But it's not easy anymore, Lord. I don't know what to do," she gazed up into the dark sky. "Why won't my own father love me? Am I so unlovable?"

Reaching for the family Bible, she flipped it open to a random passage, hoping to find a verse to comfort her to sleep. Her gaze fell on the book of 1 John chapter four. *God is love; and he that dwelleth in love dwelleth in God, and God in him. Herein is our love made perfect, that we may have boldness in the day of judgment: because as He is, so are we in this world. There is no fear in love; but perfect love casteth out fear: because fear hath torment. He that feareth is not made perfect in love.*

Her heart stirred. Had she really intertwined her worth so tightly with her wealth and being society's darling and her family's solution that she had forgotten that the Lord's love wasn't earned? She bit her lip. *Maybe I've been placing my worth on something worthless . . . my inheritance and when I lost that, I've been doing whatever I can do to make myself worthy of being loved. And Father is afraid. His fear is making his treatment of me, not an action of love but fear.*

She bowed her head. "Lord, forgive me for allowing my fear to rule—fear that if I don't obey, my own father won't love me. Please, cast out my fear. Give me a boldness that I have never before possessed. Let me love as You do. Help me forgive Father for the way he sees me—uses me for his gain."

Her tears flowed as she allowed the words to bathe her injured soul. "I am not worthless. I am loved by You. I am Yours and You love me." She bowed her head and prayed, *Lord, thank You for reminding me that I am treasured, You love me and that, because of You, I have worth. Forgive me for placing my identity in my family's wealth.* She sniffed and wiped her cheeks as her stomach rumbled. She had missed dinner.

WADE WORKED on another set of horseshoes, enjoying stretching his muscles as he had missed taking Raven for a ride today. There were more people needing his services than he thought. But he was glad for Mr. Hill, given that the business was picking up. He stoked the fire, grabbed the horseshoe, and pounded the iron against the anvil. He pounded the next and the next until his chest heaved and he could do no more. He sank into a pile of hay beside Raven and lay back just for a moment, fully intending on finishing the orders of horseshoes. The rustling of hay beneath boots alerted him that he was not alone. But when someone didn't call out for him, Wade's senses blazed to life.

Someone was trying to be stealthy. *And there is only one reason to go sneaking around. Someone is trying to steal a horse.* He grabbed the pitchfork lying next to him and rose, keeping to the corner of the stall where the shadows would shield him from view, and watched as the man approached each stall as if looking for a particular horse. Wade kept his grip ready, and mouth closed, curious to see which horse this man was trying to steal, but in his gut, Wade knew that the horse could be none other than Raven, or the horse that Austin had given Jane as a wedding present.

The man turned and, spotting Raven, opened the stall and reached for a bridle hanging on the stall door. The intruder held his hand out to the horse, who pranced back a bit. "Here, Raven, calm down," the man whispered. "Come with me—there's a good girl."

Wade charged from his corner, pitchfork raised. "Who are you, and what do you want with my horse?"

The man shouted, dropping the bridle as

he shot backwards, tripping over his own feet and falling into the breezeway.

Wade flicked up the wick of the lantern that was hanging from the nail on the wall. His jaw dropped. "Mr. Cady? Why were you trying to steal my horse?"

Mr. Cady rose, brushing off his pant legs with a laugh. "No, no, I was confused. I thought that I was getting my daughter's horse. She boards her horse here a-and I heard that Mr. Austin gave her the thoroughbred called Charleston. I-is this Charleston?"

"You called Raven by name and Raven and Charleston look nothing alike. You were trying to steal my horse. Why?"

Mr. Cady licked his lips, his eyes darting to the exit. "Look, Mr. Sterling, I know you are interested in my daughter. How about I convince you to just sell Raven to me, and we can call it even?"

"As I have told every other buyer, Raven is not for sale. Her offspring will be in a few years, but she herself is not for sale. Her mother will be having a foal in a few months, and it is already claimed. I have a waiting list as long as my arm for horses." Wade set aside the pitchfork and crossed his arms. "And I believe Jane would agree with me that it is not fair of you to use my relationship with her as a means to your gain. I would be losing years and years of work if I agreed to your demand. So, I'll ask again, why do you want my horse? Why are you stealing her? You don't race horses, and from what Jane says, you don't even really like them too much, which means that you are trying to steal the horse for someone, or sell it for some quick cash," Wade guessed.

"You think you're so smart, don't you?" growled Mr. Cady. "You think you're so high and mighty because you have one thing that everybody in this town is mad over. Well, if you were in New York City, you know who would be the big man? It would be me, not you. Me."

"Well, we are not in New York City, and out here, stealing a man's horse is a serious crime. I should know," Wade crossed his arms.

"Are you really going to turn in the father of the woman that you claim to love?"

Mr. Cady snorted. "Jane gave up everything to be with you. I wouldn't even be in this mess if she had actually obeyed me in the first place and decided to marry Austin, or Graham Bank. You owe me for her."

Wade stepped in front of the stall and closed the door. "Jane is no object to be given or taken. She is a woman with a will and mind of her own. I owe you nothing, sir. However, I wish someone had shown me clemency many years ago, and because of that, I will grant you mercy and not tell anyone about this incident. I will chalk it up to a man who is desperate. And if you are desperate, I can loan you money."

Mr. Cady sneered. "You lend me money? I doubt you have more than a couple hundred dollars to your name."

Wade shrugged. "Well, what I do have, I can offer you some of it."

"I don't want your charity," Mr. Cady spat. "I want Raven."

"No." Wade put a hand on Mr. Cady's shoulder and squeezed, guiding him to the door. "Do not come back here, Mr. Cady. I may offer you mercy now, but I am no fool.

If my horse turns up missing, I will know who to tell the sheriff to go look for in finding her. I will not report you to the sheriff this time. There's no need for that. If you change your mind and want a loan, you know where to find me."

Mr. Cady shrugged him off and stumbled through the door. "You will regret this."

"I certainly hope I will not." Wade followed him and leaned against the door as Mr. Cady ran straight toward the Harvey House.

CHAPTER 19

*H*er back ached from cleaning her parents' kitchen, but her heart felt a little lighter after her conversation with the Lord. But, as she missed dinner, she hoped to snag a pastry from the kitchen before bed to still her rumbling stomach. *I am already breaking curfew—might as well break a few more rules.*

She waved to the night chef, but upon approaching his chair, she found him sound asleep. She peeked into the dining room and found Jean May on duty, serving Lawrence at the lunch counter and, hearing Jean May's laughter, she didn't wish to interrupt. So, Jane tiptoed down the hall to her father's office—hoping to make amends. As she approached, she didn't see light streaming under the door. She turned to leave, but hearing a metallic click from inside her father's office, she pressed a hand to her mouth. The Harvey House safe was in there. It had all the cash from the day's earnings as well as the hotel guests' valuables. The blood fled her cheeks and her knees knocked.

Not daring to face the robber herself, she hurried upstairs to the room where Mr. Perkins lived and knocked on the door, barely containing her whimper.

The door jerked open to reveal the former manager in a striped nightdress and nightcap. "What? I am not the House Manager anymore—"

"Mr. Perkins," she panted, pressing a hand to her heart. "I-I can't find my father, but there is someone robbing the safe! I'm almost sure of it."

His eyes widened and he turned away from the crack in the doorway, the sound of a drawer opening. He joined her in a dressing robe with the sash tied tight at his waist and a pistol in hand. "Tell the night shift girls to leave and go get the sheriff."

She tiptoed down the stairs and hurtled into the dining room where Jean May was bringing a dish from the kitchen. She raced to join her behind the counter, whispering, "Jean May! There's a robber in my father's office. Quick. Is anyone on staff with you?"

"Just Pierre tonight," Jean May looked to Lawrence.

Lawrence rose, his guns already in his hands. "I'm on it." He sprinted forward when a shot rang out.

Jane screamed and Jean May dropped the plate of food as she clutched Jane.

"Get down!" Lawrence shouted and disappeared to the hall.

Jane pulled Jean May under the counter, her friend trembling beside her. Broken china bit into her stocking and she sank onto her backside. With a hiss, she pulled the piece from her shin and watched as the blood dripped onto the tiles.

"Miss Cady! You best come," Lawrence's deep voice boomed in the hallway even as the murmurs of guests swelled from behind their doors and in the halls.

She shot to her feet, her pain forgotten as she hurried to Lawrence. Lawrence stood in the doorway of her father's office and turned to her.

His massive build, so like his brother's, hid the sight behind him. "I sent the bellhop for the doctor and the authorities. But, before you enter, I must ask if you are squeamish at all, Miss Cady?" He glanced over his shoulder. "I'm afraid that there's been an accident."

"A-accident?" Jane peered around his shoulder.

"There's no accident! I caught Mr. Cady stealing from us all red-handed." Mr. Perkins called from the floor where he was kneeling and pressing a rag to a limp form on the floor.

"W-what?" She gripped the doorframe.

"He's a thief. Why, if you check his pockets, I have no doubt that you will find the jewels from the guests." Mr. Perkins sneered. "Imagine, you wishing to take my position. You are nothing but a thief."

Jane cried out and surged around the desk to her father's side, clasping his hand in hers, relief flooding her as his lashes fluttered. "You shot my father, Mr. Perkins?"

"That was before I recognized him, obviously," Mr. Perkins interjected.

"He's going to be alright, isn't he, Lawrence?" She whispered.

He knelt and checked the wound, sending her father to moaning. "The bullet went clean through his leg."

"Obviously, I didn't shoot to kill. I'm not a murderer," Mr. Perkins scoffed at Lawrence. "Check his pockets."

Lawrence sighed and sent Jane an apologetic look and slipped his hand into Father's pockets, retrieving several diamond and pearl necklaces and two stacks of bills, along with what she guessed was a guest's purse of gold.

Mr. Perkins gasped. "The bills were supposed to be delivered to the bank this afternoon. He told me that he delivered the funds. You can ask Miss Dolly. She overheard the entire conversation."

Jane's stomach sank as she cradled Father's hand. *How could he fall so low?*

The room began to fill with curious guests, the sheriff, and the doctor, and Jane felt her head begin to swim when a hand rested on her shoulder.

Wade knelt beside her, concern in his eyes. "Jane, I am so sorry."

She turned from her father and leaned into Wade's embrace as the sheriff had the doctor and his orderly place Father onto a stretcher and carted off to jail.

"What can I do, Jane? Tell me. How can I make this better?" He drew her from the room and into the empty dining room.

She shook her head. "I need to tell Mother . . . but I think we should wait until the doctor is free." She was so numb that she sank into a chair in the dining room and the noise faded, sounding almost like she had her head underwater. She felt herself being scooped into strong arms and she rested her head against his shoulder. Wade was here. He would take care of her. She closed her eyes, lulled by the rocking of his walk.

She started when he lowered her.

"Whoa now. The doctor said you were in shock," he murmured as he set her on a settee.

She blinked, finding herself at her parent's home. "I-I didn't even realize you carried me this far. I'm so sorry."

"Nonsense." Wade ran his hand down her shoulder to her hand. "Jane, I'm going to make some tea for you. Do you think you can go upstairs to check on your mother? The doctor's apprentice, Doctor Kent, already went up to check on her."

She should be embarrassed for being trapped in a fog, but she couldn't bring herself to care, and she had a feeling that Wade would not wish for her to be embarrassed. "Already?"

He nodded. "And I believe I heard Theo stirring too."

"Theo!" Renewed energy coursed through Jane as she found Mother's favorite hurricane vase lamp with the painted roses still lit atop the parlor table. Turning the wick, she climbed the stairs to Theo's room.

Theo sat up at the burst of light in her

dark room. "Jane!" She gave a little cry and surged into Jane's arms. "What's happening? Why are you here? And what is all that noise downstairs?"

Jane clutched Theo's hand. "You must be brave for me. Can you do that?"

Theo nodded and reached for her doll, clutching it to her chest.

Jane drew a deep breath and filled her in on the story, Theo's hand grasping hers tighter and tighter as the story went on. She released a cry when Jane came to the worst of it.

"And now, you see, we must be brave for Mother. The doctor's apprentice is seeing to her now. Can we go check on her together?"

For her answer, Theo lunged out of the bed and to the door, slowing her steps only when she pushed open Mother's bedroom door.

Jane joined Theo and closed the door behind them, finding Mother sound asleep. "How is she, Doctor Kent?" Jane whispered as she placed the lamp on the nightstand, hoping its cheerful glow would bring comfort to Mother.

Standing, the young doctor mopped his forehead and neck. "She is resting for the moment. When she wakes, give her a good strong broth. If she is inconsolable, give her this," he handed her a small brown bottle. "It's an herbal remedy that will help settle her nerves for a few hours, allowing her to sleep, but only a small dose. You might wish to take some as well if you are unable to sleep. But I'm more concerned about her. In her condition, there is the balance of keeping her calm, but also, not giving her too much medicine."

"Her condition?" Jane's heart rate plummeted.

"Is-is she ill?" Theo whimpered, wrapping her arms about Jane's waist.

His lips parted. "You don't know then?" He looked to Theo and back to Jane. "Normally, we would allow the parents to give such news, but as this is an unusual circumstance—"

Jane rubbed Theo's back, trying to keep her little sister calm. "Please, just tell us."

"She will be having a baby around Easter."

A baby? Everything clicked into place—Mother's mood shifts, Father's unusual desperation and the doggedness for Jane to marry for wealth. She looked down at Theo.

"I'm going to be a big sister?" Theo's smile appeared through her tears.

Doctor Kent sighed. "Given how ill your mother has been, it is surprising that you two didn't know. And given how difficult her pregnancy has been thus far, and difficult in the past, I highly recommend removing her from this situation created by your father. The West does not suit her delicate nature. Is there anyone in New York that you can ask to take you in?"

Jane pocketed the bottle, her mind spinning at this news that changed everything. "My mother's parents."

"Good. I doubt they would turn away their pregnant daughter." He nodded. "I'll send our bill for both your father and your mother."

Jane bit back a groan at the amount but now was not the time to focus on something like money . . . not when Theo and

Mother were needing her to be their stronghold.

Theo lifted her hand to Jane's ear and whispered, "Can you step out in the hall for a second?" She blinked, Theo's puffy eyes making it hard not to burst into tears herself.

"Theo?"

Her scrawny arms wrapped around Jane's neck. "What are we going to do?"

"It'll be okay."

"I don't think it will," Theo whispered, her tears wetting Jane's shoulder. "How will we take care of ourselves and a baby?"

"God will take care of you just like He did with me," Jane whispered, stroking back a lock of Theo's tangled mass of hair.

"You mean how God gave you Wade even after you thought your life was over?"

Jane smiled and retrieved a handkerchief and proceeded to wipe her sister's cheeks, smearing away her tears. "Exactly. Now, do you wish to come with me? And step away for a few moments before Mother wakes?"

"Where to?"

"To send a telegram."

Wade appeared from the kitchen with two steaming cups of tea. "At this hour?"

Jane shrugged. "The telegrapher lives above the telegraph office, and we will throw pebbles at his window until he opens up for us." She dropped her gaze to the floor, "But, even if he opens the door for us, I don't know how I am going to write the words, saying our father is a thief and that Mother is with child."

Theo slid her hand into Jane's and helped her to her feet. "Then let's go together. That's how you made it through Graham leaving you at the altar—together with your Harvey Sisters."

"When did you grow up, little Theo? Yes, that is exactly how I made it through and how we will make it through this."

Wade set the cups on the table. "Well, if you are both determined, let me get my coat."

"Since you went through the trouble of making tea, let's have a bracing cup before we send the telegram." *The telegram that could change our lives all over again.*

WADE SAW the girls returned to each of their homes after the telegram was sent, but he couldn't head to his own bed yet—not without checking on Mr. Cady. He paused on the porch of the sheriff's office, gathering his thoughts. What could he say to him? Should he say anything, or just check on the man? He pushed open the door and nodded to the sheriff, Cash Maverick.

"Howdy, Cash."

"Wade." Cash nodded. "Not surprised to see you as Lawrence told me that you and Miss Cady were courting." Cash rose from behind his desk with a ring of keys and moved to the cell. "I can give you ten minutes, but Mr. Cady's got to rest after having that bullet hole patched." He shook his head. "He will have plenty of rest though soon enough. The judge was already scheduled to arrive in two days. His trial and judgement will be swift, given his pockets held evidence of the stolen funds as well as the jewelry from the guests."

"Thanks, Cash." He waited as the sheriff unlocked the door and let him inside.

Mr. Cady laid sprawled out on the cot, his leg bandaged, and his eyes closed.

"Mr. Cady." Wade cleared his throat. "How are you doing, sir?"

Mr. Cady's nose twitched. "Come to file a report, have you, boy?"

"You need to file a report against Mr. Cady, Wade?" Cash crossed his arms. "Is there something you need to tell me?"

Wade frowned. "No. We settled that matter." He turned to Mr. Cady. "I'm here to ask if there is anything I can do to help your wife and daughters. I have a good lawyer."

Mr. Cady pushed himself to sit up and lean against the wall, grunting in pain. "I don't want your help . . . but I guess I need it. Summon your lawyer. I don't want to spend the rest of my children's lives in prison for a crime I committed for them."

"How is this for them?"

Mr. Cady lifted his palms. "Everything I do is for them. I build dreams out of air and sell them, making a profit that we live off of for years. I work hard to prove that I am worthy of their mother and to make certain they are kept in the height of fashion and that they want for nothing." His voice broke. "Seeing my wife suffer this past month has been nearly unbearable for me. I had to do something to make a difference. I would have never gotten ahead by being a House Manager. I had to take action."

Wade pressed his lips together, listening to the man regal tales of his past successes and his ultimate failure which led to this moment. *At least his ill-gotten scheme was motivated by a desire to provide.* He could understand that, even if he didn't agree by the means and degree Mr. Cady was willing to go. "Besides the lawyer, what else?"

Mr. Cady frowned at him. "Why do you want to do this for me?"

"Because I love your daughter and I want to marry her, which means her family will be my family. And I come from a family that helps one another."

Mr. Cady snorted. "Well, I certainly don't. But, if you want to help, make sure my family doesn't end up on the street."

CHAPTER 20

The next morning was spent consoling Mother and attempting to make plans. Wade had been marvelous, contacting his lawyer and even bringing a basket of food to her mother's home, as if he knew the cupboards were bare. She wished she could tell him about the baby, maybe that could help explain away her father's actions, but Mother insisted that no one else know. Jane agreed but shifted uncomfortably at the thought that she had spilled the news to her grandparents before this promise. But she could not distress her, not when she was in so delicate a situation.

By the time four o'clock rolled about,

Jane's shin ached from the glass cut and she felt as if she had been completing the same task and having the same conversation with Mother over and over again. She needed to return to work and clear her head. With a kiss to Theo's head, she hurried to change into her uniform at the Rawlins building.

She just finished dressing when Dolly blocked her bedroom door, keeping Jane from heading out.

"I wish you wouldn't overdo it, considering everything you went through last night. You really should rest."

"Thank you, Dolly, but I did rest. I need to work. I already missed my morning shift, and the least I can do is take the afternoon to night shift from one of the girls."

Dolly pinched the bridge of her nose. "Yes, it did create quite an argument as the one girl who covered your shift was supposed to be having her day off."

"Then give her mine that is coming up. I need to make it up to her. I have broken so many rules it is a wonder they don't all dislike me." Jane shook her head. "It would be difficult to like the girl who gets to break all the rules you have to keep."

"I wish I could counter your argument." Dolly grimaced. "Well, let's just say it hasn't helped win you any friends . . . I wish I could say different, but Jean May and Vera are the only ones that were truly worried about you. The others were just appalled that their House Manager would steal."

"And I am sure they are wondering if I will take after my father. I have no idea if Mr. Harvey will press charges, or if I even have a job at the end of all of this, but I must finish this contract—for once in my life, I need to finish something." Jane clenched her fists.

"Well, I don't know about Mr. Harvey, but the guests are most certainly pressing charges. The rules state that only the guest may have their jewels, or property, *removed* from the safe for any reason. With the jewels, pearls, and hundreds of dollars in gold found on his person, he *will* be found guilty." She rested a hand on Jane's shoulder. "You'll have to be strong if you go into the dining room. The townsfolk will be gossiping. People will stare. It's going to be a hard first shift back. Are you certain you can handle it?"

Jane lifted her chin. "Let them stare. I have a family to provide for—what do I care what they think when I know the truth of my own character?"

"You remind me too much of myself sometimes, Jane." She stepped aside and led the way out. "But you must be prepared. Pernilla is Mr. Perkins' niece, and she has already stirred some of the girls against you staying here." She glided down the stairs. "But never fear, the House Mother has returned, and Miss Trent and I will block anything they try to do." She frowned. "Pernilla has already cost me one Harvey Girl, and she won't have another."

Jane strode alongside Dolly into the dining room, smiling as she nodded to any Harvey Girl she passed.

Vera hurried to her side, clasping her hand. "Oh, Jane, I am so sorry for everything. I'm sure it was horrible." She shook her head. "Jean May told me everything. It was a good thing Lawrence was here to step in before anything worse happened." She bent to whisper in Jane's ear, "They are saying that Mr. Perkins actually knew it was your father, which is why he only shot him in the leg. Pernilla is very upset by that rumor, understandably, and girls are taking sides."

"Mr. Perkins wouldn't—" She tamped down her volume as Pernilla caught her gaze from behind the counter and frowned at her. Jane cleared her throat and reached for a notepad as a couple entered the dining room. She plastered on her best smile. "Welcome to the Castañeda! Would you like a table or seats at the counter?"

The wife murmured something behind her hand to her husband and clutched her amethyst brooch, giving Jane a sneer.

The husband reddened and cleared his throat. "I'm sorry, Miss Jane, but my wife would like to have another girl serve us."

Jane felt the blood drain from her face, but she kept her smile up. She was a socialite after all—trained in the art of being stabbed in the front by social climbing husband hunters. "Of course. I shall send Miss

Jean May. She is one of our very best. Excuse me." Jane hurried to Jean May who was wiping the counter. "Can you see to the couple? I'll clean off the counter."

Jean May sent her a sympathetic nod and handed over the rag.

Jane scrubbed the counter, blinking furiously. *Lord, help me through today. Let me not focus on the rumors. Renew my heart, Lord, and give me hope for my family's future.*

"Good afternoon, Jane."

"Wade!" She gasped, chucking the rag in the bin beneath the counter. Certainly, they had only been apart for a few hours, but the sight of him was a balm to her soul. "Coffee?"

He plopped his Stetson on the chair beside him. "Yes, please." He smiled at her, opening his mouth as if he wished to tell her something before snapping it closed.

She filled up a fresh pot and brought it out to him, placing a china cup and saucer before him. "Thank you for coming to see me."

He nodded. "Of course. I tried the Rawlins building first, thinking that you were asleep there. The House Mother wasn't there to speak with me, so I threw pebbles at your window. I considered climbing the building to the second floor to try to get to you when you didn't answer, but I knew there would likely be other girls about and I didn't want to shock anyone . . . or myself. Thankfully, one of the girls told me that you were already working."

She giggled, slapping a hand over her mouth. How could she giggle when her life was in shambles? Her countenance fell as reality crashed over her once more.

"How are you doing?" Wade spun his empty cup in the saucer.

"Not well." She admitted, resting a finger on the cup handle and then slowly pouring a second cup of coffee. "I fear the town will never trust me after what my father did."

He nodded. "People can get mighty judgy, but don't lose heart, there are plenty of good folks in Las Vegas who will understand that you are not your father." He glanced up at her. "Did he tell you that he stopped by my stable before he—?"

"He came to the stables?" *Before he robbed*

his own hotel? Her heart dipped in realization. "No? He didn't try to—Oh, Wade, did he come after Raven, or did he find out about Charleston and try to take him? I didn't tell him about the gift from Mr. Austin."

"He tried to steal Raven, but I stopped him and told him that I wouldn't say anything the first time."

She reached out and squeezed his hand. "You are a good man, Wade Sterling."

"I'd be a hypocrite if I didn't give him another chance after what I did as a boy."

"Well, I appreciate it. Did he ask for Charleston?"

"He tried to pretend Charleston was the one he wanted, but I think Raven was the only one that would free him from debt."

She topped off his cup when a cluster of ladies entered. Her stomach sank at the sight of Eliza's friends. But, as Jean May was seeing to the other couple, Jane set the pot on the workstation behind her, excused herself, and hurried to greet them when Eliza Brady joined the group as well. "Welcome, how many will be joining you?"

Eliza smiled. "Just the five of us, but you'll have to forgive me for asking, but is Miss Dolly here? We'd rather *Miss Dolly* serve us." She gestured to the cluster of town girls, a few blushing furiously but keeping their mouths closed. "We have far too many precious gemstones on us at the moment, and well—you understand."

Jane clenched her fists, but her tears were already spilling onto her hot cheeks. She spun on her heel and fled the dining room. *Horrible, detestable people.* Jane tore off her apron, swiping away her tears, not caring where she was going, but halfway around the block, she heard shouting from behind.

"Jane! Wait!"

Turning, she spied Wade jogging toward her. She slowed her flight.

"What on earth are you doing?" He demanded as he dropped her cloak about her shoulders. "You are going to freeze."

"I can't go back in there and face them. Did you hear her?"

"No, but I can imagine." He rubbed his forehead with two fingers. "If you won't come back to the hotel, at least allow me to escort you back to the dormitory, or to your mother's?"

"I don't want to see anyone right now."

"Then let's walk." He pulled her hand through his arm and she allowed him to guide her. "Will you tell me what happened to make you leave without fetching me at the lunch counter only paces from you? You make it very difficult for me to keep track of you."

"You don't have to keep coming after me every time I run away in distress." She laughed without mirth, "Which seems to be quite often these days. I never used to be so dramatic."

"It's been a trying week. And you should know by now that I'll always come after you, Jane."

Her lip trembled as her eyes welled anew. She twisted her hands, desperate to calm herself.

"Please?" He asked, drawing her to a stop beneath the cedars by the pretty blue chapel and reaching out to stroke away a tear with his rough thumb.

"It's a lot of things—secrets that press upon me." She sniffed back her tears. "Secrets that I can't tell you." *If only you knew how much you mean to me. I can't allow myself to think of you, but now that I have, it's the only dream I will ever want in life . . .a dream I can never have and it's killing me. Eliza has so much more to offer you than I do.* Despite everything, Jane felt herself lean into his hand as if being drawn by a lead rope. She closed her eyes as she willed herself to stop crying when she felt his warm lips press against hers. Her eyes flew open as she drew back, gasping.

He stared into her eyes with a fierceness that sent her heart to skipping as he wrapped his hand around hers. "I love you, Miss Jane Cady."

"You love me?" She pressed her hand against his chest.

He smiled at her genuine surprise. "Why do you think I've gone to the dining room every spare minute I could manage?"

She tilted her head, her brow creased. "Hunger?"

"At first, yes, but now my shirt is getting a little tight."

She glanced at his shirt. "All I see is muscle—" She sucked in her lips, her cheeks flaming.

He laughed. "It was the kindness I saw in your heart that kept drawing me back for more. As a child, I never knew such kindness and I couldn't fathom that such a sweet woman could exist until I met you. I see how you treat your father and mother when they do not treat you the same. There is so much goodness in you. I know that we have not known each other long, but it's as if my soul recognized yours the moment we saw each other. Your beauty from within radiates to without and when I leave your side, the world isn't as warm or bright." He tucked a lock of her hair behind her ear as he leaned closer. "I want to keep you with me. I want to make you mine and I want to belong to you. Please, please let me love you and care for you all the days of our lives," he whispered, slipping his arm about her waist and drawing her into a deep kiss.

The touch of Wade's lips made her head spin with such ferocity that she felt for a moment that maybe she could have her dream, but then, she remembered how much her mother needed her, more now than ever. And he deserved to know—no matter that her mother wished for privacy. She gently pulled away, hating the distance, but feeling as if she must have it before she did something reckless. "Wade," she whispered, his name feeling delicious on her tongue.

His eyes captured hers as he leaned in for another soft kiss. "Say it. Say we belong to one another—that you will marry me."

The tenderness in his voice made her tremble and feeling faint at his touch, she barely managed to say, "But my family—there have been some new developments."

"I'll provide for them too." He stroked her palm with his thumb. "I can help them manage their accounts—get back on their feet. Unless . . . you don't care for my own past?"

She shook her head. "The sins of your father and mother are not yours—you are their complete opposite."

The creases in his forehead melted away. "Then, if you don't mind having a man with a past, what's stopping us from marrying?"

She brushed away at her stubborn tears. Closing her eyes, she took a deep breath before meeting his earnest, love-filled gaze. "The thing is . . . you haven't known me for that long. Your dream has always been to raise and sell horses, but if you take me and my family on—you might care later when things get rough. I now know what it's like going from having everything to having to watch every single penny I spend. I know what it takes to run a growing family like mine and if—" a furious blush crept into her cheeks. "When children come along, I would further tie you down."

"Tie me down?" He shook his head. "Don't you know that all I've ever wanted in life was to be loved and tied to someone who loves me in return? It would be the greatest gift of my life to have you by my side and all the responsibilities that come with marriage."

Her heart broke at his confession, but she pressed a finger to his lips to stop him before she lost her courage to speak and will to stand strong against his pleas. "Let me speak, please, for if I don't say it now, I may never be able to again." She straightened her shoulders. "I fear you would grow to resent me and the financial strain I will bring with my family, and we will prove too much for your love. For myself, I don't care one whit about money. I could stand everything because . . ." she drew in a jagged breath. *Because I love you.* "Because I care for you more than anything, but my family—"

His eyes softened at her declaration, but the hurt was still behind them. "Don't you think that I can be selfless like you?" He raked his hand through his dark hair with a growl. "Don't you know I would give up everything if only it meant I could have you as my wife?"

"Of course I do," she whispered. *And I love you for it.* She longed to lean into those full lips of his again. "But I don't think I could bear destroying your future with my lack of fortune."

"I'll take care of you, and I'll provide for your family as well," he promised, desperation to be understood edging his voice, "and I could never resent you for providing for your family."

"With Father's arrest, there will be a trial and, no doubt, a conviction. Mother will not be able to bear to live in town anymore." She bit her lip. "Mother is going to have a baby."

His brows shot up. "A baby?"

She nodded. "It would not be the easiest transition to wedded bliss."

He grinned. "A baby is always a cause for celebration, Jane." He cupped her cheeks. "Is that what was worrying you?"

She nodded and released a sigh. "You are sure?"

He nodded. "Absolutely."

Hope bloomed in her chest at his willingness. "There is a chance that she might not live with us. With my father out of the picture, I suspect my maternal grandparents will read my telegram and ask us to return to New York. So, they may wish to see to Mother and Theo's comfort and if they do offer, I will need to accept and escort them."

"If they don't wish to return, I will provide for them and do so with joy. However, if they do wish to return to New York, then I'll wait for you." He stated, his voice gruff. "I'll wait as long as it takes until they get on their feet and I can put away enough savings to build a home for us and we can wed." He squeezed her hand. "We can do this, Jane. You just need to trust me and trust that my love is strong enough to withstand the darkest of storms, or the greatest of distances."

She swallowed, the confession of her love for Wade ached to be free. "Can you give me a month to see them settled? And then, I will return and become your wife, my darling Wade."

WADE LEANED over the glass counter at Rudy's Mercantile, studying the small array of rings in the display below. Mrs. Angelique Smith leaned over as well, pointing out the ones she thought he'd like.

"Now, I know we don't have a lot of choices for engagement rings, but these are our most popular stones for the ladies." Angelique, as she insisted on being called, tapped the glass over a ruby.

Wade shook his head and straightened. "No, I'm not seeing the one yet. Do you have anything else, something more unique?"

Angelique tapped her lip before snapping her fingers. "Oh, I just got a shipment of jewelry in from Santa Fe. It's not your typical engagement jewelry, so I didn't bring it out for you to see yet. But, if you'll wait a moment, I'll fetch it." Angelique disappeared into the storage room behind the counter and returned with a medium box in hand, lifting the lid to display the jewelry within. There was a necklace, a silver comb, earrings, bracelets and . . . a ring, "Now, these are stones that were uncovered just south of Santa Fe in the Cerrillos Hills. They are absolutely beautiful."

He ran his finger over the oval turquoise stone set in silver with a beautiful filigree on the wide silver band. "Yes. This stone reminds me of the dress she was wearing when I first met her."

Angelique let out a little squeal and

clapped her hands. "Oh, I do love, *love*. I'll put this in a pretty little ring box for you, Mr. Sterling. It has been a pleasure doing business with you. I feel like I've had a hand in your courtship of Miss Cady since you came in and picked out that corsage for the Mistletoe Maiden dance not long ago at all." She hummed to herself as she readied the ring.

Wade paid the shopkeeper's wife and with the polished ring box in hand, he barely kept himself from running to the Castañeda. He burst through the doors and found Jane where she always was, working the dining room floor. He spied the table where she had first kissed him, and it was miraculously free. He sat down at it and waited for her to notice him. She gave him a little wave and hurried to his side. He grasped her wrist and pulled her onto his lap and kissed her soundly.

She gasped and attempted to sit up. "Wade Sterling! You can't do that here."

"Why? I might be trying to avoid the advances of former lady friends." He chuckled at her shocked expression and released her, letting her stand up. He knelt in front of her and held out the ring box. "Jane, I know I've already asked you once, but I want to make sure we make this as official as possible, given our history. I want there to be absolutely *no* doubt for anyone that you and I are meant to be together forever." He lifted the lid and her eyes widened at the beautiful turquoise ring with its intricate design.

She pressed her hands to her lips. "Oh, Wade."

"When I think of you, I think about you in that brilliant turquoise dress when I first met you, and the stone just seemed fitting for you. Jane, will you be my bride and allow me to love you with my whole heart forever?"

"Wade, I never thought I could love again, but then, I met you and everything became clear. I never loved anyone like I love you. You are good, and kind, and gentle. You make me feel safe and protected and special. I would be honored to call you mine." Jane's tears spilled over as he slid the ring onto her finger and rose, wrapping her in his arms. He gave her a little twirl, careful not to knock the tables. The dining room filled with cheers, and Dolly hurried over to give Jane a hug.

"I knew it! I knew it. I am going to have to replace you after all." She smiled as she shook her head. "Wade, are you certain you can't wait to marry her until after her contract is up?"

Jane held up a hand. "You won't be getting rid of me that easily. But I will have to ask you a favor, Miss Dolly." She lifted a telegram out of her apron pocket and handed it over to Wade, explaining, "I got an answer back from my grandparents today, and they wished for me to return with my family to New York. I can be back in a month's time and finish out my contract then, if that is all right with you, Miss Dolly, for me to take a leave of absence for my family."

"I will have to ask Miss Trent and Mr. Perkins, but I don't see it being a problem given the circumstances," she lowered her voice and leaned toward Jane and Wade, saying, "It actually might be for the best for you to take some time away from the girls and let them cool off after this incident. Your contract was only for three months, so you only have about two months left to go, and then you can marry."

Jane grasped Wade's hands in hers and squeezed them. "Is that all right with you? Will you be fine to wait until I return?"

He lifted her hand and pressed a kiss atop it. "As I said before, Jane, I will wait for you as long as it takes to become my bride. And while you're gone, I will set us up a house that will be just yours and mine."

CHAPTER 21

*D*espite the next week being difficult with her father's trial and conviction, Jane's heart was at peace. No matter what happened, Wade would be by her side as he had been through the trial and sentencing. Father had been given a gracious sentence of only a year, given that he had not made it out of the building with his stolen goods. Mother was resigned and Theo surprisingly happy to return home as long as she could bring her newest collection of New Mexico bugs.

Jane had packed the house quickly and the journey to New York had passed blessedly without any trouble. But, the moment

Jane, Theo, and Mother stepped onto the train platform in New York, Mother became painfully aware of their dresses and of the little changes in style since last season. As Jane turned to alleviate her mother's worries, Grandfather's arms were around them and Grandmother was cupping Mother's face, gushing over the happy news of the coming baby.

"You have been greatly missed, my dear Jane. Few can match your quick wit, and I must admit that I sorely regretted being unable to help you and your family out due to missing you so much." Grandfather's white mutton chop whiskers trembled with every word as he ushered his family into the awaiting carriage and out of earshot of strangers. "And with all that has happened in your absence, it does my heart good to know that something good will be coming to this family soon."

Grandmother leaned forward and, with her free hand, stroked Mother's cheek before patting Theo on the knee. "I'm grateful you were willing to come home. From Benjamin's descriptions, one would think you were living in a home as grand as the one you left, but when Graham came by the house to tell me that you lived in a shabby little cottage . . ." Grandmother shuddered. "It is such a weight off my mind and heart knowing you are home. I am only sorry that we could not help you sooner."

"I cannot express our sorrow over our Benjamin's desperation that led to such measures," Grandfather continued with his eyes on his daughter. "If there is anything, great or small, that will help you, you need only tell a maid, and it will be done."

Grandmother nodded. "Yes, and while we are alone and away from the servants, we might as well get out the uncomfortable bits."

Grandfather cleared his throat. "We don't usually discuss such things as money, but I can no longer avoid it and now is the best time to inform you that you all are to live in the fashion you were accustomed to before your, uh, move to Las Vegas and I have already deposited funds into an account I created specifically for your use, Theo and Jane. There is an express clause that under no circumstances may the funds be used for or by Benjamin. As for you, dear Mildred, you have small credits under our name at any store. I'm afraid with your marriage to Benjamin, I cannot give you any funds in the event that they will likely be claimed to pay debts or be used by the man himself. You have a tender heart, you always have, but that is also your weakness. If you need a greater sum, just let me know and I will have the funds released to you when I know what it is intended for."

"Thank you," Mother replied, breathless at his generosity.

"There is no need to bring it up again," Grandfather lifted his palms to stop the flow of thanks from Jane and Theo. "We cannot have our family going about New York in anything but the finest of clothing."

Mother bit her lip, something she never did, and the action betrayed her nerves. "But won't everyone be well aware of our circumstances due to Graham's visit?"

"Graham swore he would not tell," Grandfather replied, his eyes going dark as he adjusted to lean back on the tufted leather seat of the carriage. "I've seen to that."

Grandmother pressed her lips into a thin line and focused her gaze on Jane.

What aren't they saying? Did they have to bribe him into silence? Jane fidgeted with her handkerchief that she kept at the ready for Mother. "We are indebted to you."

Grandfather waved his hand dismissively. "You are here and that is all I could ever want. If your father had only explained about the baby, I would have taken you all in instantly, but," he added when Grandmother nudged him in the ribs, "I understand his motives for wishing to provide for his family—even though I do not approve of his choices on how to accomplish that feat."

"And," Grandmother interjected with a sparkle in her eyes, "we have set aside the east wing for your use, which has three bedrooms, a parlor and," she looked at Jane, "a *music* room."

"All that space?" Jane's eyes grew wide at their kindness. "But when Uncle comes for a visit—"

"Your uncle is never in New York now

that he has a lovely French wife and sons abroad, so there is plenty of room to spare," Grandmother answered. "No. Those rooms are yours for as long as you wish to stay. He can stay in the guest rooms."

Jane smiled at the thought of playing a piano again, her fingers stretching in anticipation of playing while she was here. The light caught the little turquoise ring on her finger.

Grandmother gasped. "Is that—"

"You are too good to us." Mother dabbed her soiled hanky to her eyes, effectively distracting Grandmother.

"Nothing is too good for my girls!" Grandfather beamed, seeming happy that he could ease their burden through the comforts of old. "Here we are," he announced as the carriage rolled to a stop in front of their mansion on Fifth Avenue.

The sounds of the city greeted Jane as she descended the carriage with her dirty, travel-worn skirts trailing behind. Feeling the need to escape prying eyes, she stepped inside the grand foyer and was immediately swept up to a decadent violet and gold leaf trimmed bedroom by an overenthusiastic maid who introduced herself as Fiona. Now understanding how difficult it was to work for a living, Jane appreciated the maid's zeal and introduced herself before Fiona bobbed into a curtsy and went to draw the water for Jane's bath.

Not wanting to soil any of the furniture by sitting, Jane walked around the Persian rug to examine her room and found that her ever thoughtful Grandmother had already sent for three new sets of gowns, a riding habit, and a dinner gown that were now hanging in her walk-in closet. No doubt, she had obtained her measurements from their former seamstress. Lifting the hem of a day gown, she touched the fine bits of lace.

"Miss?" Her maid interrupted her reverie.

"Yes, Fiona?" Jane asked, turning away from the finery.

"Your bath is ready." She held the bathroom door open.

"Thank you. Such luxury to have a bath drawn for me." Gazing at the tub with rose petals floating on top of the scented water, Jane almost felt guilty over how much she enjoyed returning to a life of luxury. After a good long soak, she wrapped herself in a deliciously soft towel that held the lightest aroma of roses from the perfumed sachets. *Grandmother hasn't forgotten my affinity with that blossom.* She smiled as she removed her ring to coat her hands in lavender cream, hoping to soften her callouses while here. She slipped on the tiny ring again, her heart aching at the thought of the distance between her and Wade, but at the thought that he had selected it because it reminded him of their first meeting, made her heart warm with his love. If she just closed her eyes, she could imagine him before her.

At the knock on the door, she tugged the tie of her dressing robe and opened it.

Arms instantly wrapped about her neck. "Oh, Janey! You're back!" Meg squealed.

"Meg!" Jane embraced her friend, her soul feeling anchored again. "It's so good to see you."

"We have so much to do and talk about and how society is buzzing with how you broke Mr. Austin's heart." She pressed a hand to her heart. "Are you back for him?"

Jane grimaced. "Actually, I am only back for a month at the most. I had to obtain special permission for such a long family leave from the Harvey House."

Meg's countenance dropped. "Oh. But I thought that now you have returned, and you don't have to worry about providing for your family, you would wish to marry?"

"I do, but I am already promised." She held up her left hand, giggling.

"Janey! I am so happy for you." Meg clapped her hands and embraced her again. "I knew it. From your letters, I didn't know how you couldn't possibly be head over heels in love with such a handsome and thoughtful cowboy who rescued you from a herd of Longhorn cattle. And who *loves* you from the first moment he met you. And surely now that your grandparents are looking after you, won't they offer you an inheritance as a wedding present?"

Jane shrugged. "They have already given me so much that it would be ungrateful and rude to expect more. No. I am quite content to remain a Harvey Girl until my contract is up and then marry Wade. I can't believe my future husband doesn't care about money. I used to feel worthless without my fortune, but I don't now. However, I haven't broken the news to my grandparents, but I better before they have a score of suitors ready for me." For the first time, she noticed that the dress Meg was wearing was a riding gown. "Are you on your way somewhere?"

"I thought we'd go for a ride in the park." She moved to the closet and shoved open the doors, pulling out a riding habit. "Your grandfather has a horse ready for you."

Her heart soared at the thought, and it was like old times dressing for a ride with Meg perched atop her bed, eating a box of chocolates and by the time Jane was dressed in her new habit, she felt more like her old self than she had in weeks. And yet, she couldn't help but wonder what was going on at the Harvey House even as she reached the stables and mounted her grandfather's impressive dapple gray. The horse was handsome, and she knew Wade would love the stallion.

The two friends rode through the park, soaking in the beautiful sunny day when another rider approached them on a red roan. Jane's heart squeezed as she recognized the mount. *Graham.* She sent a panicked look to Meg, who grimaced. Jane had not told Meg all of Graham's visit—she hadn't had time and now, she desperately wished she had.

"Miss Jane Cady! Miss Meg Leopold." Graham called to them from atop his mount, tipping his hat.

Jane stiffened in the saddle. "What are you doing here?"

"Riding, which is not a crime." He bowed his head. "I spotted you from across the park and I am merely here to greet you and welcome you back to New York of course."

Meg frowned at him. "And yet you are the reason she left in the first place."

He cleared his throat. "Yes, and well, could you give us a moment, Miss Leopold? I need to clear the air with her."

She looked pointedly at Graham before leaning to Jane, "If you need anything, such as knocking him out of his saddle, I'll be just ahead on the path." She gestured to the direction with her riding crop, making her horse dance to the side before trotting off.

"Mr. Bank, what is it you want? I seem to recall our last visit ended poorly." Jane held her chin high and wished her glove was off so she could display her engagement ring. Perhaps she could pick up a glove with a slit for a ring while she was in the city.

"I wanted to apologize for leaving so abruptly on our last visit. I am sure I don't know what came over me."

And I'm sure you do. Wade's fists come to mind. "Think nothing of it. Now, please excuse—"

"But I do, especially when Austin told me that he lost your hand to that *cowboy*," he fairly spat the word.

"Which is his business and not yours." Jane turned her horse to move around Graham, but he kicked his mount to sidestep and block her way.

"You see, I think it is my business. So, tell me, are you indeed promised to that horse breeder?"

"Mr. Bank," she pursed her lips, "it is

highly irregular to ask such an intimate question."

"Not when I was the one to ask you to marry me first," he retorted, "so I don't think it is out of line to expect an answer, especially when I am owed an heirloom engagement ring."

Jane's jaw dropped. "You know the rules of polite society. You forfeited the right to that ring when you jilted me. I gave it to my father."

"Which means it is long gone." He sighed and rested his hand on his mount. "I apologize for my bitter comment about the ring. I simply want us to go back to the way things were between us before you left me to help your father. I want us to court, to become engaged and marry."

"Mr. Bank—"

"Jane, it's Graham, not Mr. Bank."

"Mr. Bank, thank you for your offer, but I can't." She scowled, remembering how he had grabbed her arm, and there was no Wade here to defend her now. But she had her riding crop and was an excellent rider.

"Why not?" His shoulders stiffened as if

not expecting to be turned down again, his eyes blazing with passion. "Do you know how it feels to be rejected after I went all the way to New Mexico for you and then saw the kind of place your father had you living in?" He snorted. "You said no, and I still kept your secret because despite everything you believe, I love you."

"Love as in you love chocolate? Or love horse riding?" She countered. "And you seem to forget that you did tell my grand-parents."

"I confided in them to help you," he whispered, his eyes filled with longing. "And they did and that's why you left that miser-able little hovel. They knew it was no place to leave you while your father was in jail. No one in New York except your grandpar-ents, Meg, and I know about your real cir-cumstances for it was I who kept his name out of the papers." He pulled his horse alongside hers. "Don't you think it would be advantageous to marry the one man who knows your secret and can protect it from ever getting out?"

Is he blackmailing me? The wind picked

up and, glancing to the darkening sky, she surmised, "I best return home before it rains."

"What is it? What's keeping you from saying yes this time?"

"Besides Wade? Maybe your attempts to blackmail me into marriage? The only reason you *didn't* spread it around was because you wanted this secret over me."

His jaw clenched as he dropped his hand. "Call it back-up."

She pursed her lips and took a deep breath to avoid saying something she would regret. "My answer is still no." She turned her mount and kicked him into a trot.

He kept pace beside her. "Jane, it doesn't have to be this way between us. Just agree to be my wife."

"I certainly will not," she fumed. "Tell whoever you want. I do *not* care. Just because I've lost my fortune, it doesn't mean you can treat me as any less of a lady. You cannot buy my affections, Graham."

"I'm not treating you unfairly. You know as well as I do that, like any marriage in our social circle, there is a certain element of business," he stated as a matter of fact. "And while you may not care about your standing anymore, I can guarantee your grandparents do," his eyes narrowed. "They care a *great* deal about their reputations and place in society. Your father being a convict will bring them all down if it's not hushed up at once and that's what I did. You owe me."

Her cheeks flamed with his insults against her father. She was finished with pretending to play by society's polite, rigid rules. "Listen very closely, Graham Bank. I will print the story in the papers myself before I allow you to blackmail me into marriage," Jane hissed.

"Blackmail?" He scowled. "I offered to marry you and care for you all your days. What more could you want in exchange?"

"*Exchange?*' What happened to love being enough?"

"We do not have that luxury," he answered, "but fortunately, I do love you, so why do you feel the need to reject me?"

"No, Graham, you don't love me. Your actions do not show love. They show lust and I know that once you married me, and the dowry my grandfather would likely give, you would tire of me! I have a value above money. I know what I'm worth and it is far more than a loveless marriage to a tyrant." She lifted her chin. "I deserve to be truly loved for who I am and not the amount of money, or prestige, I can bring into a marriage. I am to marry Wade Sterling upon my return."

He nodded, frowning. "And that hasn't changed with your grandparents' offer of help?"

"Why would it?"

"Because you have a choice to return home now."

"Which is why it is so precious to me. I wouldn't marry Mr. Austin because I did not love him, and I will not marry you because you want me back. I will return to Las Vegas and finish out my contract and then marry Wade Sterling."

"If you say no, I won't take you back when you regret it in the morning," he warned as thunder rumbled.

"I'm counting on that," she shouted over

her shoulder as she kicked her mount into a gallop.

"You are making the greatest mistake of your life, Jane Cady."

If I stay here for a month, I will be making a mistake. My mother and sister are taken care of and don't need me. I need Wade. I need to see him now. She laid low in the saddle. She had to find Meg, pack her bags, and get herself home to the Harvey House and to Wade.

CHAPTER 22

Wade surveyed the land surrounding the old hunting cabin on the far side of the *Sanctuary*. There was already a clearing on this side of the ranch, and it had easy access to the fenced area where he kept his horses. It would take some time to build a new stable alongside the small cabin, but as he had lots of brothers, they could tackle this pretty easily. Their cabin wouldn't be anything like the houses Jane was used to, but they could make it their own home. Thankfully, Lawrence had taken over the stable in town, giving Wade enough time to make plans and then have the brothers start building.

"What do you think, Wade?" Tanner pushed the brim of his Stetson out of his eyes as he stood with his bride, Corinna.

"It needs a little work, but it will give us the privacy we need as a couple and still be near to the family." He pushed open the door to the old hunting cabin that Gray used in the winter when he had to travel away from the ranch to get meat. Gray kept it tidy, but if Wade added some plaster to the logs, and painted it, it would look more like the houses Jane was accustomed to.

Corinna followed him inside the cabin, exploring the one room kitchen, dining area, and living area. She poked her head into the small bedroom and nodded. "Oh yes, this will do quite nicely." She clasped her hands to her heart. "I can already see little Wades and Janes running about the place. And the east wall would do nicely for adding on in the future."

Wade grinned at his petite sister-in-law. Ever since those two had gotten married, it was babies this and babies that. And with Tanner and Corinna both having golden hair, Wade could easily picture his nieces and nephews. As for his own children, he hoped for a whole passel if the Lord chose to bless them with little ones. "Corinna, I could use your help to get the place furnished for Jane." He ran his fingers through his hair. "I don't want to shock her too bad to mountain life if she walks into a cabin with nothing but that cot in the single room." He knew there was more to Jane than fancy things. Their love would carry through any storm, but it would be nice to have a table and chairs and a settee to rest on at night.

Corinna clapped her hands. "Oh Wade, I would be so happy to help and, if you will let me, I want to purchase you something extra special as my wedding gift."

"Your help would be gift enough, but as I know you won't take no for an answer, thank you, Corinna and Tanner." He rubbed his hands together. "We better head down the mountain with the wagon and get to shopping before she comes to town in a few weeks. I'm sure Lawrence is already itching for me to take back over the stable."

JANE STOOD on the train platform in Las Vegas with her umbrella open as rain poured, soaking her skirts and trunk. She glanced about for Wade. She'd sent him a telegram and hoped he had received it in time.

"Jane!" He called out racing toward her, skidding on the slick brick platform. She reached for him and was instantly tugged down by his weight, tumbling atop him as the freezing rain plastered them both. He released a groan but that didn't stop him from claiming a kiss.

"Did you miss me?" She laughed, kissing the tip of his nose.

"More than anything." Laughing, he righted them, snatched up the umbrella, and wrapped his arm about her and closed the distance between them, the world around them fading into the rain. "Did you miss me?"

She pressed her face into his chest. "Once you've felt the warmth of the sun, you never wish to return to your old life, and you would do anything to keep it near. All the riches in the world cannot make up for its absence."

He pressed his lips to her forehead before holding her back to gaze into her eyes, "Jane, be my warmth forever?"

She rose onto her tiptoes and, with her hand behind his neck, she pulled him down toward her into a deep kiss. "I will."

"You are certain?" He asked with bright eyes, his half smile tempting her for another kiss. "You will marry me now and break your contract?"

She giggled. "I only signed a three-month contract, and I took a week off to see my mother and sister to New York."

"How about Valentine's Day? That would be my first Valentine's Day with a girl and quite the marker."

She lifted her lips to brush a kiss to his jaw. "I wish I could, but my contract is up mid-March."

He sighed. "Well, I suppose the boys and I have some work to do on our home before we wed. It would be nice to spirit you away

to the mountains to a house that is put together and not in shambles."

"I'd live in a tent with you, Wade Sterling, but if I am honest," she smiled up at
him, "I would prefer a real bed with a cozy
comforter and curtains in the windows
with windowpanes to keep the wild animals
out."

He kissed the top of her head. "Very
well. Consider my comments as temporary
insanity."

"I prefer the term hopeless romantic."
She laughed as her heart soared in the
freedom of their future together. "And the
moment my contract is up, we shall have a
wedding with all our friends there to celebrate with us. How does March eighteenth
sound?"

With an elated whoop, he dropped the
umbrella and enfolded her into his arms and
spun her around. Passersby stared openly at
their display, commenting on their perfectly
good umbrella going to waste beside them,
but Jane didn't care as they embraced, happy
they were together at last.

Lightning cracked overhead, jolting Jane from their joyful reverie and grabbing his hand, she gathered her skirts and dashed down the walk and up the steps of the Castañeda. Under the colonnades, she gasped with laughter as she pressed back her drenched hair.

Wade delicately cupped her face in his rough hands. "I can't believe you are to be my wife in March. Marrying was a dream that I had long since buried, but now, my heart is springing to life again."

EPILOGUE

M arch 18, 1899

JANE TWIRLED in the mirror that Jean May had taken from one of the girls' rooms to the front parlor of the dormitory. Jane smoothed her hands down the lace bodice that once belonged to her mother, knowing Wade would love it just as her father had adored seeing her mother in it on their wedding day. She wished her family could be here to celebrate, but with Father serving a year in prison, and Mother's baby due soon, all her family needed to stay in New

York. Meg was already abroad on her Grand Tour, but Jane knew she was thinking of her this day as much as Jane was thinking of Meg. She rested her hand on the gold locket that Meg had sent her with their pictures inside. Near, or far, she knew her dearest friend was praying for her and wishing her well.

Graham certainly isn't, but at least his making me "regret" my decision was only a suit for breach of contract and not revealing the truth about Father. His desperate suit was thrown out at once given the entire church had been filled with guests that saw *him* throw her over on their wedding day. Her grandfather's lawyer suggested a counter-suit against him, but Jane had pleaded that he reject the idea. She wanted to focus on her future now.

Her heart pounded. *And my future begins in only moments.* She set the veil into place atop her low coiffure, affixing it with a silver comb with stones that matched her turquoise engagement ring. Hearing the giggling from behind the parlor door, she called out, "I'm ready."

Her Harvey Sisters, Dolly, Jean May, and Vera burst into the room, giggling and oohing over her dress.

"You look beautiful," Dolly's eyes glistened as she handed her a small bouquet of wildflowers bound with an emerald ribbon. "We used your floral dictionary when searching the fields." Dolly pointed to a golden poppy. "This symbolizes love." She shifted the bouquet to showcase a cluster of white flowers. "These are yucca flowers, and they represent loyalty and purity." She pointed to a lovely cluster of purple flowers in the shape of a foxtail. "And these are hyssop blooms, which I'm not sure what they symbolize, but they certainly are beautiful." She hugged Jane and sighed. "Why is it that every Harvey Girl I grow close to is snatched away by some handsome cowboy with a smile that melts knees?"

"Thank you for the flowers. They're perfect," Jane smiled at her friends. "I'm going to miss you all so much."

"The trail up the Gallinas Mountains isn't too bad. I'm sure I can visit . . . eventually." Dolly grimaced. "With Mr. Perkins moving to the Montezuma tomorrow, I received a bit of news."

Jane gasped, squeezing Dolly's hand. "Dolly! Did they name you the new House Manager?"

Dolly bit her lip as if trying to contain her excitement. "I didn't want to say anything on your big day—"

Jane threw her arms about Dolly as Vera and Jean May squealed for her. "I am so happy for you. You deserve this. You have worked so hard for years and anyone can tell that you are a born leader. Not many Harvey Girls have the drive and dedication to their jobs like you."

"Thank you. I'm hoping the rest of the girls will think so too. Now, enough about me. Let's get you to the church so you can become Mrs. Wade Sterling!" Dolly thread her hand through Jane's left arm and Jean May linked her right arm, as Vera picked up Jane's train and together, Jane's bridesmaids escorted her down the street to the blue chapel nestled in the cedar trees.

Jean May kissed her on the cheek. "May the Lord bless your marriage. I hope that one day we may be sisters too—Lawrence has been awful keen on having a cup of coffee every night during my shifts. I think he may come courting soon."

"And if he doesn't, I'll give him a hint that he should—as his new sister, I'm sure I'll have a little sway," Jane smiled up at the closed chapel doors. "So many wonderful things await us, ladies. God has bright futures planned for us."

The ladies climbed the steps and Dolly and Jean May pulled open the doors as the old organ in the corner sounded the wedding march. It was nothing like her last wedding—and it was perfect.

As she stepped through the threshold, the guests rose, her Harvey Sisters and townspeople giving her warm smiles. Former Harvey Girls and their spouses beamed at her and at the front rows stood Corinna and Tanner and the rest of the Sterling brothers. At last, she dared to raise her lashes to the man who would be her husband. Her breath caught at the sight of Wade in a black suit with a golden poppy in his lapel. Did he know it meant love? The man took her breath away in his plaid shirt and Stetson, but in a suit and silk cravat— she feared she might faint.

She couldn't help her giggle from escaping as the elation of her future filled her being as she strolled through the petals strewn down the aisle. Giving her bouquet to Dolly, she placed her hands in Wade's and together, they vowed never to be apart again. At last, Wade swept her into his arms and kissed her, leaving her no doubt that this love was real.

WADE SPUN on the dancefloor with his beautiful bride in his arms as his brothers danced with the Harvey Girls. Lawrence was looking awful star struck over Jean May and Wade couldn't be happier for him. *There may be another Harvey Girl bride for another Sterling brother yet.* He twirled Jane under his arm, and she laughed as she collided into his chest.

"Seems to me that a New York Four

Hundred socialite should know how to dance." He grinned down at her.

"How else is a girl supposed to get a fellow's attention than to fall into his arms?"

"Kissing comes to mind. That worked right well for us," he chuckled. His chest swelled that this long held dream had come true—that the Lord had not only cleared him from horse thieving but also gave him a bride beyond his wildest dreams and a woman who would make a mother that a child deserved. She was kind, determined, fiercely loyal, and beautiful inside and out. *And she's mine.* He bent and kissed her lips as the song ended, bringing cheers from the guests. *All mine.*

She smiled up at him, eyes sparkling. "What a fine husband you are turning out to be."

Wade laughed and gave her another quick kiss on the cheek. "I'm glad you are easy to please, my dear. But I have a little surprise for you," he said, drawing her off the dancefloor and reaching into his jacket and pulling out a small, velvet box. "By means of a peace offering, Eliza Brady sent you this."

Stiffening at her name, Jane opened the lid to find her great-grandmother's beautiful pearl necklace. "She gave it back?" She gasped, stroking the familiar pearls.

He shrugged. "I may have bought them from her, at an inflated price, but even by her being willing to part with the pearls, I think it speaks volumes that she wishes to move beyond the past." Wade pointed to a small card tucked in the lid of the box. "What does it say?"

Clearing her throat, she read, "'Jane, blessings on your marriage.' Well, it's not the grand apology I had hoped for, but it's a start." She winked at him and folded up the note before lifting her curls and veil and turning so Wade could fasten it about her neck. "Thank you for my necklace, darling. It means the world to have it back."

"I feel the same way about you, my sweet little wife. That time with you in New York was torture."

"But that was months ago." She giggled and rested her head on his chest.

"Yes, but the memory is still fresh." He laughed.

"Thank you."

"For what, my darling?"

"For making this real when it started out with a fake kiss." She stood on her tiptoes, pressing a light kiss onto his cheek.

Wade laughed and drew her onto the dancefloor once more. "Mrs. Sterling, you and I both know that there was *nothing* fake about our first kiss and I'll go on proving it for years to come because every kiss from you makes my heart soar just like the first time."

Author's Note

Dear Reader, thank you so much for reading Book Five in the Aprons & Veils series! I had such a fun time writing Jane and Wade's whirlwind romance!

I know the timeline of Wade's love at first sight may seem rushed to some readers, but I took the inspiration of their insta-love from my own. I met my Dakota in September 2011, was engaged by June and wed in December. So, yes, I do believe in love at first sight. (Absolutely shocking with my being a romance writer, I know.) The moment we saw each other, everything faded away and we've been together ever since and are still as sappy as day one.

If this is your first time reading about the Harvey Girls, know that they did indeed exist. In the 1890s, there were not many respectable jobs for women, so when Englishman Fred Harvey created his chain of fine dining restaurants along the Atchison, Topeka, and Santa Fe railroads, single women without an education, or in need of earning their own way, were given a chance to earn an honest wage without the speculation that they offered anything else but food as a service.

With Mr. Harvey's strict rules about the waitress's code of conduct, the women were given their independence while still maintaining their good name and place in society under the protective, fatherly arm of Fred Harvey. These extraordinary, brave women became known as the Harvey Girls, the ladies who tamed the Wild West with fine china, good pie, and exceptional service with complete propriety.

For the purpose of my story, I did take some small liberties with the Castañeda, such as the opening date of the hotel. Sources claim different years, so I decided to begin this series the year the Castañeda was built. I also changed the hotel's dining room floor appearance. I did attempt to stay as accurate as possible with the Fred Harvey system and layout of both Harvey buildings based on the historical pictures and references available. The Castañeda Harvey House is one of the few still standing and has been fully restored to operate once more and you can stay as a guest in the Hotel Castañeda, today.

If you want to read about Corinna and Tanner's enemies to lovers romance, check out *The Vanishing of Miss Victoria* today!

If you enjoyed *The Courting of Miss Cady*, I would love if you could please take a moment and leave a review, or rating. Happy reading, friends!

Grace Hitchcock is the award-winning author of multiple historical novels and novellas, including the American Royalty, Best Laid Plans, and Aprons & Veils series. She holds a Master's in Creative Writing and a Bachelor of Arts in English with a minor in History. Grace lives in South Louisiana with her husband, Dakota, sons, and daughter in a farmhouse that is always filled with the sounds of sweet little footsteps running at full speed. When not writing, chasing her toddlers, or tending to her chickens and golden and labrador retrievers, she's baking something delightful and can usually be found with a book clutched in her fist.

APRONS & VEILS
BOOK ONE

The Finding of
Miss Fairfield

GRACE HITCHCOCK

VALMONT

CHAPTER ONE

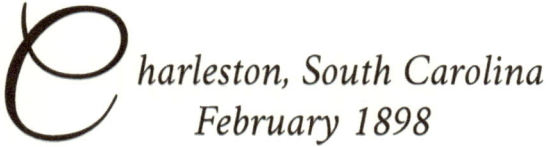

harleston, South Carolina
February 1898

SOPHIA FAIRFIELD'S heart skipped at the sight of Mother holding a damp handkerchief to her eyes as Father and his business partner, Prescott Payne, stood before the floor-length windows facing Charleston Harbor with their heads together, speaking in low, somber tones over the crackling of the fireplace. They halted their whispering when they caught sight of her standing in the second-floor East drawing room doorway, her reticule dangling from her fingertips with her box of new poetry, papers, and pencils propped on her hip. "Mother? What's wrong?"

Mr. Payne stepped forward, his emerald eyes capturing hers in a most disconcerting fashion. Grinning down at her, he ran his hand over his neatly trimmed gray beard. "My dearest Sophia, I've spoken with your father and mother, and they have whole-heartedly given us their blessing to wed."

Sophia's stomach dropped, her limbs aching to bolt from the parlor as the grand-father clock in the corner sounded the noon hour. Her gaze darted to Mother's elated face. Sophia had only accepted Mr. Payne's suit last month as a courtesy to her father, intending on ending things once Mr. Payne saw that they were ill-suited for one an-other, given he was over twice her age, but he had apparently not understood her subtle hints for him to cease his efforts. *Or not even cared, given he sought my father's an-swer instead of my own.*

"Is my darling bride-to-be speechless at last?" Prescott held his hand out to her, inviting her to join him.

Bride-to-be? The box slipped from her grasp, the items scattering about the floor. She dropped to her knee to retrieve them, but Father crossed the room and seized her arm.

"Leave it for Belle." He waved forward the petite maid standing beside the tea service.

Sophia sent her friend an apologetic smile as Father drew her away into the gilded parlor. Though a small room, gold leaf adorned the crown molding and the ornate medallion with the gold and crystal chandelier in the center of the room that illuminated the platinum wall coverings that perfectly matched the opposite West parlor room. Mother had to have a matching set of French chandeliers of her own after her visit to her sister's in New York.

"I have already accepted his hand on your behalf, daughter. You will wed as soon as you choose the day. We were just discussing the arrangements right before you returned home from your little shopping expedition on King Street."

Perhaps I can reason with Father when Prescott departs? But one glance at the pride radiating from her father, she knew it would be hopeless and she would never have the courage to stand against him. Like every time before, she would wilt beneath his crushing will despite her best arguments. She glanced down at her ring finger. She had been fortunate he had never pressed her into a marriage before now . . . but she supposed being the seventh, homeliest child of nine had something to do with it, and now that her youngest and prettiest sisters had wed at Christmas, she should have suspected she was next.

Mr. Payne captured her hand and slid a gold ring with a ruby cushioned by a pearl on either side onto her shaking finger. "What a lovely bride you will be, my dear. I am a fortunate man indeed to have found three women in one lifetime whom I have loved." He kissed her fingertips, his bushy mustache brushing against them and making her jerk back her hand. He narrowed his gaze for a half second before laughing.

Her? A lovely bride? She had been told far too often to keep her bangs trimmed and tidy to hide her high hairline and scolded more often than not for reading too late as it made her eyes habitually shadowed. No one in this family had ever accused her of being a beauty, except perhaps her youngest sister Jane. But Jane was the sweetest of the Fairfield daughters. Maybe it was because of her plainness, Sophia had never thought she would be required to marry. It would have required too much financially of her father to make a good match with a handsome suitor. She worried her bottom lip. Prescott, though twice her age, had retained his charm and could have had any of the society widows. *What has Father offered him to lure him into a match?*

"My second wife was a widow, so I have forgotten how you young brides can be with your wedding nerves," Mr. Payne said to her, conspiratorially elbowing Father.

Mother had the decency to blush while Father joined in the bawdy laughter, slapping Mr. Payne on the shoulder.

She swallowed back her protest over

their assumption that she would marry Mr. Payne, but she could not broach the subject while *he* was in the home. She would have to do battle in secret. She had never stood up to Father's demands before, but her parents had not set their sights solely on marrying her off before. She studied the ruby and all that was tied to it. She twisted it around her finger.

Mother grasped Sophia's hand and admired the gem before turning her bright smile up at Prescott. "It is magnificent. Well done, Mr. Payne. We will make the announcement at Sophia's birthday dinner party tonight. My daughter's engagement to Prescott Payne on her twenty-fifth birthday will be a surprise and delight to all who attend. I would love for Sophia to have a June wedding, but it is rather far away."

Sophia gripped the back of the settee to ground herself. *Please Lord, give me the courage to speak with my father and be victorious just this once. I cannot lose when there is so much at stake.* Now that her siblings were married, she was supposed to have this time to herself—to enjoy being the only daughter in the Fairfield house, to spend her days studying and tutoring her nieces and nephews, as well as the dear girls at the orphanage.

"Two months will be more than sufficient to plan a wedding fit for American royalty," Prescott replied, dismissing Mother's suggestion without so much as an apology. He snatched up his burgundy planter's hat and cane from the settee and turned on his boot's heel to face Sophia. "I must depart to dress for our engagement party, but know that I am counting the minutes until we wed, my sweet girl."

Then you will be counting forever if I have my way. She managed a weak smile, willing herself to be silent until they were alone. For if she did indeed lose this battle, she did not want Prescott to think of her as a spineless woman, even if everyone else in this family thought it was true. She waited for the downstairs front door to close behind him and crossed the drawing room to the window, watching the happy couples and families in carriages passing below her on East Bay Street. She closed her eyes against the sight, silence greeting her ears. She ached for the days when the house was filled with the sounds of her siblings running up and down the stairs, laughter filling the home—no matter how much they teased her for her looks and her nose always being stuck in a poetry book.

"Don't you think it is a little soon for me to consider marriage to Mr. Payne?" Sophia looked tentatively up at her father. "Not that I am not honored by having a gentleman in such high standing interested in me, but we hardly know one another."

"It certainly is not. For some reason, he considers you attractive even though you are practically an old maid and well," he motioned at her with one hand.

"Ernest." Mother cleared her throat. "What your father means is that he's far more established than any other suitor you have ever entertained."

"At fifty-five, one would hope for establishment, but I've only entertained the suitors my sisters rejected who only wanted to call upon me in order to become better acquainted with Father and his shipping industry," Sophia mumbled, running her fingertip over the wavy glass, longing to be out of doors, even if it was freezing, to be away from his oppressive gaze. At least on the portico she could breathe and pretend not to be trapped by her parents' expectations.

Father sighed and gently grasped her wrist, turning her toward him. "You are trying my patience with your protests, my dear. You must admit I have been more than indulgent of your sisters' choices in suitors, and your lack of interest in suitors in the past, but you cannot stay in my household forever. And if you will not pick a gentleman who suits your fancy and who actually wishes to marry you, I will."

Mother rested a staying hand on Sophia, quieting her protest. "Sophia, you know Prescott could have his pick of any widow in Charleston and yet, he has chosen you, and we couldn't be happier with the match."

She lowered her head, her cheeks flaming with suppressed anger at her helplessness. "I am well aware of that fact, but you see, I didn't choose him. *Father* did. And how on earth he could expect that I would be happy with a man better suited to be my aging uncle than my husband, I'll never know."

Mother gasped. "Sophia Bird Fairfield! Such an outburst is not to be borne. Apologize to your father at once."

Father held up his hand, the diamond in his gold ring on his little finger shimmering. "No, she's right. I was the one urging you to accept my friend as a suitor in the first place, and I'm the one who has accepted his hand for you." He took Sophia's hand in his with a tenderness she had not felt in years. "I've always had your best interests in mind, which sometimes means I have to make the difficult decisions for you. As a little girl, you trusted me to take care of you, but after that bout with scarlet fever that weakened you, I had to be, what appeared at the time, callous in my choices for you." He stroked her cheek with the back of his hand. "All I ask is that you trust me again, Sophia, and know I will do what is right for you."

"I do trust you, but am I never to have a voice? Or would you have me follow your will on this as I have done for everything else in my life because it's easier than disagreeing with you?" She bit her lip at the hardness returning to his eyes. Sophia's will wavered as it always did in the face of his disapproval, and he knew it.

"Your siblings have all made marriages of advancement. This would not only make me happy, but I've spoken with your brothers Elton, Thomas, *and* Robert. They all agree that Prescott is a most advantageous match for the family. As my business partner, and a gentleman of great means in his own right, I know Prescott has stature among not only all of Charleston, but nationally. He will take care of you in the manner you are accustomed to and will give you all that your heart desires." He gave her a little smirk. "I imagine he would provide you with a library full of every poetry book you have ever dreamed of possessing."

Mother nodded, placing her arm about Sophia's petite waist. "And more importantly, Prescott expressed to me how much he adores you."

"We have only been seeing each other

for a month . . ." Sophia shook her head, incredulous at the news. She could count on her right hand the weeks he had called upon her. "No, it hasn't even been a month because he was out of the city for a week, so how on earth could he possibly *adore* me?"

"Sometimes, it only takes a day." Mother smiled up at Father. "It only took a moment for us to fall in love." She stroked Sophia's cheek, tucking a stray flaxen lock behind her ear. "A love for Prescott will come. Trust us. Just give it time."

SEATED in the middle of the massive mahogany dining table with Mr. Payne on her left, Sophia felt on display in her copper silk creation from Worth with its daring neckline, which Mother had insisted upon. And seeing as Mother would broach no argument, Sophia defiantly had her bangs braided back to reveal her high hairline, despite her mother's expressed disapproval.

Sophia glanced to her right where Mother was making small talk with her dinner guests across the table, her siblings and their spouses sprinkled throughout the group of close friends. Sophia struggled to keep her expressions from reflecting the dread she had been attempting to mask all evening in the flickering light of the Girandoles, their four candlesticks further illuminated in the convex looking glasses.

Smoothing her silk skirt, she attempted to slow her racing heart and focused on the melodies of the string quartet. Mother hated lulls in conversation, so she always had soft music flowing through the foyer from the downstairs parlor during dinner parties, which sometimes made for a noisy dinner, but for once, Sophia did not mind as it gave her time to collect her thoughts. How had this afternoon gone so differently than she had hoped?

When she had broached the topic of becoming an English tutor for the other young ladies of Charleston, as well as continuing her work at the orphanage, both her parents scoffed at her offering—even though she had been the one to teach her nieces and nephews how to not only read but enjoy the study of poetry. While her parents saw her tutoring in the orphanage little more than wasted charity, Sophia knew she was making a difference as two of her charges, who were aging out of the orphanage, obtained positions as English teachers.

If she wasn't allowed to tutor, what other choice did she have? According to her father, she needed to have her own home at once—to be provided for as a gentlewoman. Without the option of a position, she was left with no other choice. *Lord, give me direction. Send me someone else! Or give me a way out of this marriage.*

"You are radiant this evening, my darling."

His deep voice awoke Sophia from her reverie, and she looked to her intended. He was a well-preserved gentleman for his age and if they had time together, perhaps she could indeed become friends with him even if the thought of sharing a life with him made her stomach turn. "Thank you, Mr. Payne."

"I believe it would be appropriate now

for us to address one another by our given names. After all, we are betrothed," he grinned, his eyes sparkling in the candlelight that further shadowed his crow's feet.

"Very well, Prescott." She took a substantial bite from her sweet potato roll to avoid saying anything else. The sweet bread caught in her throat, and she released a series of strangled coughs that had her reaching for her water glass and her mother shooting her a scowl.

"I wish you did not feel so nervous around me, *Sophia*." Prescott chuckled, returning his attention to his mushroom soup.

"Nervous? Why ever would you think that?" Sophia cleared her throat and took a spoonful of soup but missed her mouth slightly. She snatched up her napkin and dabbed her reddening cheek.

His hand slid over the tablecloth and encased hers. "Because, besides almost choking on your bread, I can feel your hand trembling." He smiled. "A sweet trait for a bride-to-be, but as your future groom, I would like a bit more from you than a chaste kiss on the hand."

"More?" Her voice cracked. *What is he asking?*

He leaned toward her, his eyes rolling appreciatively over her gown. "A kiss at the end of the evening is more than proper . . . and I do not mean on the cheek." He slowly ran his finger over her wrist in small circles. "You have no need to fear me. I will be a good and gentle husband to you."

A kiss. Simple to a man with two wives before her, but she had always longed to share her first kiss with a man she loved. She carefully withdrew her hand and dipped her head, sensing Prescott stiffening beside her at her silent refusal.

Father rose from the head of the dining room table, clearing his throat and lifting his glass. Prescott caught her hand under the table and Sophia's cheeks flamed as she once more slipped her hand away and folded them demurely on her lap. They were not married yet and she had no such intentions of allowing him *any* liberties, no matter his disapproval. *You can do this,*

Sophia. She glanced across the table toward her childhood friend, Beatrice Hawthorne, and sent her a small smile, wishing she had the chance to tell Beatrice before the announcement even though she had no intention of following through with the match.

"Ladies and Gentlemen, may I please have the honor of your attention?" Father clinked his glass with a spoon. "I have asked you here tonight, not simply as a gathering of friends and family, but in celebration of a long-anticipated matter." He smiled down at Sophia and Prescott, sending murmurs throughout the dinner party. "Most of you know, the Payne family and the Fairfields have done business together for many years and tonight, our bond deepens. Tonight, it gives me great joy to announce the engagement of my daughter to Prescott Payne."

The room erupted with applause and cheers. Chairs scraped against the oak floor as her sisters and friends rushed to wish her well and congratulated Prescott. Despite her tumultuous heart, she smiled and accepted their warm wishes, endeavoring to catch the eye of Beatrice, but her friend remained seated, her gaze fixed on her crystal glass with heated cheeks. Sophia thought she could detect tears glistening in Beatrice's eyes, but before she could reach her, Prescott threaded Sophia's arm through his and led her up the curving stairs to the entertaining rooms, only pausing once they were in the center of the East drawing room. The Persian rug had been rolled up and stowed away, allowing for dancing. With a nod of his head, he signaled the quartet, who must have taken the servant's stairs during the announcement to meet them.

He bowed to her as they began to play a waltz. "May I have this dance?"

Feeling all eyes trained on them, Sophia curtsied, allowing him to take her into his arms. His gentle touch upon her waist brought forth a sigh from a group of ladies as Prescott guided Sophia past, her skirts whirling as he effortlessly moved them about the floor in perfect time, his eyes never leaving hers. His attentiveness almost made her think they had a chance of happiness, if this was somehow the Lord's will. But as the music faded into silence, Prescott led her off the dance floor and the spell vanished from his eyes as guest after guest came up to reiterate their happiness of the couple's coming nuptials.

Jane drew her into an embrace, her eyes bright with unshed tears. "Dearest sister, I am ever so happy for you both." She rested her hand on her abdomen. "Marriage is such a boon, and children are a blessing that fills one to overflowing with joy." She kissed Sophia's cheek, whispering, "I know you are uncertain of the whole business, but truly, I think you will be happy."

"Thank you, Jane." She squeezed her sister's hands as the next couple pressed forward. She longed to have a talk with her sister, but if she approved of the match, she might inadvertently give away Sophia's true feelings on the matter. No. It was best to keep her feelings tucked away.

But with every well-wisher, Sophia's heart grew heavier. *Lord help me to get through tonight. Give me direction.*

"Sophia." Beatrice hissed, tugging her arm from behind.

Sophia was about to excuse herself from Prescott, but found he was so engrossed with a fellow businessman, she could easily slip away without notice. She grasped Beatrice's arm and accepted the silk shawl from her ever-attentive maid, Belle. Sophia smiled her thanks and guided Beatrice out onto the portico, inhaling the gentle breeze from the bay rustling through the magnolia leaves and palmetto branches. She leaned against the thick rail, drawing in the lights dancing in the harbor from anchored vessels. Perhaps there was a captain in need of a ship's boy? She was scrawny enough. Or perhaps a handsome captain who needed a bride and wouldn't mind if she wished to spend her time teaching and reading?

"I should have been told." Beatrice crossed her arms against the chill.

She reluctantly turned away from the ships and the wealth of imagination they offered her. "Please forgive me for not telling you sooner, Beatrice. I would have . . . if I had known of my family's intentions."

Beatrice pinched the bridge of her nose, scowling. "Didn't you just tell me three days ago you were going to dismiss him?" She motioned toward Prescott and his ring on Sophia's finger. "And now you are to marry him in a matter of months. What happened?"

Sophia drew her silk shawl over her arms. "What I always feared would happen. My entire life I have been groomed to be a wife. I am not allowed to work. I cannot even travel alone without a maid to accompany me and even to travel *with* a maid, I must have my father's blessing, which he never gives." She met her friend's gaze. "I'm trapped by society and my father's rules. I have no other option because, in my father's eyes, I'm his frail little girl that needs to be looked after by a strong, wealthy man."

Beatrice shrugged, pulling at her gloves to return them to above her elbows. "I could've told you that, but I knew the only way you'd realize the truth was for something like this to happen, or better yet, you'd actually fall in love." She nodded toward

Prescott. "But I thought if you didn't become madly in love with Prescott, I wouldn't have minded so much as I would've enjoyed consoling him."

"Beatrice! Some things should not be jested about."

"I am not jesting. I would be honored if he came to call on me. He's everything you could ever want in a man," Beatrice sighed as she gazed hungrily at Prescott. "If you'd only open your mind, you'd see what a good man he is and that he's been trying so hard to capture your hand this entire month. You cannot do better than Prescott Payne, and I suggest you take your focus off of yourself and your *feelings*. We aren't all as fortunate as you to have a wealthy suitor. So, try not to make any impetuous decisions, Sophia. Think of your family and your future." She glanced across the room, "Now, if you'll excuse me, I need to make my own future secure."

Stunned, Sophia followed her friend inside and leaned against the fireplace mantel as Beatrice wove through the crowd to Mr.

Steward's side, an elderly single gentleman of seventy with considerable means.

"My stepfather is the most favored man alive to have captured another angel for a bride," a deep voice murmured behind her.

Sign Up for Grace's Newsletter!

Keep up to date with Grace's news on book releases and giveaways by signing up for her email list at GraceHitchcock.com

FREE from Grace Hitchcock

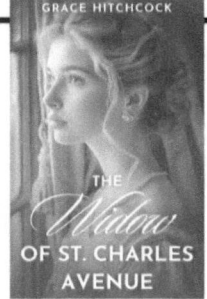

New Orleans, 1895

Colette Olivier, a young widow who married out of obligation, finds herself at the end of her mourning period and besieged with suitors out for her inheritance. With her pick of any man, she is drawn to an unlikely choice.

The Widow of St. Charles Avenue by Grace Hitchcock
a Second Chance Brides Novella
GraceHitchcock.com

Scan to Claim Your FREE Novella

More in your favorite series . . .

With a hope for belonging, Belle Parish leaves her position as a maid in Charleston to travel to New Mexico to become a mail-order bride. Colt Lawson's letters hold great promise, but something does not add up. Belle flees straight into the Castañeda Hotel Harvey House. Giving up the prospect of marrying, she focuses on her role as a Harvey Girl waitress until a strong Texas Ranger rides into her life.
The Pursuit of Miss Parish by Grace Hitchcock
Aprons & Veils #2
A Mail-Order Bride RomCom

Of all the dares Lorna Elliot had accepted, becoming a Harvey Girl waitress was by far the dumbest. And she had done it to herself in a fit of pique over a Texas Ranger who was mooning over another woman, but now that Ranger Reid is the new sheriff in her hometown, it's going to be impossible for her to move on unless she takes control of her heart—for better, or for worse.
The Enchanting of Miss Elliot by Grace Hitchcock
Aprons & Veils #3
A Friends-to-Lovers RomCom

Tanner Sterling has hunted his last bounty. As a new foreman, he wasn't expecting to rescue a sweet Harvey Girl from a raging river his first day. But, when he sees her on a wanted poster, he knows hunters will be coming for her. Despite wanting to hang up his past along with his gun belt, Tanner will do anything to protect her from the coming storm . . . even if he has to claim the bounty himself.
The Vanishing of Miss Victoria by Grace Hitchcock
Aprons & Veils #4
An Enemies-to-Lovers RomCom

www.ingramcontent.com/pod-product-compliance
Lightning Source LLC
Chambersburg PA
CBHW020923020726
47495CB00002B/321